8

Our Price

No Return

Murder on Ice

Murder on Ice

Alina Adams

BERKLEY PRIME CRIME, NEW YORK

MURDER ON ICE

A Berkley Prime Crime Book / published by arrangement with the author

PRINTING HISTORY

Copyright© 2003 by Alina Sivorinovsky.
Cover art by Teresa Fasolino.
Cover design by Lesley Worrell.
Text design by Kristin del Rosario.

ISBN: 0-7394-3907-3

Berkley Prime Crime Books are published by
The Berkley Publishing Group,
a division of Penguin Group (USA) Inc.,
375 Hudson Street, New York, New York 10014.
The name BERKLEY PRIME CRIME and the BERKLEY PRIME CRIME design are trademarks belonging to Penguin Group (USA) Inc.

PRINTED IN THE UNITED STATES OF AMERICA

Prologue

Prior to starting her first season as a figure-skating researcher for the 24/7 network, Rebecca "Bex" Levy received an iceberg-high load of advice.

Some of it was concise.

"Don't screw up," Gil Cahill, 24/7 Sports' Executive Producer told her.

Some of it was obscure.

"A cheated triple Axel is not a quadruple toe loop," coach Gary Gold lectured.

Some of it was obvious.

"I need all my research prior to the start of the event," commentator Francis Howarth intoned meaningfully, while his wife Diana stood nearby, rolling her eyes and needling, "I think she knows that, dear. I hardly think Bex was planning to give you your information after the closing credits rolled."

But only one piece of advice turned out to be actually useful.

"Remember," 24/7's veteran skating director told Bex before their first production meeting for their first event, "The
skating season is not a sprint. It's a marathon. Ration your
energy accordingly."

He wasn't kidding. The skating season, which had once
encompassed the European and U.S. championships in Jan-
uary, followed by the world championships in February, and
once every four years an Olympics followed by ten months
of getting ready for next year, now stretched from early September to late March, with senior and junior eligible competitions, ineligible competitions, pro-ams, exhibitions,
Grand Prix events, a Grand Prix final, nationals, Europeans,
world championships, and once every four years an
Olympics followed by a five-month, thirty-city tour of
champions. And then three whole weeks to relax, regroup,
and get ready for next year.

The killer schedule—if it's Tuesday, it must be Biell-
mann spins—took its toll on everyone connected to the
sport. Not only the athletes, who dutifully packed up their
sequined costumes practically every weekend for yet another jaunt to Europe, to Asia, to Canada, to New York and
California and back again, but also on the coaches, parents,
team leaders, doctors, judges, choreographers, skate sharp-
eners, nutritionists, agents, publicists, makeup artists, seam-
stresses, hair stylists, print journalists, Internet journalists,
and assorted other hangers-on. And then there was the television media: commentators, directors, producers, cameramen, technical directors, tape operators, sound mixers,
editors, production managers, production coordinators, production assistants, and researchers—let's not forget the researchers!—all of whom arrived days before the
competition commenced to set up their crews and command

centers and stayed days after the event ended to edit and transmit and clean.

Naturally, as a result of jetting off every few days to yet another time-and-strain-of-flu zone, by the time the world championships rolled around, everyone, from skater to entourage to media hack, was exhausted. And even though the world championships were currently being held in the U.S.—San Francisco, California, in point of fact; home of the Golden Gate Bridge and record-breaking earthquakes, but not, Bex made a point of highlighting in her research notes, Rice-A-Roni—which at least meant less travel time for the American delegation, everyone was still dead tired from seven months of globe-trotting and eating strange, greasy foods and sleeping in strange, greasy beds and bathing in strange showers with drains that somehow seemed to be perennially clogged. Everyone, as a result, was operating on a very, very short fuse.

That was why, in only ten days of competition, they'd already seen eleven hysterical meltdowns, eight formal complaints about biased judging, seven countercomplaints about biased refereeing, five screaming matches, four out-and-out fistfights, two reporters getting their credentials pulled, and one arrest (disturbing the peace; Belgium's ice dancer decided to celebrate his bronze medal win by doing a naked Yankee polka on the roof).

And this was all even before the Italian judge turned up dead.

One

Prior to the Italian judge, Silvana Potenza, turning up dead, Bex already had a homicidal situation on her hands. When she first signed on as 24/7's skating researcher, she hadn't realized that the job description included not only collecting, transcribing, photocopying, and presenting every piece of information and/or minutia that might become even vaguely relevant during the course of a skating broadcast—information that ranged from how many quad jumps the men's champion planned to attempt to the year any given arena was built and every sporting event, plus results, held within it since construction concluded—but also the vital responsibility of keeping 24/7 commentators Francis and Diana Howarth from killing each other. On the air. And off.

Alas, Bex was way, way, way out of her league. At the age of twenty-four, she was younger than most of Francis and Diana's ongoing arguments. Although, to be fair, just like with the origin of God, the universe, and mankind, no one was exactly, precisely sure when the infinite vitriol initially began. According to Bex's research, Francis and Diana Howarth had started off their public lives as perfectly matched skating partners. No one before or after them had ever mastered pairs skating to such an extent that, in the words of one charmed reporter, "they even breathe in sync off the ice." However, something about singing "The Star-Spangled Banner" as the second consecutive set of pair Olympic gold medals were hung around their necks must have driven them over the edge. Because, to hear it told, it was the last time they ever verbally agreed on anything—or even faced the same direction.

This schism, however, did not prevent the marvelously photogenic pair—both of them blond, fit, energetic, and so all-American that when they smiled, their teeth audibly sparkled—from getting lavishly and ostentatiously married, complete with four thousand of their closest and dearest friends in attendance and an ice sculpture perched upon every reception table, each individually hand-carved to mimic a different, world-famous Howarth skating pose. The spectacle earned them the cover of *Time* magazine and a six-page color photo spread inside. The same week their issue (number seven on the all-time best-seller list) hit the stands, Francis and Diana performed the first show on their ninety-six-city tour of the optimistically titled, "Romantic Harmony on Ice." For eight years, they crisscrossed the country with "Harmony." Their gushing PR agent insisted that, in that time, America's sweethearts got showered with enough flowers to approximate the weight of nine city buses.

When their performing days ended, Francis and Diana continued to produce the show with an ever-changing roster of talent and in their free time spawned three now-grown children, Francis Jr., Diana Jr., and Frances Dyana (Bex shuddered to imagine the arguments that must have raged to determine first and second billing on that last moniker). Their show was the most successful tour in the world, and the children, as far as Bex could tell, had turned out well enough. So, in the end, the only thing their seeming dissent about every issue known to mankind really prevented them from doing was occupying a room, any room, without launching into a diatribe.

Of course in any random room, there were at least other people to talk to and/or run interference. In a broadcasting booth, it was just Francis and Diana. And Bex Levy.

The night of the ladies' long program at the world championship, Bex entered the booth knowing she was doomed to spend the next four hours sitting between the Liz and Dick, Siskel and Ebert, Sam and Diane, fill in your own cliché, of the skating world. She brought her research manual for protection. The manual, a three-ring, green binder filled with every skater's biography and the elements of both their short and long programs, plus details on their music, costumes, choreography, and coaching, was half a foot thick. Bex figured, considering how meticulously she'd slaved over putting it together, she'd be able to mediate any and all Howarth tiffs with a quick riffle of the pages and a well-documented citation. Or, if worse came to worst, she could smack them with it.

The 24/7 research broadcast booth was built, as all 24/7 structures were mandated to be, as quickly and cheaply as possible. As a result, sitting rink side, there was only room for the ultranecessities: a table, lots of wires and cables, one camera, and three chairs, one for Francis, one for Diana, and one for Bex. At the start of the season, Bex had sat to the side, leaving Francis and Diana next to each other. Big mistake. They'd spent one entire event in December (granted it was the junior worlds, which meant there wasn't much to say beyond, "He/She/They need a little more seasoning and experience under their belts before they can confidently land all those jumps") practically arm wrestling for space to lay out their open binders. Now, Bex sat between the Skating Bickersons. It kept them from arm wrestling. But that put Bex, whether she wanted to be or not, smack in the middle of all their . . . discussions.

As they prepared for the ladies' broadcast, the ice was still being diligently Zambonied in preparation of the first skater, and Bex was still fiddling with her headset, making sure she could hear both Francis and Diana in the booth, and Gil Cahill and his director in the parking lot production truck from which they actually broadcast the live show, when Francis and Diana proceeded to live up to their reputations. And lucky, lucky Bex got to be the one to hear it all.

"We're showing the medal contenders and then the third American girl?" Francis stared at his show rundown, a listing of every skater, commercial, and announcer stand-up scheduled to go on air, as if it were the first—rather than the umpteenth—one he'd ever seen.

"That's what it says, doesn't it? Erin Simpson, Jordan Ares, Lian Reilley, and the Russian girl, Xenia Trubin." Diana lingered over the last name, pronouncing it perfectly—Zeh-knee-ah True-bin—and cattishly grinning to drive home the point that, all season, Francis had inevitably stumbled and pronounced it Eks-ee-knee-ay.

"Why show the Reilley girl?" Francis ignored his wife and zeroed in on the point he'd actually wanted to make all along. "She's in seventh place, no chance for a medal. And she skates like she's having a convulsion."

"She's got a triple-triple," Bex pointed out, initially thinking he was asking a legitimate question before realizing that he was actually setting a trap with which to beat Diana over the head and her presence and/or answer was unnecessary. That resolved, Bex went back to twisting the headphone knobs and wearily listening to Gil scream in her ear, "Can everybody hear me? Speak up if you can't hear me!"

Francis challenged the world at large, and Diana in particular, by idly remarking, "A philosophical query, my dear: If a skater only lands her triple-triple in a forest with no little woodland creatures or judges around to see it, when she falls on it every single, single time in competition, does the splat make a noise?"

"Oh, shut up, Frannie." Diana took her seat in the booth and channeled her distaste with Francis's world-famous convoluted metaphors into glaring at her headset, trying to figure out how she could slide the clunky, offending black plastic band and dangling microphone onto her head without disturbing the meticulous French braid she'd spent all afternoon bullying out of the hotel's hairdresser. "Lian Reilley is the designated up-and-comer, she's the U.S. bronze medalist. Besides, we always show the Americans, no matter what place they're in after the short. People want to see Americans."

"You know, of course," Francis said as he crossed both arms behind his head, terrifying Bex into thinking that he was settling in for a long, leisurely argument instead of getting ready for the show, "she doesn't even deserve seventh place. The child was severely overmarked. I fear the judges were so dizzied by those teeny-tiny revolutions of hers, they couldn't focus their Barney Google with the goo-goo-googly eyes enough to notice those choppy little strokes of hers or the fact that her footwork pattern was barely an earthworm, much less a serpentine."

"Serpentine isn't a noun, Francis." Diana clucked her tongue at him in a gesture of either marital affection or extreme hate. Bex had spent a whole season with the couple. She had yet to figure it out.

"Lian Reilly—and listen closely to this, Ms. Bex, you might want to write it down—Lian Reilley is precisely what's wrong with women's skating today. She does these tiny jumps that barely leave the ground and then lands in the same place they started from. She can't spin, and she most certainly can't coordinate a movement with a beat of music."

"She's young." Diana didn't look at him, but she obviously couldn't resist the rejoinder. "Give her some time. She'll improve her presentation."

"She's the same age as Jordan Ares," Francis invoked the U.S. silver medalist, "And that girl has music oozing out of her fingertips. Watch Jordan on a practice. Watch her, watch her, I dare you. Any music that's playing, that's the beat she skates to. She doesn't even think about it, she just does it. That's an artist, a true figure skater. And that Russian vision—what's her name again, now?"

"Xenia Trubin." This time it was Bex's turn to break down and answer Francis, even though she'd sworn and promised herself she wouldn't encourage him.

"She's the same way. Even when she was little Ms. Reilley's age, goodness, could that girl skate. Couldn't jump to save her life, of course. Back in the old days, Bex, we used to take bets on whether she could actually fall more times than she had jumps planned in her program. But, her skating? Her skating was divine. She can cross the rink in five strokes and not break a sweat. She's a classic skater. A skater's skater. The fact that that wonder hasn't won a world championship in eleven years is a travesty. She's the only one out there who can actually skate!"

"Do you think the fact that Xenia Trubin hasn't skated a clean program since Yeltsin was president might have something to do with that losing streak of hers?" Diana opened her research manual with an exasperated thunk and thumbed through the pages. "Now, I grant you, she's excellent at waving her arms around to portray Russia's grief over Stalin's five-year plan or some other such high-concept nonsense, but then she friggin' falls down! Now, if she had half of Erin Simpson's consistency—"

"She'd be as dull as our little home-fried jumping bean. Erin Simpson can jump. Jump, jump, jump, jump." Francis tucked his elbows into his sides and fluttered his fingers not unlike Tweety Bird. It was a most disturbing image, and Bex whole-heartedly wished he'd cut it out. Putting on a falsetto voice, Francis added, "And she's so gosh-darn adorable I just want to squash her like a bug." He dropped his arms and, thankfully, the voice, to add, "Adorable is one thing, but the girl is not world champion material. If she wins here, we might as well all slit our wrists and go home. Call it the Jump-O-Matic World Championships, that's what it's become. It's an insult to everyone who ever actually took the time to learn to skate!"

"The judges disagree with you, and no one seems to be slicing their wrists over it. Erin Simpson has beaten Xenia Trubin four times this year—fair and square, I might add— and I doubt that's going to change at this event."

"Erin didn't outskate her. Not once."

"No. But, she outjumped her."

"You mean she out-stood-up her. Xenia may fall on her jumps, but at least they leave the ground and complete a full rotation. Erin is as bad as Reilley. Who cares if she lands on her foot, when the jump barely left the ground in the first place? It's not figure skating, it's hopscotch!"

"Landing it is all that matters. You're out of touch, Francis. Face it, deal with it, and shut up about it."

"You know, my dear, no one's hair actually grows out of their head that color," was Francis's idea of a witty retort to his spouse as he indicated her newly dyed, blonde coiffure and wrapped his headset around both ears, thus effectively ending the conversation.

Or so he thought.

Even as Gil was counting down, "Ten, nine, eight, seven . . ." to their live broadcast, Diana reached behind Bex's shoulder, pulled one earflap off of Francis's head, and hissed, "You just wish you still had something left to dye," before letting it snap back against his cheek.

A split second later, over the television airwaves, viewers were being treated to the cultured, dulcet tones of Diana Howarth, America's sweetheart, sweetly welcoming them to tonight's broadcast of the ladies' long program at the World Figure Skating Championships, even as her husband winced and rubbed his newly bruised cheek.

"It's wonderful to be here," her tone was all big smiles and perfect, white teeth.

"Indeed," Francis beamed back, scowl notwithstanding. "We're in for a night of incredible skating. All four of the ladies we're going to show you tonight are incredible artists and technicians, and any one of them could skate away with the gold. . . ."

Bex took a deep breath. *Let the games begin. . . .*

She didn't have to wait long for the fun to start. Lian Reilley was the first broadcast-worthy skater up. As the barely five foot tall, sixteen-year-old, Chinese-American skater in the golden yellow dress with matching ponytail holders and gloves entered the arena, every available 24/7 camera whipped around to capture her awkward, plastic skate-guards-over-blades trudge toward the ice. While Lian looked straight into the lens nearest her, grinned, waved, and shouted, "Hi, everyone back home, I love you!" Bex opened her research manual to the Lian Reilley page and, looking from right to left, made sure that both Howarths had done the same. On the right-hand side of the document was Lian's name, her age, her hometown, her coach, her choreographer, her parents' names, her competitive record to date, her height and weight (at least the height and weight she was willing to commit to), the name of her music and all of her elements listed in order of performance. On the left-hand side of the document was her name again (Bex had learned she could never write the skater's name often enough as, at her first competition, Francis accidentally turned to the wrong page and was busy waxing poetic about Erin Simpson as Jordan Ares was skating), the correct pronunciation of her name (another thing she couldn't count on Francis to remember), her record to date written in full sentences instead of numbers this time, and such fun biographical data as the fact that Lian had been adopted as an infant from China, that her favorite color was gold, and that "ten years from now I'd like to be a two-time Olympic gold medalist, Harvard graduate, and touring with my own ice show as I finish medical school."

The future Dr. Skating Star stepped onto the ice and assumed her opening position, arms raised, looking heavenward, her face a mask of deep meditation.

Francis turned off his mike and mumbled, "She looks like she's surrendering."

On air, Diana chimed, "Her costume is quite one-of-a-kind and lovely. It took fourteen man-hours to bead it all!

Lian told us earlier that she always wears gold at competition because it inspires her and makes her work harder!"

Lian set up for her alleged triple-triple. She did a triple-double, instead.

Neither Francis nor Diana said a word. Mr. Howarth was too busy raising his thumbs to his ears and wagging the remaining fingers at Mrs. Howarth.

Lian set up for her next triple-triple. Another triple-double.

Dead silence from the announcers.

"Damn it, guys," Gil thundered over the headset. "Let's get some chatter going. I want to hear commentary. Come on, the people at home are dying to hear what you think of this kid, it's what they tune in for. Talk! Talk! Talk!"

Diana winced at the decibels of Gil's encouragement. She looked at Francis. He looked at her. They played a round of "I can stare without blinking longer than you can." Nobody said anything. What's more, nobody looked like they were planning to say anything until the other person said something.

"Bex!" Like the band mates of *This is Spinal Tap*, Gil seemed to have found the eleven on his amp switch. "Make them talk!"

Bex flipped a mental coin. And kicked Diana in the shins. America's sweetheart glared at America's overworked researcher. But she got the message and flicked on her mike. In a burst of inspiration, she said, "Lian Reilley's jumps are still awfully low and close to the ground. I don't know if she'll get full credit for completing them. What do you think, Francis? Will the judges reward Lian's jumps just because they were landed, despite the quality?"

She thought she'd been clever. She thought that by asking a question instead of simply making a statement, Diana had manipulated Francis into not only talking but answering her on the air and thus somehow proving . . . proving . . . proving . . . something apparently very important in the Howarth household.

Mistake Number One.

"Diana," Francis began, the *you ignorant slut* part unspoken but nevertheless rather forcefully implied. "What a ridiculous thing to say. If you truly understood skating, you would realize that the most important parts of a jump are the number of revolutions and the landing of them on one foot. Clearly, Lian has completed both of those requirements. Everything else is merely lip service. Unlike you, I wholeheartedly support this spunky up-and-comer and fully expect our wonderful national bronze medalist to get total credit for all of her jumps."

If Diana's ears weren't trapped beneath the headset, Bex fully would have expected to see steam emerging from both orifices. Instead, the trapped steam seemed to transform Diana Howarth's body into a pressure cooker as, instead of her ears, all that anger appeared to coagulate in her foot. In response to Francis' verbal smack-down, Diana raised her leg and kicked Bex in the shin. A combination payback for Bex's earlier action and, presumably, a "pass it on" to Francis.

Bex declined to pass it on.

Yet.

She wasn't intending to do anything to disturb the relative peace that had descended upon them as, for the rest of Lian's program, the Howarths made it a point to speak around, rather than to each other, a fact that Gil didn't seem to notice. At the end of the routine, he absentmindedly told them, "Good chatter, guys. Keep it up."

Why, oh, why, Bex cried internally, did he have to encourage them like that?

Xenia Trubin was next on the ice. Bex checked her notes.
The twenty-six-year-old Russian and European champion
was skating to a selection by Shostakovich and, contrary to
Diana's earlier sarcasm, she wasn't portraying Russia's grief
about Stalin's five-year-plan. She was portraying man's in-
humanity to man in an age of commerce and globalization.

By doing a triple Lutz–double loop combination.

Bex presumed her lack of understanding of what one had
to do with the other was probably a cultural difference.

This time, Diana didn't wait for Gil to scream and Bex to
kick her before picking up the slack. When Xenia's music
entered the slow, lyrical section, the one wherein she ran
backward on her toe picks with a look of abject terror on her
face, symbolizing her fear that commerce and globalization
would crush her with its mighty weight right there in the
middle of the rink, Diana announced, "Despite her numer-
ous titles—though, I must point out, those are mostly European—Xenia Trubin is nowhere near the jumper her main
competitor tonight and for most of this season, America's
Erin Simpson, is. In fact, even if she lands everything here
tonight, Xenia only has six triples planned in this long program, whereas Erin Simpson will be doing seven, including
two in combination. Erin's program has a great deal more
difficulty in it, and, as a result, I'd say that this world championship is Erin Simpson's to lose. Don't you agree, Francis?"

Once again, Bex guessed that Diana thought she had
Francis figured out. Since, with Lian's program, Diana had
parroted an opinion Francis expressed earlier only to see
him turn on a dime, disagree completely, and embarrass her
on air, she must have thought that by expressing an opinion

she knew he didn't agree with, she would at least be prepared for his inevitable attack on her. Bex was rather proud
of herself for figuring it all out. With this being the last event
of the season, she felt like she was finally getting somewhere in her decoding of the Howarths.

Mistake Number Two.

For both Bex and Diana.

After a half-century partnership, Francis was inevitably
one step ahead of his wife. Instead of giving her the vehe-
ment denial she expected, he once again pulled the rug out
from under her by—go figure; Bex figured she might as
well give it up—agreeing wholeheartedly.

"Absolutely, my dear. Absolutely. Xenia Trubin may be
the best Russia has to offer, but she is no match for America's one-two-three punch of Simpson, Ares, and Reilley.
Her technical skills are weak, and no amount of arm waving,
rushing from place to place, or rather unseemly—if I do say
so myself—spinning positions will be able to cover that up."

Even as Francis was speaking, Xenia finished up another
of her so-called unseemly spins, nose pressed to her knee,
bottom in the air, arms—well, Francis was right about
that—flapping by her sides, and collapsed on the ice, breathing heavily. After a dramatic respite on the ground of either
recuperating rest or ongoing fear of capitalism, she slowly
stood up and, after bowing to the judges, waved to the
crowd, her face an unreadable mask of not happiness, not
sadness, not relief, but determination. Xenia knew that her
biggest battle was still ahead. She didn't appear to give a
damn that the crowd's applause was perfunctory and luke-
warm while they strained their necks to get a glimpse of Erin
Simpson, warming up rink side. When Xenia skated, she
gave the impression of not even noticing that the audience
was there. All she cared about were the judge's marks.

Her numbers came up rather quickly. She'd barely sat down in the kiss-and-cry area and taken a parched sip of bottled water and kissed the indifferent flower girl who dumped an armload of limp roses at her feet, before they popped up on the scoreboard, indicating uniform votes. And, indeed, every judge on the panel but one gave her a 5.8 for technical merit, and a 5.9 for presentation. The Russian gave her two 5.9s.

"Those are a little high," Francis mused, stating the obvious for the service, Bex guessed, of the blind in the audience.

"But, there's still plenty of room on top for Erin," Diana bolstered.

"Oh, absolutely, no doubt about it. Erin Simpson is certainly capable of earning straight 5.9s and maybe even some 6.0s for her technique, her jumps are that solid. And, to be honest, her presentation is equal, if not superior to Xenia's."

And, Bex mumbled to herself, don't forget the "perky" mark. Erin Simpson could easily outscore anyone on that all-important, "perky" mark.

Bex guessed that "perky" kind of came naturally when you were nineteen years old but barely an inch over five feet tall. No hips, no breasts, no body fat. With those dimensions, Erin was hardly a candidate for a "sultry" performance, or even "non–pedophilia-inspiring." Perky was all she had. A huge, huge, huge smile, cosmetically twinkling lids beneath blue eye shadow, a sprinkling of freckles across her pert little nose, and a blonde, bouncy ponytail. Adorable.

If you were twelve.

To Bex, this umpteenth case of arrested development actually looked kind of creepy. Sure, Erin Simpson may have been a four-time U.S. champion with over a million dollars worth of endorsement deals, her own television special, and an official Web site, "Erin Excitement!" but would a college guy want to date a Girl Scout?

Granted, at the World Championship, dating wasn't really an issue. It wasn't even about looking attractive, although Bex had heard enough people over the course of the season whisper that "So-and-so should really get her teeth fixed if she expects that artistic mark to go up," and "So-and-so is going to get his nose fixed so it matches his partner in profile," to think that looks had nothing to do with the final results.

But, the fact was, Erin Simpson looked the way skating liked its champions to look. Cute. Innocent. Wholesome. Erin at nineteen going on twelve was much more the world champion ideal than Xenia, who'd dyed her usually mousy brown hair an orange red that, to paraphrase Francis, truly never, ever grew out of a human head that color, and, for her costume, wore shredded black rags dripping from her arms like sludge.

In comparison, Erin's dress, a sparkly robin's egg blue with sequins across the bodice, lace trim around the skirt, and puffy party-dress sleeves, was a blast of good taste and restraint.

Erin wasn't taking any chances with her look this year by trying something cutting edge or new. She knew the stars might never align so fortuitously again. Thanks to the serendipitous retirement of the defending gold medalist, this year was her first real, odds-on-favorite chance at a world championship. Erin had finished third for the past two years in a row, both times behind silver medalist Xenia Trubin. For her part, Xenia had finished second for five years in a row.

These were two women, Bex knew, who both wanted the title very, very badly.

Xenia out of frustration. She'd been competing on the world championship scene since she was fourteen. She'd worked her way up from twenty-first place to second. And then she sat, entrenched there, watching younger girl after younger girl pass her in the ranks.

And Erin . . . Erin wanted the title because she'd been born to it.

Literally.

Her mother was Patty Simpson. Seven-time U.S. champion. Olympic bronze medalist. Four years later, Olympic silver medalist. Never Olympic champion. Never world champion.

That, Patty proudly told anyone who would listen, would be Erin.

Patty put her little girl on the ice at fourteen months. With Mommy as coach, Erin's first competition was at age three. She was the youngest U.S. novice champion, then the youngest U.S. junior champion, then the youngest World Team member all by age twelve. Her career, to date, was identical to her mother's. They looked so much alike (since there'd never been a father around that anyone knew of), that people whispered that Erin had been cloned, not born.

But this was the year Erin Simpson was scheduled to break her mother's pattern. She'd beaten Xenia all season in their Grand Prix head-to-heads. This was the year Erin was scheduled to win the world championship.

She started her program off strong, taking the ice and, right off the bat, landing her (albeit tiny) triple-triple combination to an explosion of partisan cheers from the arena.

Her next jump, however, a triple loop, was only a double.

"It's all right, it's all right," Francis chanted like a hypnotic mantra. "Remember, the long program has no required elements. You don't lose points for the things you don't do, you only accrue them for the things that you do do."

"And that was a beautiful double loop," Diana chimed in. "She'll get full credit for it."

"It doesn't matter, anyway," Francis insisted. "Remember, now, Xenia Trubin completed only six triple jumps, whereas Erin Simpson has seven planned."

"And she's already landed her beautiful triple-triple."

"It was a marvelous triple-triple. Certainly worth more than one of Xenia's spins.

Erin's music slowed down. Now, Bex presumed, it was Erin's turn to make funny faces and run from rampant capitalism. Although, according to Bex's research, the theme of Erin's program was actually *Happiness.*

And apparently happiness was neither—"Peanuts" style—a warm puppy nor learning to whistle. To Erin Simpson, happiness was a look of deep longing into the stands, followed by a furrowing of brow and a shaking of her head as if trying to clear it, then a look of constipated pain in the other direction before a sudden music change was followed by her breaking into a trademark grin and performing a move wherein Erin hippity-hopped across the ice, going round and round in circles. Bex liked to call it dog-chasing-own-tail.

"Oh, oh, oh, isn't that wonderful?" Francis all but clapped his hands together with glee. "Such sensitivity to the music, such spirit, such life."

"It's almost as if the music is transporting her, isn't it, Francis?"

"You know, Diana, the theme of her program is *Happiness.*" Francis looked at Bex and winked, as if expecting her to congratulate him for actually having read his research material. "And I can safely say that not only Erin Simpson but the entire judging panel should be very, very happy with this program."

"Did we just witness a world championship performance, Francis?"

"I'd bet my Olympic gold medal on it!"

"Hey, you be careful! That's *our* gold medal you're gambling with there!"

"Do you disagree?"

"Oh, no, not at all, my dear."

Bex's tolerance level for cutesy dialogue reached gag proportions. Meanwhile, from the booth, Gil cheered, "Excellent, guys, excellent! Keep it going! We'll go to commercial before the marks come up; that'll really keep the tension high!"

Bex gritted her teeth—and not just to hold back nausea. Holding the marks for commercials was a practice she hated. Whenever television bought the rights to an event, they also bought the right to keep the scores from being announced until the time was convenient for them. To Bex, it didn't seem fair to make an athlete who'd worked their whole life for this moment wait an extra five minutes to find out if they'd succeeded or not, all in the name of ratings.

And Erin Simpson didn't seem to think it was too hot of a strategy, either. As soon as she dropped her closing pose, she was looking at the scoreboard. She was looking at it as she waved to her standing ovation. She was looking at it as she skated around to pick up the teddy bears and flowers thrown on the ice. She was even looking at it as she jumped off the ice and into the arms of her nearly hysterical with ecstasy mother.

And still, there were no marks.

The wait whipped the crowd into even a greater frenzy.

As Erin sat in the kiss and cry, waving her arms above her

head and grinning even more broadly than usual, the fans began chanting, "Six! Six! Six!"

Patty joined in the chant, then hugged Erin, then looked at the scoreboard.

But they were still in commercial.

Patty hugged Erin again. Erin hugged her back. They kept hugging tighter and tighter, until, at risk for suffocation, both awkwardly let go and, running low on patience, looked around as if the scores might be playing hide-and-seek with them. Starting to get pissed off now, they looked down at the ground, then up again at the scoreboard. Erin jiggled her knees. Her mother put one hand on her thigh and shook her head. Erin quit it and chewed on a cuticle. Now Patty's knees started jiggling.

Finally, Gil Cahill told the referee, "TV's good. Release the scores."

The scores came up: 5.8s and 5.9s for technical.

Erin and Patty hugged again. The fans screamed.

And then the presentation marks: 5.7s, 5.8s, and a 5.6 from the Russian judge.

Erin's perky grin turned into a furrowed brow. Her mother's brow furrowed, too.

The ordinals came up. A five-four split. Four votes for Erin, five votes for Xenia.

Xenia Trubin was the world champion.

"Impossible!" Francis sputtered.

"It's a travesty!" Diana almost beat him to the punch.

"This makes no sense." Francis's finger poked the monitor in front of him. "Both skaters landed the same number of jumps, but Erin had a triple-triple combination!"

"She seems to have lost this event on the artistic mark!"

"Ridiculous!"

"I agree! Her program was lovely. Youthful and joyful

and carefree, it's everything one can hope for in a skating performance."

"You know what the problem is." Francis was peering closely at the marks now. "Take a look at this panel, Diana. We have one, two, three, four judges from America, Canada, France, and Australia giving the win to Erin, and four judges from Russia, Ukraine, Kazakhstan, and Latvia giving the win to Xenia. The interesting decision is right here, by the Italian judge. By all rights, she should have voted with the West."

Bex's mouth dropped open. Was Francis saying what she thought he was saying? Was he honestly going live on national television and explaining that Western judges were obligated to vote with their Western counterparts?

"You're right, Francis," Diana concurred. "The Italian judge seems to have voted with the ex–Soviet bloc. That doesn't make any sense."

"You know, Diana, as a citizen of the world, it was my sincerest hope that with the dissolution of the Soviet Union we would finally see an end to block voting. And yet, here we are again, the ex-Soviets all voting together and, clearly, somehow swaying the Italian judge, too."

Bex's mouth could no longer drop open. If it dropped open any further, she would be licking her shoes, and in this booth, there was no room for it. What the heck were Francis and Diana saying? Could they even hear themselves? Could they hear what they were suggesting? What can of worms were they opening?

"Gil," Bex whispered into her headset. "Gil, we can't let them say this. Stop them, please. We have no proof. It's libelous. And it doesn't make any sense—

"Be quiet, Bex, it's good television," Gil flicked on his

switch to the announcers. "Great chatter, you two, keep it going, keep it going."

"I wonder how they did it," Diana mused. "I wonder what they offered the Italian judge to ignore that beautiful performance by Erin in favor of that avant-garde mess of Xenia's."

"This is horrible. Just horrible." Francis's voice had dropped to funeral dirge mode. "I offer my sincerest apologies to everyone watching at home, but, for the life of me, I can't think of any way to explain this decision. I am embarrassed for our sport, Diana. I don't know what to say. Poor Erin Simpson. Poor, poor, lovely Erin Simpson. She won the world championship tonight. And the Italian judge stole it from her as surely as if she'd ripped the gold medal from that sweet, brave child's neck. . . ."

Jordan Ares was the last skater of the night. She skated well and won the bronze medal. But, by that point, nobody cared. Even before the competition was officially over, the local radio station was announcing: "Corruption at the world championships!"

By the time Bex followed Francis and Diana out of the announcer's booth, the media, both print and television, was camped outside like a salacious throng, demanding that the pair comment on the travesty that had just occurred.

"Travesty," Francis said. "That's the perfect word for it. It's a travesty. Obviously, some sort of fix was in, some sort of deal was made, to keep our beautiful and talented, dear American champion from winning the gold medal."

"It's the Italian judge,"Diana repeated. "Look at her marks. She voted for Xenia over Erin, and there was no rea-

son for her to do that. The Italian judge isn't part of the Soviet bloc. Clearly, she had to have been coerced."

"How can you say that?" Bex waited until she'd se-
questered Francis and Diana in their 24/7 dressing room before unleashing all the comments percolating in her mind
earlier. "Don't you realize that by suggesting there was a
conspiracy on the part of the Soviet bloc, you're also imply-
ing that there was a conspiracy on the Western side? I mean,
yes, all the ex-Soviets voted together, but so did all the
Western countries. How is that not a conspiracy on both
sides?"

Francis and Diana looked at each other.

"Hmm," Francis said, "I never thought of it that way."

"What an interesting point you've made, Bex."

And then they refused to say another word on the subject.

$\mathcal{E}$rin Simpson's defeat, plus a fetching photo of her
tearstained yet bravely smiling face, made the front page of
every major American newspaper the next morning.

Her quotes, "I skated my very best. I'm happy with my
performance. My job is to skate, and the judge's job is to
judge. This silver medal is the silver lining on my cloud,"
made her seem simultaneously modest and plucky. Erin did
five satellite interviews, seven cable talk shows (both news
and sports), and called in to every national morning show to
express her utter satisfaction with the decision.

Meanwhile, as Erin insisted how content she was and
how she wouldn't trade her hard-won silver for a trunk of
gold, her official Web site, "Erin Excitement!" launched a
petition to strip Xenia of her gold medal and award it to Erin
instead. By nine A.M. the morning after the long program, it
had seven thousand signatures, including one poster who

listed their address as Sierra Leone, Africa. Gee, and here
Bex had assumed the people of Sierra Leone had bigger
things to worry about—what with the machetes chopping
off limbs and all—than the outcome of the World Figure
Skating Championships.

Obviously, not all was sunshine and lollipops in the
Simpson camp. Because, for every brave-trooper smile Erin
offered the media, five minutes later there was Patty,
snarling.

"Anyone with eyes could see that Erin won last night.
She and Xenia landed the same number of jumps, but Erin
had a triple-triple combination. And if you want to talk
about the artistic mark, well, just listen to what Francis and
Diana Howarth said on the air! And their judgment is beyond reproach. They were Olympic champions, for Pete's
sake. They truly understand artistry. I'd like to know what
the Italian judge was looking at. Actually, no. I'd rather
know whom she was listening *to!*"

Xenia, for her part, was also besieged with interview requests. Her quotes, though, were less pithy. "I win gold
medal. I am best."

Her coach, Sergei Alemazov, elaborated, "The judges de-
cided that Xenia is the winner. Yes, the vote was very close.
But, very often in the past, the vote was very close. Erin
Simpson is a nice skater. But Xenia won on the artistic mark.
Xenia is terribly artistic. Xenia is a grown woman. Erin
Simpson is a child. And Erin Simpson skates like a child."

In fact, the only person not getting airtime was Silvana
Potenza, the Italian judge.

Though that wasn't due to the media's lack of trying.

They'd practically camped outside the poor woman's
hotel room door, screaming questions and flashing lights in
her face whenever she stepped outside. But Silvana Potenza,

a fifty-something woman who either was rather round or simply looked it due to perpetually being wrapped in a russet floor-length fox coat, refused to say a word.

Gil Cahill was in heaven.

"Is this terrific or what?" he raved at the production meeting Friday morning. This was a daily event when they were in the middle of a show. The entire cast, staff, and crew got together so Gil could explain to them why they were the most useless people on earth and how he "could pull a dozen, non–English speakers in off the street and they would do a better job in each and every position." The only lucky sons of guns exempt from the daily enlightenment were a rotating series of cameramen, who had to miss the fun because one cameraman was on duty at all times, shooting all the skaters' practices, lest something exciting happen while the rest of them were absent.

Gil went on, "You know, I thought we might get a little ratings bump with worlds being in America this year, hometown crowd and all, people love that shit. And then, when we had two girls in the top three, I thought, yeah, that should pick up a couple of extra households. But, this! This is freaking, friggin', fucking fantastic. We're raking in free publicity from every newspaper, radio station, and TV station in the country. Everyone's talking about Erin Simpson. I've got a source telling me she's on the next cover of *Time* and friggin' *Newsweek*. Can you bums imagine what kind of numbers our exhibition show is going to get on Sunday? Everyone wants to see this kid and the Russian who stole her medal. We're going to go through the roof!"

"Uhm . . ." Bex wanted to raise her hand, but Gil Cahill had a problem seeing anything outside his own ego. She settled for shouting. Or, as they called it at 24/7 production meetings, business as usual. "Gil! Gil! Gil, you know, I was thinking. Maybe during the Sunday show, we could do an element-by-element comparison of Xenia's and Erin's program, and show how they broke down and why some judges may have valued technical merit over artistic, and vice versa. I think it could be really informative."

Gil looked at Bex for a moment. Then he faked falling down on his chair and snoring.

"I take it that's a no?" Bex asked politely.

"You're new, Bex, so I'm going to share with you a little 24/7 rule, kiddo. We don't bite gift horses on the ass around here."

"I'll keep it mind."

"Good kid."

Bex changed tacks, addressing Francis and Diana. "So let me get this straight. Just so I can put it down in the research notes for Sunday. You two claim that Erin lost last night because the panel was stacked against her."

"Well, actually the panel wasn't stacked against her. It was five to four, pro-West. She should have won, if only the Russians hadn't gotten to the Italian judge and made her change her vote," Diana patiently explained.

"So you're saying that if the Italian judge voted with the West like she was supposed to, Erin Simpson would have won, no matter how she skated?"

"Erin Simpson skated beautifully last night. No mistakes. No falls."

"But you're saying that it doesn't matter. That how the two women skated is irrelevant. You make it sound like all victory is dependent on the panel. That it's preordained."

"The results were certainly preordained last night. The Soviet bloc wanted Xenia to win, and win she did, even with that mediocre performance."

"But, doesn't that mean that all the times Erin beat Xenia

at the Grand Prix this season, she only won because the panel was stacked in *her* favor?"

Diana and Francis looked at each other.

"Hmm," Francis said, "I never thought of it that way."

"And does that mean that when you two won your Olympic gold medal, it was only because the panel was stacked in *your* favor?"

"What an interesting point you've made, Bex," Diana said.

And stood up to leave.

With Francis by her side, she was barely to the door, when Mark, the lucky cameramen assigned to shoot the ladies' practice for the exhibition, burst into the room, breathing heavily. He'd run all the way from the arena to the hotel, lugging his heavy camera on his back, and now he could barely get the words out between his gasps.

"Did you hear?" he demanded. "Silvana Potenza! She's dead! Murdered!"

TWO

"What luck!" Gil Cahill exclaimed, offering the 24/7 version of condolences for the deceased and, in the next moment, whipped around to point a finger at Bex. "Bex. What are you still doing here? Why aren't you at the arena, researching this thing?"

Because just like two objects can't occupy the same space at the same time, one object can't be in two places simultaneously, and/or *Because I lack the twinkling ability to transport myself through the air,* Star Trek *style,* were just two of the snappy-if-she-did-say-so-herself rejoinders that flashed through Bex's mind.

What she actually said was, "I'll get right on it, Gil."

Of course, Bex wasn't alone as she gathered up her things and ran across the hotel's parking lot toward the arena. The entire staff of 24/7 was right behind her. But they, the lucky bums, were just going to gawk. Bex was the only one expected to actually get some work done.

Bursting through the arena's side door, Bex followed the murmur of gossip toward the body. The more certain it grew, the closer Bex figured she was getting. When the buzz around her was, "I think something happened, like some skater or coach got hurt or something," Bex knew she was heading in the wrong direction. When she heard a murmured, "Someone's dead. An accident near the rink," she knew she was getting closer. And, naturally, when she heard a voice stating with confidence, "It was the Italian judge, Silvana Potenza, and I'm sure it was something to do with the whole Xenia Trubin/Erin Simpson situation, you know how the Russians hate to lose, I bet the police are questioning them right now as we speak," Bex knew she'd hit the gossip mother lode.

Yup, this was definitely the place. Bex's incredible research skills had cleverly led her to the heart of the action. Well, Bex's incredible research skills, and the sight of a chattering crowd huddled around the door to the refrigeration room; yellow police Do Not Cross tape practically blinking like a beacon. That last part kind of helped, too.

She attempted to elbow her way to the front of the throng, boldly proclaiming, "I'm a researcher, I need to get in there," adding, "Stat!" for emphasis. It was, incredibly for someone who'd watched as much television as she had growing up, the only emergency type situation word she could think of.

Even more incredibly, it seemed to do the trick.

People moved. Well, their bodies moved. Their pupils stayed glued to the crime scene, which, only an hour earlier, had gone by the more plebian name, *door.* It must have been a heck of a fascinating sight, too, because the crowds kept rubbernecking long after it became obvious that, just like perennially promised, there really was "nothing to see here."

That is, if you followed the rules and did not cross the police Do Not Cross line. But Bex worked for television. Television had very quickly taught her that rules and lines and sex-segregated locker rooms only applied to other people. Television folks got to walk in any old place they wanted. It was a rule. Really. Some kind of Constitutional Amendment or something.

The memo about which, apparently, hadn't been passed on to the San Francisco Police Department. Go figure, but they actually looked surprised to see Bex duck under the tape and boldly enter the refrigeration room.

There were two cops in the room, both standing over a puddle (in lieu of a chalk outline?) and staring at it rather intently. The entire room was illuminated by a single, multi-watt lightbulb dangling from the ceiling like the penultimate shot in *Psycho*, and, in addition to some old tables with broken legs, chairs with broken arms, and a garbage bag over-filled with old programs someone had obviously dumped there because it was closer than the designated storage room, the bulk of the place was occupied with rusty, brownish pipes that sang a variation on "clink, clunk, groan, drip." Bex presumed they delivered the coolant to keep the arena's ice frozen and that the dripping water was either condensation or actual holes in the metal.

"What the hell do you think you're doing in here?" Cop Number One demanded of Bex.

"I'm with 24/7. We're covering this event." I.e., *We bought the media rights for a heck of a lot of money, and that gives us access to every inch of this arena, including murder scenes.*

"Cool," Cop Number Two said.

It earned him a look of disgust from Cop Number One, which Cop Number Two ignored.

"Where's the body?" Bex asked, looking around, wondering if it, too, had been dumped in the corner to keep from having to schlepp it outside.

"Medical examiner took it away." Cop Number Two looked to be in his mid-thirties, with neatly combed brown hair, linebacker square shoulders, and front teeth so white and uniform they could only be very expensive caps. In Bex's narrow world, there was only one reason for a civic servant to have capped teeth. Either they'd all been knocked out in a ferocious fight to protect truth, justice, and the American way, or the cop also did a little acting/modeling/commercials on the side. Considering his glee at hearing she worked in television, Bex was betting her money on the latter.

"Was it actually Silvana Potenza?" She directed her question exclusively at Cop Number Two. Cop Number One, though at least a decade younger and thus presumably more in Bex's league, did not have capped teeth or even so much as a hint of a nose job. Ergo, she had no use for him.

"That's what her ID said. Silvana Potenza. She's Italian, right?"

"So how did she die?"

"Electrocution." Cop Number One spoke up. Maybe he was of the if you can't beat 'em, join 'em school? He indicated the dangling lightbulb above their heads, complete with pull cord. "She was standing in a puddle when she tried to turn the light on. Zap."

"Zap?"

"That's a police term," he offered helpfully. And smiled. So the guy wasn't impressed with television, but he did have a sense of humor. Good to know.

"It's just one of those things. A freak accident." Cop Number Two wasn't about to let his nontheatrically minded

friend steal the spotlight. He stepped in front of his col-
league, effectively blocking him from Bex's view, and even
made a big theatrical gesture with his arms.

"An accident?" Bex repeated. "But, I thought ... I
heard—"

"It was an accident, Bex." A voice behind her made Bex
jump. Apparently, she wasn't the only one who knew how to
yell "Stat" to shove through a crowd. Because, standing in
the doorway, was Rupert Newman of Great Britain, the current president of the International Skating Union. That
would be the union that ran the championships. Perhaps
24/7 had bought the broadcast rights, but the ISU and thus
Rupert Newman owned them in perpetuity.

"A tragic, tragic accident."

"Bullshit!" Gil Cahill thundered. "This press release is
total bullshit."

Bex hadn't written the press release. She'd merely dutifully photocopied it and distributed the ISU document
among the 24/7 staff, as per her job description. So, naturally, this made her responsible for its contents.

She had, however, written the summary of the press release, which she distributed along with the original. In Bex's
experience, Gil, Francis, and Diana, among others, got
bored reading an entire page of something and needed the
Reader's Digest version if Bex had any hope of their actually retaining even a fraction of the information. So, for the
page-long challenged, Bex had neatly compressed the following: "The ISU mourns the (SFPD-ruled) accidental
death of Silvana Potenza, an Italian judge of twenty-six
years' standing. Potenza was electrocuted on Friday morn-

ing when she walked into the arena's refrigeration room and attempted to turn on a light while standing in a puddle."

"And what," Gil demanded, "was Silvana Potenza doing wandering into the refrigeration room in the middle of the ladies' exhibition practice?" They were both squeezed into the tiny corner at the back of the production trailer euphemistically dubbed Gil's office. Of course, the only thing separating Gil's office from the production area was a line of black tape on the floor. And the space wasn't even big enough for a functional desk. So Gil's computer was propped up on a card table. His rolling chair was tucked underneath it. Whenever anyone tried to sit on the chair, it caught the slope of the trailer and proceeded, indiscernible increment by indiscernible increment, to roll downhill until the computer was still in the office, and the person typing on it was out. This annoyed Gil to no end. He couldn't stand insubordination, even from furniture. Actually, especially from furniture. So his idea of punishing an underling was not to stuff them into a windowless trailer corner and yell at them. Gil's idea of punishing an underling was to stuff them into a windowless trailer corner and make them sit on his perennially rolling chair.

Bex sat on it now. She was supposed to be listening to Gil. She was actually mostly concentrating on keeping her toes dug into the wooden floor so she didn't roll away.

"Now, I'm not a researcher like you, Bex, so you tell me. Are judges generally famous for their unquenchable curiosity about any and all refrigeration rooms, or is this more of an Italian interest? Like painting on ceilings and having people whacked while they eat cannoli."

Goodness, but there was so much for Bex to reply to in that query. She could start by pointing out his incredible lack of political correctness. Or she could remind him that in *The*

Godfather (seemingly Gil's sole source of info), Pete Clemenza was not actually killed while eating cannoli, but rather after his wife had yelled after him not to forget them. She could also note that Mrs. Potenza was truly Italian, not Italian-American, and thus not covered by the stereotype. Or she could just keep her mouth shut and let Gil carry on, since, obviously, it was all he really wanted to do in the first place.

"I don't like being played for a fool, Bex."

"I'm not playing—"

"Oh, I'm not talking about you, for God's sake. I'm talking about someone important. The damn ISU has been on my ass every day since we got these championships. You'd think paying an organization a barrel of millions for their precious world championships would buy you some cooperation, wouldn't you, Bex?"

Oh, this was tricky. Rhetorical or actually in need of an answer? And, if the latter, in need of an honest answer, or just a rote one? And if the latter-latter, which rote one to whip out?

Thankfully, Gil spared Bex further deliberation. He answered his own question. Less chance of getting it wrong that way.

"It buys you nothing! All I asked was for a couple of reasonable things, to make it a better show for all of us. That random draw thing they do for the short program, right? Who needs it? I mean, they've already done the qualifying rounds, so they pretty much know who's a contender for this thing and who's going to stink it up big time. So would it be so awful to just group 'em like that? Put the good ones together, so it's easier for us to shoot? But they wouldn't go for it! Can you believe they wouldn't even put the three

American girls last, so we could get some tension going? They're killing my show, here. They're friggin' killing me!"

"You and Silvana Potenza." Bex couldn't help it. Sometimes her mouth worked ahead of her brain. She really, really needed to work on that.

But, then again, who'd have guessed it was just the right thing to say?

"Exactly!" Bex had worked for Gil since the season started in the fall. In seven months, this was the first time he'd ever smiled at her. "Exactly, that's my point. This stonewalling about Potenza is just another way for them to screw my show. They know it's what the whole country—hell, the whole world!—is talking about. They know that our exhibition ratings are going to go through the roof as soon as people find out we're going to blow this judge mess wide open."

"But," Bex offered timidly, "doesn't the ISU want the ratings to be high? I mean, it's their world championship we're promoting. The more people who watch, the more people—"

"The more people will plant their eyeballs on all that ISU dirty laundry! Are you kidding me? Those droopy pinkies in the ISU are flaking in their sequined panties about the kind of dirt a real investigation could dredge up!"

Again, most, most politically incorrect. Though, this time, not factually inaccurate. Gil, in his bellicose way, did seem to be on to something, here.

"But, without ISU cooperation, I don't know how we could find out any—"

"Did Woodward and Bernstein get cooperation out of Tricky Dicky?"

"Well . . . to this day no one knows who Deep Throat really was."

"Did Upton Sinclair get help from the cows when he wrote about that bad beef?"

"Now you're just testing me, right? To see if I know who Upton Sinclair was?"

He waved his hands in the air. "All right, all right, we all know you went to college. This isn't the time to be showing off, Bex."

"Right. Sorry."

"Here's the deal: Those ISU bastards want to kill my show. I've got no intention of letting them get away with this crap, not with the money we're paying them. They can put out all the press releases they want, and scream "accident" until each and every one of them sounds like Harvey Fierstein—and I especially mean the women. But, we're going to cut them off at the ice skates. You with me, Bex?"

"Uhm . . . Gil, you mean you want me to—"

"Find out who the hell killed this Silvana Potenza. Damn it, Bex, do I have to draw you a figure eight?"

"Gil, I'm not sure if I know how. . . . I mean, even the police are saying it's an accident."

"Are the police figure skating experts?"

"I would be willing to bet no on that one."

"Are you?"

"Am I what?"

"Are you a figure skating expert?"

Oh, goodie, another possibly rhetorical question. And this time, an even stickier one. Because, the truth was, Bex wasn't exactly sure what to call herself. Not that she'd lied on her résumé or during her job interview or anything. Bex had been totally up front about how her bachelor's degree from Sarah Lawrence was in "general knowledge," which did include a heavy research component. But not in figure skating. Upon graduation, Bex would have been hard-pressed to tell an Axel jump from a Salchow, much less a Mohawk from a Choctaw. But then, in a year of bumming

around as a freelance writer, selling her skills to the highest
bidder and waxing poetic on topics ranging from "How a
Bill Becomes a Law 2002" (this time with no singing) to
"Your Tractor & You: A Guide to Regular Oil Changes for
the Small Farmer," Bex met an extraordinary senior citizen
named Antonia Wright. Bex profiled Toni for *Maturity* magazine, detailing her World War II–era battle to break the
color line in professional figure skating and her subsequent
success as the first African-American ice show star. Along
the way, Bex also learned about Axels and Salchows. And
Mohawks and Choctaws. And lasso lifts, and serpentine
footwork sequences, and the fourteenstep and Charlotte spirals. And, also along the way, when Toni recommended her
for the 24/7 research job, praising Bex's writing and research
ability, not to mention her ability to learn fast and work cheap,
Bex added up her student loans, her car payments, and the
cost of renting in New York City, and accepted the position.

Which all neatly brought them to the question at hand.

"Are you a figure skating expert, Bex?"

"Well, Gil, I—"

"I don't think so."

Okay. That solved that. It opened up a whole other can of
worms, but it certainly did solve that.

"Your work this season, I have to say, has been less than
stellar. For instance, remember when we were broadcasting
the Europeans live from Nottingham, and I asked you how
many English women had ever won a medal of any color at
the world championship, and that include ladies' singles,
pairs, and dance? I think it took you until we'd come out of
the commercial break to get that statistic for me. That's
sloppy work, Bex, very, very sloppy. Frankly, at this rate, I
don't know about hiring you back next year, I really don't.

My announcers need to be confident in the information that they're given. And if you can't provide that info—"

"Gil?"

"Yes, Bex?"

"I'll find out who killed Silvana Potenza for you. You'll have the information in time for the exhibition broadcast on Sunday."

"Why, thank you, Bex." Gil actually put his hand out to stop her chair from rolling away. "That's very kind of you to volunteer. Shows real team spirit. We like that here at 24/7. We like that a lot."

Bex's first plan for figuring out who lured Silvana Potenza into the refrigeration room and/or toward her puddle of slushy doom involved getting her 24/7 credential, the one that said Bex Levy—Researcher next to her sleep-deprived picture, and walking up to every single person in the arena with the polite query, "Hello, my name is Bex Levy, I'm the 24/7 researcher, as you can clearly see by my ID. Excuse me, did you kill Silvana Potenza? No? Do you know who did? No? Well, thank you very much for your time."

She gave up the notion when she realized its impracticality. Like anybody would ever tell the truth to a researcher. Why, people's tendency to lie was what made this job the profession of kings! So, that left Plan B.

Go to the police. Ask them stuff.

Bex had never been to a police station before. Honestly, why would the opportunity have come up? She'd seen an awful lot of them on TV, though.

Hence, her extreme sense of disappointment when Cop Number Two, who turned out to have a name, Stace Hale Jr., as a matter of fact, and a small office in the back, which looked, not like the set of *Hill Street Blues* or *NYPD Blue* or even *Barney Miller,* but like a messy college dorm room, complete with a trash can full of coffee cups and MacDonald's wrappers, a three-hole binder on the desk, and a school—University of California at Davis—flag on the wall.

"What can I do for you, Bex?" Stace gestured for her to take a seat. When he realized that the folding chair, which presumably usually stood there, had been seemingly requisitioned for other purposes, the gesture turned more into a *Please feel free to lean against my wall.*

Bex asked, "Silvana Potenza. You said her death was an accident."

"Yes, ma'am."

"How can you be so sure?"

"No sign of foul play. If someone tried to force her to stand in that puddle and turn on the light switch, they'd have gotten electrocuted, too, just from touching her."

"Couldn't they have held a gun on her or something? Make her do that?"

"I suppose it's possible. But the position of the body is consistent with someone just walking in and reaching for the light. It's automatic, don't you think?"

"What if someone lured her there? Told her to meet them. Isn't that possible?"

"Yes, it surely is."

"Aren't you going to investigate?"

"What would you like us to do, Bex, walk up to everyone in the arena, flash our police badges, and ask, "Excuse me, did you kill Silvana Potenza? No? Do you know who did?"

"Would you, please?"

Stace smiled. "I like TV people. You're funny."

"Listen," Bex was now falling back on her many years of detective training: undergrad by Nancy Drew, master's by Columbo, Ph.D. by Agatha Christie. "Can I ask you a favor?"

"No sales tax on asking."

"Except for her clothes, did Silvana Potenza have anything with her? Like maybe an appointment book, or a diary, or . . . or . . . a list of people out to get her?"

"I've been watching TV, Bex, your 24/7, in fact. Sure sounds to me like everyone in that competition was out to get her."

"You're not helping, here, Stace."

"Sorry."

"So, did she have anything with her?"

"A purse."

"Really? Great! What was in it?"

He hesitated.

"Look," Bex said, "You just told me her death was an accident."

"That's what the department decided."

"Which means it wasn't a homicide. Which means her belongings aren't evidence."

"No, but they are *her* belongings."

"Isn't being alive possession by nine-tenths of the law if the other party, well, isn't?"

"Now see, there you go being funny again."

"Come on, Stace." Bex gave up logic and went straight to the last refuge of the truly desperate: whining. It never worked when she was a child. Bex wasn't sure why she thought it could abracadabra some magic now. Except for the fact that an alleged grown-up whining was much, much more annoying than a child. "Just let me see what was in her bag, and I'll—I'll—" Bex didn't know what to offer him, sex or money. Not because she had an aversion to either, but because she honestly couldn't guess which he might prefer and she didn't want to guess wrong.

"I've got an idea," Stace said. He stood up and left the room.

Bex didn't know if he was going to get her Silvana's bag or come back with a warrant for her arrest on the charge of trying to bribe an officer. Even if she hadn't quite gotten around to the actual bribing yet.

Neither, as it turned out. Stace came back with a manila envelope. He sat back down behind his desk and riffled around in the middle drawer. Finally, he withdrew a glossy white sheet of paper and slipped it into the envelope. Only then did Stace pass it on to Bex.

She looked at him, all sorts of scenarios swimming through her mind, all of them scary, all of them from television. Was she supposed to open the envelope? Was it some kind of coded message he wanted her to deliver to another officer? Could it be incriminating information for another case that he wanted her to destroy? Was he testing her? Was he—?

"It's okay. You can open it."

Well, at least the test was getting easier. Bex slid her hand into the envelope, expecting everything from a booby trap to illegal narcotics to the aforementioned arrest warrant.

It was a head shot. An eight-by-ten, black-and-white, glossy headshot. Of Stace Hale Jr. And all of his perfectly capped teeth.

Stace said, "You think you could pass it on to someone at 24/7? In case they, you know, ever need an expert witness for one of their news shows. That's a pretty good way to get your face out there, isn't it? I figure, any exposure is good exposure, right?"

Bex said, "You're an actor." It wasn't a question. She'd guessed as much back in the refrigeration room.

"Not exclusively. I also do stand-up."

"Bet this place gives you lots of material."

"It's an angle. And everyone's afraid to heckle me. That's a nice bonus."

"You'll let me look in Silvana Potenza's purse if I pass on your head shot?"

"What do you call that in show business? Reciprocity?"

"Actually, we call it blackmail," Bex said, then brightened. "Not that there's anything wrong with that. Stace, I would be happy to pass on your head shot."

He smiled. "I'll be right back."

This time, Stace returned with a plastic bag tucked loosely under his arm. Inside was a brown suede bag with a golden clasp and a strap long enough to throw over your shoulder. Now that she was looking at it, Bex recognized the bag as a part of Silvana's ensemble. She never went anywhere without it.

Bex eagerly flipped open the clasp and reached inside. Her first discovery was an empty tissue packet. Oooh, Bex, alert the media, this is earthshaking stuff.

The sarcastic retort flitted through her head before Bex realized the irony. Hey, she *was* the media. Well, better alert herself, then.

Her next discovery was even more exciting. A half-eaten packet of lemon-flavored hard candy. Now, in a traditional murder mystery, Bex might have insisted on having it checked for poison. But, as far as she knew, the pharmacology world had yet to develop an elixir which, when mixed with sugar and food coloring drove otherwise sensible women to fling themselves into puddles while clutching electric light cords.

Next came a tube of lipstick. Same issues as the candy.

A bottle of ibuprofen and a bottle of aspirin, both extra-strength. Obviously, the previous night's accusations had taken quite a physical toll on Silvana, and she wasn't expecting the new day to be any better.

A stack of twenty postcards. Bex flipped through the scenic imagery of the Golden Gate Bridge, Fisherman's Wharf, cable cars, cable cars in front of the Golden Gate Bridge rolling by Fisherman's Wharf. . . . Two of the postcards seemed to be missing. Oh, boy! Bex's first clue! She wondered what it meant. Clearly, it suggested that Silvana Potenza liked to send postcards.

Bex mustn't forget to write that down.

At the very bottom of Silvana's bag, Bex found a cell phone. It was the standard ISU-issued one, with their sticker on the back. Desperate to keep close tabs on their judges at every competition, the governing body made a practice of handing out local cell phones, then collecting them at the end of the event. Bex didn't know how the judges felt about the phones, but she personally found them very helpful. If she needed an unexpected question answered, all she had to do was refer to the handy-dandy phone sheet issued by the ISU and call the judge or official she wanted.

Except that, at the moment, the only question she really wanted answered was who killed Silvana Potenza. And she didn't think calling her would do the trick. Absently, Bex flipped open the dead woman's phone. For a moment, she even seriously contemplated dialing M for murder, to see what would happen. For the next moment, she seriously contemplated the stupidity of her impulse. And then, for the first time that day, Bex actually did something clever. She punched *69 to find out where the last call Silvana ever received had come from.

The phone rang. And rang. And rang. No answering machine, no rollover to a voice mail. Just ringing. It gave Bex time to contemplate what exactly she was expecting to hear.

"Hiya, Murder Central, here."

Okay. Now, she definitely wasn't expecting that.

"Uh . . . hello?" Bex's gift of gab, so sparkling as long as the conversation sparkled exclusively in her head, wobbled like a skater landing on a bad edge. "Who—who is this?"

"Who's this?"

"I'm Bex."

"Hiya, Bex."

"Uhm . . . hiya. Can I—can I ask you a question?"

"Shoot."

Interesting choice of words. "Why did you answer the phone Murder Central?"

"Oh, was that in bad taste? I didn't mean it. I was just making a joke. You know, because of the judge that died and everything."

"You know about the judge?"

"Well, yeah. I'm standing right here."

"Where's here?"

"I'm standing like five feet away from the room where they found her."

"You're in the arena?"

"Yup. I work here. I run the scoreboard. Name is Corky."

"Corky . . ."

"It's a nickname. For Zachary."

"I see."

"I couldn't pronounce my name when I was little, and so it came out sounding like—"

"Corky?"

"Right. It came out sounding like Corky."

"No. I mean, yes, I'm sure it did. But, Corky, what I meant was—is this an office phone at the arena that I called?"

"Pay phone."

"It's a pay phone?"

"Right. I was just walking by and the phone was ringing, and then I walked by again and it was still ringing, and I figured boy, somebody really needs to talk, so I picked it up and made that joke about Murder Central, 'cause I happened to be looking at all the police tape and all, but I didn't mean anything by it."

"Thank you, Corky," Bex said.

"No prob."

"It was very nice talking to you."

"Double the pleasure on this end."

"Well . . . bye."

"Bye, Bex."

She hung up the phone and told Stace, "The last person Silvana talked to called her from the arena pay phone right across from the refrigeration room where she died!"

"Is that a fact?"

"It is." Bex waited for him to say something. When he didn't, she prodded, "Well?"

"Well, what?"

"Doesn't that give you any ideas? Doesn't that prove that maybe somebody lured Silvana and that, before she got there, they fixed up the room so she'd have to step into a puddle to pull the light switch, and—"

"Zap?"

"Exactly!"

"Who did it?"

"I don't know!"

"Exactly," Stace repeated.

Bex rolled her eyes. Gil's favorite phrase popped into her mind, "You're killing me, here, guys, you're *killing* me!"

As a last-ditch effort, she reached into Silvana's purse to see if there might not be some final item hidden in its suede depths that would make everything just fall into place.

Nope. Nothing. Bex flipped her hand around and felt along the walls. Her fingers brushed against a folded sheet of paper that had escaped previous detection by lying flat so smoothly, Bex had presumed it was part of the purse.

She pulled it out. She unfolded it.

She saw the printout of an E-mail sent to Silvana Potenza the morning before the ladies' long program. Listing the ladies' finish order as Xenia Trubin first and Erin Simpson second. And signed Sergei Alemazov.

Xenia's coach.

Three

She refused to get excited about this. After all, if Sherlock Holmes had gotten excited about his first-ever, bona fide clue, the hounds of the Baskervilles might have eaten him before he ever had the chance to find a second one. So Bex remained calm. Eerily calm. Lest her premature excitement frighten the clue back into hiding.

She double-checked the date. Yup, definitely the morning of the ladies' long program. Hours before the final results were posted. And yet, here they were, the final results. Xenia first, Erin second, Jordan Ares third. Not their standings after the short program. Their standings after the long. Which had yet to take place. Yup. There it was. And signed by Xenia's coach, too. A chap with a definite vested interested in seeing his girl atop the podium.

And here was something else superinteresting. The piece of paper Bex was holding in her hand was smaller than a normal-sized piece of paper. About two and a half inches

smaller, in point of fact. Which might not have meant anything to the average amateur sleuth. But an amateur sleuth
who'd spent the last several months on the road desperately
trying to make European-sized paper match up with American-
sized hole punchers and binders knew one very important
fact: European paper was smaller than American paper.
Ergo, this E-mail had to have been printed on a European
printer. Most likely by a European.

Was it time to get excited?

Yes, Bex thought it might very well be that time.

She thrust the E-mail printout at Stace and announced, "I
need to take this with me."

"Uh . . . let me think about that . . . No." Stace had obviously been honing his delivery at the comedy clubs, because
it came out perfectly. Alas, Bex wasn't amused.

"Okay, then, not the original E-mail. But, can I at least
have a copy?"

"Still sensing a no on the horizon, there, Bex. Sorry."

"How would you like to be a TV star?" Bex asked.

And waited.

She had his attention. Bex could tell because he had yet
to utter a pithy refusal. "Here's the deal," she said. "We're
doing a special about Silvana Potenza's . . . uh . . . death on
Sunday, live during the exhibition show. Obviously we're
going to need an expert to talk about how she died and
everything."

"And who might that expert be?" Stace raised an eyebrow.

"You get me a copy of this E-mail, and I'll get you a spot
on coast-to-coast national television." Bex hoped she at least
sounded convincing, since everything following the word
"and" was a big old puff of smoke. Bex was a researcher, not
a producer. She had about as much control over who got on

the air as Mickey, the roll-tape guy. Actually, Mickey probably had more, since he was physically in the truck and had
access to buttons and switches and, if he really wanted to,
could send the whole network into black with the click of a
finger. Bex had access to nothing. Well, except this E-mail.
And right now, she wasn't about to give that up for anything
in the world. She would worry about the subsequent details . . . subsequently.

Stace said, "Deal."

Five minutes later, Bex was standing on the police station
steps, using her head, her arms, her coat, anything she could
think of to protect the precious E-mail from San Francisco's
version of a spring breeze, also known as whipping, icy rain.
In that moment, Bex sincerely believed that the single-sheet
copy, with its smudge of gray at the top where the shorter,
European page ended, its mumbo jumbo of computer code
at the bottom, and its unspeakably gorgeous list of names in
between, was truly the loveliest item Bex had ever been
privileged to lay eyes on.

Okay. Now. Job descriptionally speaking, Bex was now
obligated to scurry her tail right on over to Gil's and give
him a full report. He would then take her E-mail, put it on
the air, and promote the hell out of it. Other news outlets
would inevitably pick it up. The Trubin/Simpson controversy would return to the front page. Ratings for the live exhibition broadcast would go through the roof. Bex would be
a hero. The girl who saved figure skating from both controversy and obscurity.

Assuming she was right.

If she was wrong, if the E-mail didn't mean what they'd
all jump to conclusions it meant, and if somebody could

prove that was the case, 24/7 Sports would end up with egg on their faces, lawsuits galore would rain down upon them like locusts, the ISU would never sell them the rights to another championship, and Rebecca E. Levy (didn't legal depositions always use full names?) would go down in history as the woman who bankrupted a sports federation *and* a TV network. (Also, she doubted if, after all that, they'd let her keep her job).

Bex wiped a sprinkle of raindrops from the E-mail.

And decided to do a touch more investigating before going to Gil.

It didn't matter where any given championship was being held—Dubrovnik, Finland, or Paris, France—Bex's favorite place at a competition was always the official competitors' hotel. Not only because the sight of it meant Bex's twenty-hour day might finally be coming to an end and she might get a chance to rest her weary, throbbing head upon yet another pillow smelling of disinfectant (which, honestly, was preferable to yet another pillow smelling of rodent poison), but because, inevitably, the official hotel was where all the real action took place.

Sure, the arena was where people skated and fates were decided and tears of joy, sadness, or just plain old relief were shed. But the arena was also where competitors threw their arms around each other and posed for the press to dispel all those "rivalry" rumors, where female pair skaters and their gay partners stuck their tongues down each other's throats to prove that they really, truly were in love and engaged and no one should believe rumors to the contrary, and where coaches and former students who'd parted on the most vitriolic of terms shook hands and wished each other all the luck in the world.

Blech. Just watching that stuff made Bex feel like a tub of Crisco had been dumped over her head.

She much preferred the competitor's hotel. Namely, the backroom competitor's (and coaches and officials) lounge where neither reporters nor fans were allowed. (Bex, of course, didn't count as either.) While print media weren't allowed in the skaters' lounge, as Gil was so fond of reminding, television's purchase of the event meant they could be anywhere, anytime. And thank goodness for that. Because where else could you see the reigning men's champion (in full view of the female ice dancer who only a week earlier he'd held hands with as they strolled through beautiful, downtown San Francisco, pointedly stopping to gaze upon window displays of engagement rings as a 24/7 camera whirled in ecstasy) remove the pink feather boa from around his neck and use it to lasso one of his main competitors into a kiss and public grope? Or Canada's sweetheart, the underage spokesperson for her national antidrug campaign, light up a cigarette and follow it up with a glass of red wine? Or Russia's champion pair skaters, who publicly swore they would never, ever leave their beloved homeland no matter how bad the financial situation got, systematically walking from one federation president to another, handing out cards with a list of demands to be fulfilled before the pair agreed to switch beloved homelands?

It was the best show in town and the best place to find a skater during their downtime. Why not? The room had food, drinks, music, video games, and more intrigue than an episode of *As the World Turns*. In fact, one skater dubbed it *As the Toe Picks*.

Bex went in looking for Sergei Alemazov. She figured

the author of the E-mail was a logical place to begin ferreting out its veracity. She searched around the coaches' table. She found Igor Marchenko, Jordan Ares's coach, and Gary Gold, Lian Reilley's coach, sitting side by side, each with a plate of food in front of them, dutifully cutting, chewing, swallowing, and taking sips of sparkling water all without once looking in the other's direction. Even when they reached for condiments, which required leaning across the other person, their eyes somehow managed to always be gazing some other way. So much for that "we're all one big, happy family" line everyone from the Connecticut Olympic Training Center was always laying on.

To Igor's left sat the Russian coaching contingent (as a Russian working in the U.S., Bex guessed Igor was some sort of table no-man's-land), a half-dozen former Soviets equally divided between sour-faced men in bright red coats and matching noses sporting either bad comb-overs or really bad toupees and, in one disturbing case, both, and zaftig women with teased hairstyles as big as their shoulders and bursts of hair spray crackling when they turned their heads—not unlike the northern lights. Unfortunately, Sergei Alemazov, the one Russian coach Bex had ever met who didn't fit the stereotype—honestly, the man was such an original he didn't fit *any* stereotype—wasn't there.

All right, then. On to Step B. If the Zamboni didn't come to the ice surface, the ice surface would just have to go to the Zamboni. And if Bex couldn't find Sergei, then Xenia, the next best thing, would just have to do.

Fortunately, she was much easier to find than her coach. As noted earlier, the current shade of her hair evoked nothing so much as a carrot burning in hell. Even among the peculiar skaters who periodically streaked their hair to match their costumes—pink, purple, and blue being the most pop-

ular colors—Xenia stood out. That afternoon, she was sitting all alone in the corner of the room, staring out the
window and nervously tapping her fingers, painted to match
her hair, on the windowsill. The other skaters seemed to
be keeping their distance from her. Probably afraid that
contested victories might be catching.

"Xenia?" Bex called the (for the moment) world champion's name and instinctively recoiled, all the while wondering what she was so scared of. Xenia Trubin may have
looked tall on the ice, especially when she was performing
her dance of down-with-capitalism, but she was barely five
foot three. Which, while making her a virtual giant among
the skating Lilliputian set, still placed her at an inch shorter
than Bex. And sure, she was probably in better shape that
Bex, and stronger, but she was hardly challenging her to arm
wrestle. Still, there was something about the Russian champion, something about her air of wanting to be left alone,
that was, in spite of logic, a bit intimidating. She was
twenty-six years old, only two years older than Bex, but
she'd been competing internationally for over a decade, and
her world-weariness made her seem a half century older, and
thus more formidable.

Xenia turned her head slowly, as if still in the process of
deciding whether or not she wanted to do it. She saw Bex
and raised her palm up toward the sky, questioning, "Yes? "

"Hi. I—I'm Bex Levy. I'm the 24/7 researcher. I talked
to you before the competition started, to get information for
our announcers. Do you remember?"

Xenia looked unconvinced, but she did manage a nod.
"Yes."

"Can I ask you a couple of questions now?"

"You do not want to speaking with me."

That sure was news to Bex. "I—uh—don't?"

"No. Speaking is two people. You talk, I listen; I talk, you listen. But you do not want to listen. You only want I should to say I am sorry I win. You want I should say Erin Simpson is perfect flower in green garden of figure skating. How dare Xenia Trubin win title American Erin Simpson want. Yes? This is what you want? Sorry much, I not say it."

"You believe you won fairly?" Bex asked, not accusing, truly curious to hear what Xenia thought about the whole fiasco. On the other hand, Bex had never met a skater who, no matter how badly they'd skated, didn't think they still deserved to win, if only on the artistic mark, on reputation, or even personality. So the surprise factor here was low.

"The judges say I win, so I win. When I am fifteen years old, my first world champion competition, I land seven triple jumps, more than any other lady. The judges say I no win. I no win. Is the rules. Is the sport."

"You know, I understand what you're feeling. It really isn't fair."

"Fair," Xenia snorted. "Only in America, people say fair, fair, fair. I ask question—you born in America, I born in Russia, somebody stranger born in Africa. Where is fair?"

Bex wasn't sure how to answer her question. She'd come prepared to talk skating and maybe a little murder. Not Philosophy 101.

"In America, skating costs much money, yes?"

"Yes," Bex agreed. "It's very expensive, you're right."

"So, when you pick American champion, you pick best skater in America, or best skater in America with money?"

"I suppose you're right. . . ." How was it Bex had strode in ready to make like Emile Zola and *"J'Accuse"* everyone in sight, and suddenly here she was feeling like a Bible had been slipped under her palm and a promise to tell the truth, the whole truth, and nothing but the truth, extracted?

"They close my ice rink in Russia. Sell it to Mafia to gamble on hockey games. Now, is hockey all day. One hour free for figure skating. Ice not good for figure skating. Many breaks. And no heating. Pipes break, nobody fix. Costs money. I visit American training centers. Good ice, warm air, sunshine in windows. We come to world championship. We compete. Is fair?"

"Well, no. . . . But, if you factored in training conditions, you'd have to factor in things like injuries and genetic predisposition and—"

"For eleven years, I come to world championship. Six years ago, federation president call me to meeting. I think maybe he send me to new rink. Warmer, better ice. He tell me, "Xenia, we think you are finished in figure skating. Your results not so good. Many, many chances, no gold medals. Russia want gold medals. Is country pride. You are country disgrace.""

Over her shoulder, Bex snuck a look at the Russian federation president, he of the bad comb-over and dead-ferret–like toupee. Not for a moment did she doubt him capable of making such a blunt assessment and then sharing it with his subject.

"But, it worked out okay for you, didn't it? I mean, it must have motivated you. You won the silver the following year."

"Silver," Xenia said pointedly, "is no gold."

Alchemically speaking, she was right. But Bex had the feeling they weren't discussing merely precious metals, here.

"For six years, I work and I work and I not quit, even when my president says no more money. Even when first coach says, "I wash hands of Xenia. No more." I must to beg Sergei to take me as student, and Sergei only take because everybody else say, "Bad, bad," and Sergei, he likes to be different, yes?"

"I'd heard that about him, yes."

There wasn't a soul in skating who hadn't heard of Sergei Alemazov's . . . quirks. As an amateur skater, he'd been notorious for making up routines on the spot, often in the middle of a competition, the more major the better. He also snuck shots of vodka before stepping onto the ice. "Is good for blood vigor and manly juices," he explained. And, at his own Olympics, after getting marked lower than he thought he deserved on a figure, he'd skated over to the barrier and informed the referee he was retiring from the sport—right now, in the middle of his event.

"But, too bad for me, American media decide: if world championship is in America, then American must to win gold medal. 'And when judges disagree, media say, "Cheat, cheat!"

Bex wished she could argue. But she'd been in the booth with Francis and Diana.

"Actually, the judges are what I wanted to talk to you—"

Xenia said, "I know Mafia."

Bex wondered how one said non sequitur in Russian. And then, because her brain just happened to work that way and there was nothing she could do about it, Bex wondered how you said non sequitur in English.

And then she said, "Huh?"

"Yes. Mafia. I tell you. At rink, is all Mafia. Mafia today is same as KGB yesterday. Much money, much power. No law."

"I believe you." And Bex did. She had a standing policy to believe anyone who said they had Mafia connections. She suspected she'd live longer that way.

"I tell them to stop you, television, telling lies about me. They stop you."

There was a threat in there, Bex felt pretty sure of that. And she was also sure that Xenia, in her fury at the various large, international media conglomerates that had made what should have been the best day in her life so miserable, had decided to project a human face onto said media conglomerates. And she'd chosen Bex's mug as the scapegoat of choice.

Bex didn't think this couldn't possibly be good. Despite her mental chastising of Gil's political incorrectness earlier, she couldn't help entertaining a stereotypical thought of her own: *I sure hope I don't wake up to find a Russian herring's head in my bed tomorrow.*

Still, being a researcher, she had to make certain: "Are you threatening me, Xenia?"

"I know Mafia people." Xenia shrugged. "Friends. They not want to see me sad. They fix problems for me."

Problems like . . . Silvana Poteneza?

It was an obvious leap, and Bex would have been a coward not to pursue it directly.

On the other hand, Xenia did say she knew Mafia people, and Bex did have that policy. . . .

So maybe a little tentative hemming and hawing was in order.

"Actually, Xenia, see, the thing is, I didn't really come to talk about the fuss everyone's making about who did or didn't deserve to win. I wanted to talk to you about Silvana Potenza."

Xenia's brow furrowed. Bex bit her tongue to keep from telling her to quit it. It would cause wrinkles, and if she couldn't afford to skate at a decent ice rink, she definitely wouldn't be able to afford the necessary Botox. Life was unfair that way, you know.

Xenia said, "Silvana, she to die this morning. Sergei tells me."

"Yes. Right. She died. We're doing a story about her death. Did you know her?"

Xenia shrugged. "Judge? I see judge in hall, in elevator, I say, "Hello, how are you?" Judge says, "Fine, thank you.""

"And that's it? That's all?"

"Well, maybe . . . no. . . ."

"No?" Bex repeated.

"Sometimes she say, "Xenia, you should to work more on this jump," or "Xenia, maybe you change little piece of music at end of program to make more exciting finish.""

Oh. Hardly the stuff exposés were made of. Bex mashed down her disappointment. "And that's really all?"

Another shrug. This time more dismissive. And then, like a spotlight going on for an exhibition number, Xenia's face glowed with newfound enlightenment. She turned to fully face Bex for the first time since their conversation began. She reached forward with her right hand, simultaneously beckoning Bex closer and grabbing the power position in their discussion. Earlier, Bex had the questions and expected Xenia to provide her with answers.

Now, Xenia was in charge.

She smiled. The way soap opera characters did right before they maliciously revealed being pregnant with their brother-in-law's baby. Bex wasn't expecting a surprise nearly as juicy. But the smile did get her hopes up. And really freaked her out.

Xenia said, "Silvana is dead. ISU say was accident. Was not accident."

"How do you know that?" The words were out of Bex's

mouth before she realized that probably qualified as giving away too much. And then she wondered if Xenia had also promised Stace a moment in the sun in exchange for inside info. Or maybe her Mafia friends did.

"Accident," Xenia snorted. "Stupid, stupid ISU. What judge go for to freezing room? Is stupid. You know skating, you know accident is stupid lie."

Bex said, "I'm trying to find out who killed her."

This was the part where, Bex figured, your average Joe American would have responded with, "Since when are you a cop?" or "What right do you have to do that? What right do you even have to be asking me questions?" But Xenia the Russian, who'd in the past decade seen her country go from an iron fist where crimes were defined and undefined on the whim of a mercurial government to a virtual anarchy where crimes were defined and undefined on the whim of a mer-curial . . . something, didn't seem to find it odd at all that a middling television researcher had dubbed herself detective and was going around questioning suspects with all the au-thority vested in her by no one.

Xenia said, "Maybe ISU kill her."

Well, it was a thought . . . except for: "Why would they do that?"

"Embarrass. She embarrass them. She no go on televi-sion and say, I judge fair, I no cheat, Xenia is winner, Erin Simpson loser. Everyone say bad about ISU. So ISU fix problem."

"Maybe . . ." Bex let the thought trail off as she pondered the most delicate way to phrase her next query. "Except that I don't think anyone from the ISU was at the arena when Sil-vana died. They were all at some press conference. I know, because I was supposed to go do a report on it, but I had to be at a production meeting, and as I keep telling Gil, I can't be in two places at the same time, no matter how much he may want me to be, so . . ." Xenia's face radiated the Russian equivalent of *Now tell me why the hell I should care about your personal problems?* so Bex wisely ended her digressive trail of thought and refocused on the issue at hand. "Anyway, no one from the ISU was at the arena the morning Silvana died. But, actually, Xenia, you and Sergei were. Right? You had a practice for the exhibition on Sunday. And that's when Silvana was killed. During that practice time."

"You think I kill her." It was a statement not a question. And it came complete with flaring nostrils and cheekbones flushing almost the exact shade of Xenia's hair.

"Well, actually, I'm just trying to figure out where everyone—"

"Use your stupid head! Silvana vote me winner! Why I should kill her? I should say thank you! Erin Simpson! Erin Simpson is angry one!"

Actually, at the moment, Bex could certainly argue the veracity of that statement. Not that she really wanted to. Xenia's raising her voice had already drawn a few curious stares from the other skaters and officials. The gentleman with the boa even stopped using it as a boy-toy lasso to look over and see what the fuss was about. Comrade Ferret Head put down his wineglass and did the same thing. Bex was tempted to pull out her research credential, wield the badge, and announce, "Nothing to see here, move it along, move it along." Mainly because she wasn't interested in everyone knowing her extracurricular interests until she was ready to spring the news in a classy and clever manner. And also because she thought it would be a really neat thing to do, and, honestly, how often in life would she get the opportunity?

Having Xenia scream it to the universe was neither classy nor very clever.

"Shhhhh . . ." Bex flapped her arms like she was trying to put out a fire in Xenia's lap. Also neither classy nor clever. But, it got the job done. Xenia lowered her voice. Bex suspected she wasn't too interested in putting on an off-ice show, either.

"Why you talk to me?" Xenia snapped. "You talk to Erin Simpson! Erin is also on same exhibition practice. And Jordan. And Lian. Everybody at practice. You go to talk to them."

"Actually, the person I would really like to talk to is Sergei."

"Sergei not only coach at arena. Also Igor and Gary, and, of course, Patty. Patty look at me with evil eye. She say to Erin to bump into me on practice. Try and hurt me."

Xenia stood several inches taller than Erin and actually looked like a woman rather than an adolescent. It was difficult to imagine what sort of damage Erin could do to her. But the fact was, when people were zipping around at top speed wearing knives strapped to their feet, size really didn't matter. Intimidation came from those willing to wield it. Bex had seen a tiny ice dancer take down the hulking male half of her main competition simply by stopping a split second too late. Oh, of course, she'd burst into tears immediately afterward and defended herself by pointing to the injury she herself had sustained from that horrible, horrible, unexpected and unpreventable accident. The tiny terror had a scratch across her forearm. Her opponent's thigh was sliced down to the bone. He was out for the season. Oops.

Of course, it was a far cry from a tussle on the ice to a corpse in the refrigeration room.

Or was it, really?

These were weird people she was dealing with. They had

their own priorities, their own logic. And their own reasons for making someone else look bad.

Bex filed away Xenia's accusation about Patty and Erin and resolved to look into it. But she was far from buying the Simpsons-equals-devils scenario quite yet.

"Well, thank you for your time, Xenia." Bex attempted to back out quietly and carefully. With no clue as to when the next fit of accusation hysteria might strike Xenia, Bex figured it would be best to remove the trigger, i.e., herself.

"I don't kill Silvana Potenza." Thank God Xenia decided to whisper rather than shout that final missive. Obviously, she understood that everyone knowing about Bex's extracurricular interests wouldn't do her a world of good, either. After all, it was one thing to be suspected of winning your gold medal unfairly. Murder was a whole other thing.

Even in the skating world.

"Okay," Bex said. Because, as far as she knew, the only tangible response to such a declaration would have to be *I believe you* or *As if!* At the moment, she felt ill prepared to back up either option.

Xenia picked up on Bex's ambivalence. Because she repeated, for emphasis, "Me and Sergei not only people in arena. Erin and Patty, Jordan and Igor, Lian and Gary. You ask them. Ask them about Silvana. They know. They all know the truth."

Four

So Erin and Patty, Jordan and Igor, and Lian and Gary, they all knew the truth. Fabulous. Bex felt like she was halfway home. Now, all she needed to do was figure out what exactly the scope of their knowledge might be, and this case was as good as solved. And people went to detective school to learn how to do this?

Naturally, Xenia was no help in the matter. Following her rather cryptic statement, she simply stood up and walked past Bex to take a seat next to the Russian federation president. Considering how Xenia felt about the man (and Bex was actually extrapolating how one would feel about a man who'd called you a national disgrace and then cut your funding, to boot), Bex could only presume that, at the moment, Xenia nevertheless found him a safer and more pleasant companion. Which was very interesting and obviously meant something. The question was: What? Was Xenia afraid because Bex was on the right track about the motive behind Silvana Potenza's murder? Or was she simply trying to get away from more questions by hiding behind the ferret toupee? And if she was trying to get away from more questions, then why? Because Bex was on the right track about the motive behind Silvana Potenza's murder, or because the conversation was boring her? Or maybe she was just hungry and wanted lunch. The cold cuts and sandwich buffet did still look good, even if the Swiss cheese was starting to go a little dry and curly around the edges.

Actually, now that she thought about it, Bex could see how having done a semester or two in detective school might have helped her answer some of the questions currently swimming about her brain like blind guppies with a distinct lack of direction.

She pondered her next step. Logic dictated that this was the spot where a reasonable person might acknowledge being in over her sleepy head and perhaps pass the investigation on to someone more qualified. Which, at this point, included anyone and everyone both on and off the premises. But, if Bex had possessed a tiny iota of logic, she'd also have pursued a more reasonable major in college. Like anything with an actual title. "General knowledge," after all, could only take you so far. No one taught Homicide 101 at Sarah Lawrence. Only critical thinking. Which Bex was, at the moment, doing intensely. When her B-minus knowledge of the subject told Bex to press on with the Sam Spade I-work-alone bit, she did pause for a period to wonder if she were making the right choice. But by then it was too late.

She was already standing outside the door of Sergei Alemazov's hotel room.

When she remembered that a B-minus really meant just a fraction above average—and an average person would recognize the folly of what she was doing, wouldn't she?—then it was really too late.

Sergei Alemazov had opened the door and was standing directly in front of her.

Or maybe Bex should have used the word *looming*. Because, in skating terms, the former Russian and European champ was a giant. The problem with trying to gauge a person's height while they were standing on the ice was the fact that, out all alone surrounded just by white on either side, there was no frame of reference to compare with. And, since skaters tended to have long, fluid limbs, it was easy to assume that all the men were a minimum of six feet tall. They weren't. Most of them barely reached five ten and even that was frequently a combination of standing on skates and having really pouffy hair.

Not Sergei, though. He had to be at least six foot two, with each forearm the size of a small hippo's leg, and each thigh the size of a Communist revolution cannon. He wore a bright blue track suit circa 1970, with a zipper that once may have been gleaming white, but now showed dull, silver nicks and tears. His sneakers, however, were American high-tops, brand-new. Obviously, this was a man who had his priorities straight.

At this point, Bex was getting used to the ruddy facial tinge boasted by most Russian men. She'd even made a game out of guessing how long before the slightly sunburned look would be replaced for each by the blue-vein relief map of a bulbous nose and broken capillaries under the eyes. Knowing of Sergei's propensity towards precompetition carbo loading that came in liquid form and was good for "vitality and the manly juices," Bex had been expecting a particularly detailed cartography demonstration. That's where he surprised her. His complexion was quite clear, youthful even, and the only redness about his head came from his thick, curly hair. Bex wondered if his had been the shade Xenia was actually trying to match when she fell into the vat of hell-burning carrots. At the same time, Bex also understood why Sergei had never done as well in front of Western judges as a Russian champion might have expected to. She guessed it would be difficult to take seriously a high-concept free program about how all men were brothers under the skin who must band together to overthrow their ꞁ﹐ꞁꞁꞁꞁꞁꞁꞁꞁꞁ ꞁꞁꞁ ꞁꞁ﹟ꞁꞁꞁꞁ, ꞃꞁꞁꞁꞁ꞊ ꞁꞁ ꞃꞁꞁ꞉ ꞁꞁ꞉ꞁꞁꞁ꞊ ꞁꞁ꞊ꞁꞁꞁꞁꞁꞁꞁꞁ ꞁꞁ ꞁꞁꞁꞁꞁꞁꞁ꞊ who looked like the product of a forbidden love affair between Popeye the sailorman and Ronald McDonald. (Not that there was anything wrong with that.)

"Hello," he said. Which, under the circumstances, was a perfectly reasonable thing to do.

What a shame Bex was failing to come up with something equally pithy.

"Uh—hello. Hello, Sergei. Hello."

And here, they'd come to the crux of another burning issue. Bex was twenty-four years old. Growing up, she'd been drilled by her parents that the only proper way to address strangers who were older than you, was using Mr., Mrs., or Miss. Maybe Ms., but preferably only if the person in question either ran a magazine of the same name or was somehow related to PacMan. Calling older strangers by their first names wasn't even an option in the Levy household.

Alas, the world of skating took place primarily outside the Levy household.

And in the world of skating, first names were de rigueur. For a number of reasons. One of them was standing in front of Bex right now. A Russian. Russians had first names. Russians had last names. Often long and difficult to pronounce last names—but they had them. However, Russians were not called Mr., Mrs., Miss/Ms. and then their last names. If you wished to address an older Russian person with respect, you would call them by their first name, and then by their patronymic, which was actually a complicated distortion of their father's first name. In other words, if Bex were addressing a man named Ivan whose father's name was Peter, she would be compelled to call him Ivan Petrov. If she were addressing Ivan's sister, Marusya, she would be Marusya Petrovna. If Bex were then addressing Peter himself, and his father's name was Boris, Peter would be Peter Borisovitch. His sister, Ludmilla, would be Ludmilla Borisovna. And so on and so on, with various names having different conjugations depending on their gender and their final letters. It was all quite logical once you actually bit the bullet, knuckled down and, like Bex did her first week on the job, studied it. But it wasn't easy. And television, Gil explained to Bex her second week on the job, likes things easy.

Which was why, for skating purposes, all Russians had only first names when spoken about and addressed on the air, and only first and last names when they were Chyroned during a broadcast (the only exception being Russians who had particularly difficult-to-pronounce first names, like Stanislav or the aforementioned Ludmilla, at which point they were to be given nicknames like Stan and Millie and exclusively called that while they were skating and later while being interviewed). To show how the arrangement wasn't personal or culturally insensitive in the slightest, Gil also pointed out that 24/7 had a policy regarding the Chinese skaters as well. Even though 24/7 knew full well that in China a person's family name came first and their given name last, 24/7 would reverse the order on air and on the Chyron. Because, well, because they could.

Which brought Bex back to her current dilemma.

"Hello, Sergei," she said, knowing full well that she was being disrespectful in both his culture and her own. And knowing full well there wasn't a damn thing she could do about it.

"What can I do for you, Miss?" Oh. And one more thing to discombobulate her. Popeye and Ronald McDonald's Russian love child sounded eerily like Paul McCartney. In an interview at the start of the season, Sergei had told Bex that he taught himself English by buying bootleg Soviet Beatles records, transcribing the songs, and looking each word up in the dictionary.

"Oh, right, yes," Bex stammered, wishing that, at the moment, her English were half as good as his. "Listen, we're doing a special for the Sunday exhibition on Silvana Potenza's death. Do you think I could come in and maybe ask you a few questions?"

Did Bex imagine it, or did Sergei actually flex those head-to-toe rippling muscles of his as he considered her request? She tried to remember her *Murder, She Wrote*: Was it prudent to walk alone into the hotel room of a potential murder suspect who looked like he could crack her skull like a walnut merely by pursing his muscular lips?

"All right," Sergei said after a beat and stepped aside from the door to let her pass.

Guess Bex was about to find out the answer to her question. (For the record, she was really hoping it was *yes*.)

His hotel room was standard issue. Two double beds, two end tables, two lamps, a chair by the window, a TV, a full-length mirror, and a dresser, on top of which lay what looked to Bex like half the breakfast buffet from the competitors' lounge downstairs. There were slices of bread stuffed into plastic baggies, cold cuts and cheese, packets of tea, three apples, four boxes of cold cereal, and a bagel that looked

prechewed, as if it had been stuffed into somebody's pocket.
And then Bex remembered: while the local organizing committee made sure that skaters had tickets for their meals,
they usually didn't distribute them to the coaches. The
coaches had to buy the passes to eat in the competitors'
lounge. Most could easily afford it. Some clearly couldn't.

Sergei saw Bex looking at his hoard and swallowed in
embarrassment. He shifted from foot to foot, then abruptly
barked, "So. You wished to speak to me about Silvana?"

"Yes." Bex nodded furiously, as if vigor could wipe away
both his embarrassment and her embarrassment at causing
his embarrassment and so on and so on. "I do. I—I want to
show you something."

He crossed his arms. It looked like two jumbo jets refu-
eling. "Very well."

Bex reached into her research binder, feeling her hand
trembling and reasoning that it had a pretty good cause to do
so. After all, if walking alone into the hotel room of a potential murder suspect who looked like he could crack her
skull like a walnut merely by pursing his muscular lips was
less than prudent, what in the world would Angela Lansbury
say about taunting and/or infuriating said murder suspect by
showing him her one piece of evidence?

Bex slipped the E-mail copy out of the binder and folded
it at the top so that Sergei's return E-mail address wasn't instantly visible. She took a small step toward him and
stretched her arm forward, close enough for Sergei to see the
list of skaters' names in their order of finish but far enough
away that, if he wanted to grab it, she could still spring back.

At least, that was the plan. Bex figured it was always
good to have a plan.

Bex said, "Silvana had this E-mail in her purse when she
died."

Sergei squinted, trying to read the small print, but at no point did he make any effort to actually reach for the copy or bring it closer. Bex was most grateful for that. On top of her fear of being murdered, dismembered, and tucked away in a plastic bag next to the squished bagel, there was also her fear of Sergei grabbing the E-mail, ripping it up, Bex not being able to get another copy from Stace and, as a result, feeling most stupid. To be honest, Bex wasn't even sure which doomsday scenario she was actually most afraid of. At least, when you were dead, you didn't have to live with your stupidity.

Sergei said, "That list, it's not accurate, you know?"

"What?" Bex had been so busy imagining him stuffing the plastic bags full of her into the minibar and some hapless tourist stumbling upon them when he only wanted a ten-dollar can of Fresca, that she hadn't even bothered following along with what Sergei was reading.

"Yes, look, right here." Sergei lightly tapped the E-mail with his finger, making Bex realize that what she'd assumed to be a safe distance was actually about as safe as a stop sign at the edge of a cliff. "After the top three girls, Xenia, Erin, Jordan, the list is actually not at all consistent with the final standings."

"It isn't?" Bex hated to admit it, but she hadn't looked beyond the top three, figuring everything else was irrelevant.

"No, it's not. For instance, cast your eyes, here, at Lian Reilley. She is ninth on this list, when I believe she finished seventh overall, did she not?"

"Uhm . . ." Bex said.

"This isn't the final standing for the ladies' final."

Bex turned the E-mail to face her and finally deigned to look lower than third place—like she should have done in the first place. "No, you're right, it's not. Definitely not." But then a brainstorm slapped her, and she practically jumped in place from the impact. "Sergei, do you have the competition protocol handy?"

The protocol, a four-colored book of all the results, including every judge's marks for every skater during the course of the competition—pink for the ladies, blue for the men, yellow for pairs, and green for dance—was printed and handed out as soon as the last event was officially completed. Bex's was back at the production trailer. But fortunately, Sergei had one handy.

He handed the book to Bex, and she eagerly leafed through it, finding exactly what she was looking for in minutes. She was a researcher, after all.

This time, she actually checked closely, comparing every name on the E-mail against the one in the protocol before leaping to her conclusion.

"Aha," she said, mostly because she'd always wanted to, and those opportunities, like the ones for visiting a police station, did come up so rarely. "Look," she pounded her finger triumphantly against the pink sheets. "The list on the E-mail, it may not be the official, final result, but it *is* exactly how Silvana voted. Lian Reilley may have finished seven overall on the ordinals, but Silvana had her in ninth place."

"Oh," Sergei said. "I see. Well, then, I suppose that is logical."

Bex said, "Silvana got this E-mail the morning before the ladies' final, and that night, she voted exactly the way the E-mail told her to."

"Yes," Sergei nodded. "That would seem to be the case under consideration."

Bex asked, "Do you have any idea who sent this to her?"

Sergei shook his head. "I did not know Silvana very well.

We were acquaintances, nothing more. She judged me when I was still competing."

Bex unfolded the top of the E-mail, wishing there was music to accompany her dramatic revelation. She said, according to the return address, "You, Sergei, sent her the e-mail."

Between the word "you" and "sent," Sergei had reached over and snatched the copy out of Bex's fingers. She didn't even have the chance to react, much less stop him. Well, so much for her certainty that she'd be able to leap out of the way should he decide to kill her.

"This is ridiculous! Ludicrous! Unconscionable!" Apparently, when he got angry, Sergei's English slipped from the Beatles into *Masterpiece Theatre* land. "Where did you get this? Who gave this nonsense to you?"

"It was inside Silvana's purse. I got it at the police station. The officer in charge of the investigation will confirm that it's authentic."

"Rubbish! Fucking rubbish!" Now there was a word Bex didn't hear much of on PBS. "You think this means I was in cahoots with Silvana Potenza to obfuscate the results?"

"Yes," Bex said. "That's exactly what I think."

Only without the word *obfuscate*.

Sergei said, "Xenia told me she believed there was a conspiracy against her. She told me the American media wanted to take her medal away and give it to Erin Simpson. I did not believe her at first. I told her that is not what Americans are like. Truth and justice for all, that's what Americans believe in. They would not cheat a poor Russian girl out of a prize she deserved."

"Do you believe she deserved it?" Bex knew that the middle of a pro-American political treatise was probably not the best time to interrupt, but it did beg the question so

tidily. "Do you have no doubts at all that your skater deserved to beat Erin Simpson?"

"Don't be foolish," Sergei said. "To say I have no doubts
is to pretend skating is a sport of the clock, like horse racing
or the America's Cup. Skating is subjective, every person
knows that. Four judges preferred Erin Simpson's skating.
They are not wrong, they are merely in the minority. That is
also most American, is it not? Majority rules? Majority ruled
in this case; it always does in skating. Five judges voted for
Xenia. So Xenia deserved to win. Absolutely."

"But, if Silvana's vote was tainted . . ."

"Not by me!"

"So you do think it was tainted by someone?"

"What evidence do you have of this?"

"Well, this E-mail, for starters."

"I did not send it."

"Is it your E-mail address?"

A pause. Then, reluctantly: "Yes."

"Does anyone else have access to your account?"

More reluctance. "No."

"So who then—"

"I have no way of sending an E-mail. I have no computer."

"You have an E-mail address but no computer?"

"No." Even his eyeballs were muscular when they rolled
in his head. "I have no computer with me when I travel.
None on the premises."

"Oh." Bex looked around the room. Yup, definitely no
computer that she could see. Of course, that didn't mean . . .
"Couldn't you have used someone else's?"

"I did not send this E-mail!" Sergei thundered. Bex wondered if it would be redundant to add that even his tongue
had muscles. "If Silvana were still alive, she would tell you

this. I did not tell her or ask her or pay her to do anything for me and for Xenia!"

"Which brings me to my next point," Bex said. "If Silvana really didn't cheat, why do you think she refused to speak up and clear her name?"

Sergei's breath was coming out in gasps. Not the uncontrolled gasps of an out-of-shape weekend athlete gulping for air at the end of a mile run. But the slow, steady, controlled in and out breaths of a man so in charge of every fiber of his being that he could regulate his heartbeat and the color of his face and the timbre of his voice simply through inhaling and exhaling. Bex bet that Sergei's pulse hadn't budged since their conversation began. She bet that his blood pressure was perfectly normal and not a bead of sweat had squeaked out of a single pore. And yet, he was nervous. Bex would have bet her life on it.

Why the heck not? She was already betting her life on him being able to stay in control long enough to refrain from killing her.

"I do not know why Silvana did not defend herself."

"Did you ask her?"

"Yes." Up until the moment the word came out of his mouth, Sergei had been shaking his head side to side. And yet, in the end, he seemed incapable of lying. "Yes, I did. When she would not speak to the press corps and impart upon them her side of the story, I did ask her why."

"And what did she say?"

"She said . . . she said . . ." Sergei cleared his throat. "She said that to answer the charges against her would be to dignify them with a reply."

"And she didn't want to do that?"

"No. She did not. She said answering the charges would

make the media corps think they had the right to make the accusation."

"And she didn't think they had that right?"

"There is no proof Silvana cheated. How dare they ask her questions with no proof?"

"What about this E-mail?"

"This E-mail is a lie!"

"What a shame Silvana isn't alive to tell us that."

"You think I killed her." Like Xenia, Sergei did not so much ask a question as make a statement. Bex wondered if this was another side of the Russian psychology. After a century of borderline-psychotic leadership, they were much more accustomed than Americans to being accused of committing random crimes.

"You have to admit, you have an excellent motive. If Silvana is dead, she can never confess to colluding with you and changing the results. Xenia gets to keep her title. She's your first world champion student, isn't she?"

"Yes. Xenia is the first."

"And," Bex pressed on, "In fact, she's kind of your nyah-nyah-nyah in the face of the Russian federation, isn't she?"

Finally, Sergei asked a question. "What is *nyah-nyah-nyah*, please?"

"It means Xenia's win is a chance for both you and Xenia to stick a finger in the Russian federation's eye and tell them they were wrong about you both. Xenia told me the federation thought she was finished, that they withdrew their support, their funding."

"The federation knows about business. They do not know skating."

"They never supported you, either, did they Sergei?"

"I was national champion. Three times."

"And one of those years, they left you off the world team

in favor of another skater." Bex loved it when she got to use her research powers. Made her feel like a superhero.

"So? Past history. Long time ago." Now Bex knew Sergei was feeling nervous. His hard-earned English grammar was disappearing by the mouthful.

"The reason Xenia is your only big student is because the federation won't let anyone they consider a real contender take from you." Like Xenia and Sergei, Bex decided to give that whole nonquestion statements strategy a try.

"Not true."

"No?" *Darn* . . .

"They allow them to take from me. They just will not pay for them to take from me."

"Ah." Hoo-ha, she was getting good at this!

"I bet that's all going to change now." Bex framed her guess as yet another statement. "You've coached a world champion. I bet the money will just start rolling in. And I'm not even counting the percentage you get from Xenia."

Ever since "amateur" skaters started earning prize money along with their medals, their coaches started taking a percentage of the winnings.

Sergei conceded nothing. "Perhaps this will happen, yes."

"So you've got a lot to lose if Xenia is stripped of her title."

"You are playing pretend games."

"And you certainly had a lot to gain from first telling Silvana how to vote, then making sure she could never expose you."

"I did not kill Silvana."

"Can you prove it?" Bex gambled that a Russian wouldn't know anything about innocent until proven guilty.

"Yes," said Sergei.

Double darn. "Okay, I'm listening."

"Silvana was killed while the women were practicing, correct?"

"Correct."

"Well, I was not at the arena at that time."

"You weren't?" Bex pointed out, "Xenia said you were. She said all of the ladies doing the exhibition were there, along with their coaches."

"Xenia is confused. She is used to my always being with her on the practice, and so she forgot that this time I actually was not."

Okay. Now. A big part of Bex's job as 24/7 researcher was to interview the skaters and coaches and write down their answers. Even when she didn't exactly believe them. For instance, it didn't matter that Lian Reilley had yet to land her triple-triple combination in competition. Bex still, for every event, dutifully wrote down, "Lian will be performing a triple-triple combination in her long program." Because that's what Lian and Gary Gold told her. But this . . . this was a jump of a different edge. Bex wasn't about to take anything either Sergei or Xenia told her at face value. Even if, at the moment, she figured it was in her best interests to pretend she did.

"Fine. So if you weren't with Xenia at the arena, where were you?"

"Here."

"In the hotel?"

"In my room."

"Alone?"

"Yes."

"I thought you said you can prove where you were. If you were alone and nobody saw you, that's not what we call an airtight alibi."

"I was speaking on the telephone."

"To whom?"

"To—to a person."

"Really? Well, that narrows it down."

"To a friend. Yes. To a friend."

"Can I call this friend to confirm?"

"Absolutely, yes." Sergei fumbled in his pocket for a scrap of paper and after a moment of rifling, pulled out a folded-up, old receipt. He handed it to Bex without a second thought. A phone number was scribbled in blue pen across the back. "Here," he said. "Here is who I was speaking to. Please call and ask. He will confirm."

On her way down to the lobby in the hotel elevator, Bex felt like the proverbial cat that'd swallowed an entire shelf of Barnes & Noble self-improvement manuals. Yes, Oprah, yes, Dr. Phil, yes, the really tall guy with the infomercial, she felt that empowered! In fact, if at that moment Bex were pressed to come up with a title for her own existence, she'd feel obligated to go with "You're Okay, but I So, So Rock."

Why the euphoria? Oh, well, many reasons. Where to begin?

For one thing, she was still alive. Considering that Bex had entered Sergei's hotel room not one hundred percent certain of that result, this in and of itself was rather euphoria-inducing. Wasn't that how guys got hooked on the thrill of war or something? Wasn't that what happened to Christopher Walken in *The Deer Hunter*, when he couldn't stop playing Russian roulette? Bex couldn't be sure. She'd seen it once late at night on some obscure cable channel that kept cutting to a commercial every time the footage got too gory. But, in between the ads for Top 40 CD sets and some kind of superglue that fixed anything it touched but wouldn't get stuck to your hands, that hooked-on-the-adrenaline-rush-of-surviving had seemed to be the point.

So, yeah, Bex was definitely having some of that.

However, the really big giddiness was, in fact, coming from another source. It stemmed from the fact that, for the first time since she'd begun this psuedoinvestigation, Bex knew exactly what she needed to do next. The time for flying by the seat of her pants was over. The time for making like Columbo was now.

Sure, she had the number of Sergei's person/friend burning a hole in her hot little hand, and she fully intended to dial those digits shortly. But she also had something even better: knowledge gleaned from an entire skating season spent living out of a suitcase in hotels all over the world. Thanks to her experience haggling with snarling desk clerks at checkout time, Bex knew something even more important than the number of the person Sergei was allegedly talking to when Silvana Potenza was killed. She knew that hotels kept track of all outgoing calls, time and duration, so they could then charge you seven dollars a minute for them.

This was a majorly wonderful thing.

It meant that, just like the cops in the first half of *Law & Order*, plus all its ubiquitous spin-offs, Bex could find out exactly what number Sergei called, when he called it, and how long their person-to-person chat lasted. And she didn't have to get a court order or anything. All she had to do was charm the same snarling desk clerks who made leaving to catch a plane so difficult each and every time into showing her their records. How hard could that be?

Well, anyway, it was very empowering to have a plan.

And Bex couldn't wait to get started. Except that the elevator she was on seemed to be taking the scenic route, stopping on every floor to let in another throng of skating fans. The first group directly in front of her appeared to be a grandmother, mother, and teenage granddaughter—at least, that was Bex's guess due to their Before, After, and Much-After looks. All three wore T-shirts silk-screened with a different action photograph of the reigning men's champion, and were deep in conversation about whether he would be wearing his green or his turquoise leather pants for his exhibition routine on Sunday. Grandma laughed and said, "Oh, if only I were a few years younger!"

Mom followed up with, "You and me both!"

The teen daughter quipped, "But he's just the right age for me!"

Bex wondered if they knew about their heartthrob's tendency toward feather boas and who he used them to lasso. Judging by the infatuated sighs, that would have to be a no.

On the third floor, a group of Erin Simpson's fans got on. These days, they were easily identified by the martyrlike righteous indignation on their faces and the religious fervor glowing in their eyes. That and the fact that they were wearing buttons that said, "Erin Excitement!" (www.ErinExcitement.com)

Figuring it was part of her job, Bex tapped a ponytailed one on her shoulder, introduced herself, and asked, "How's the petition coming?"

"Great!" All four of them turned around in unison, looking like the possessed children from *Village of the Damned.*

"I talked to Jasper this morning," the apparent leader— she had the perkiest ponytail—chirped. "And he said the signature count is now up to almost ten thousand!"

"Who's Jasper?" Bex asked.

"He's Erin's Web master. He's been doing her site for a

couple of years now. He's like some computer expert or something."

"He's a grown man?"

"Oh, yeah. He's like old enough to be my dad."

It didn't matter how long Bex worked in skating, she suspected she would never get over the creep factor of grown men obsessing over little girls. This Jasper guy was hardly the only one she'd heard about who built electronic shrines, posted on fan message boards, and even traveled to competitions to see their favorites in person. Most of them seemed nice enough. They were respectful to the skaters and generally polite when you met them, and she'd never even picked up whispers of any inappropriate behavior. So maybe it was just a harmless hobby, and she was being a prude.

But it was creepy nonetheless.

"What are you all going to do with the petition when you're done?" Bex asked.

"We're sending it over to the ISU, of course. Now that we know for sure that Silvana Potenza's vote was fixed—"

"Whoa! Wait a sec. Back up." Bex wondered if she'd stepped into a black hole and come out the other side a week later. "What do you mean now that you know for sure? How do you know?"

"It's obvious." The ponytails shrugged in unison, and although only one of them spoke, the sentiment seemed to be coming from all four of them. "It's why she committed suicide."

"Silvana committed suicide?"

"Sure. Why else would a judge go into the refrigeration room?"

It was the question of the hour. But Bex had never thought to look at it like that. She felt her euphoria slowly slipping away. The current title of her autobiography: *You're Okay, I'm . . . Starting to Wonder.*

"You think she killed herself because—"

"Because she couldn't live with herself for what she'd done to Erin."

"I see."

"Also, it's a crime, you know. My dad is a lawyer, and I asked him, and he said Erin could have sued her, the judge, a civil suit, because of the, you know, endorsements and money and stuff she lost coming in second instead of first."

"Except," the brunette ponytail interrupted the blonde, "Erin would never do that."

"That's right," towheaded ponytail agreed. "She's too nice."

"She doesn't care about the money; she skates because she loves it."

"Right, otherwise, she wouldn't do it. She's not like Xenia, who's always talking about the prize money and how she bought herself this fancy apartment back in Russia."

"Erin would skate even if there was no money involved. That's how you know she's the *true* champion. She does it because she loves it."

Bex asked, "Do you guys actually know Erin?"

"We're in her fan club." This time the voices answered in unison.

"I got my picture taken with her."

"I write her a letter every week, and she answers me sometimes."

"I always throw her a teddy bear when she's done skating, and now she knows me, and she waves to me when she goes over to pick it up."

"She came to my rink once to practice, and I sat and

talked to her mom while Erin was getting changed, and she was super, super nice."

Okeydokey. Survey says . . . that would be a negative on the "Do you guys actually know Erin?" query.

But, just like with the boa, Bex decided to keep the summation to herself.

Instead, she asked, "Do you think your petition will do any good? Do you really think the ISU will change their results?"

"Totally. Jasper sent an E-mail to the ISU right after he got the first 5000 names on the petition, and they wrote back—I saw it, he forwarded it to me—saying they were going to have a hearing. At first, I was really scared that awful judge would just go in and lie her head off. But now that she's dead, it's like she practically confessed and she won't be able to say anything about it. Now the ISU will *have* to give Erin the gold she should have won in the first place because everyone *knows* the whole thing was fixed now. I mean, we're the fans, we're the ones who buy the tickets and give the money to keep the ISU going, and we all know Erin won."

"So, you're saying the ISU should award the gold medal to whomever the fans want, or you'll stop buying tickets and coming to the competitions and shows?"

Eight Erin-loving eyes stared at Bex blankly. Even the family with the silk-screen T-shirts was looking at her funny. For a moment, Bex entertained the thought of all seven of them leaping upon her, rabid-dog-style, and beating her to death with their souvenir programs. If it were hockey, her headstone could read: Sudden Death. She'd have to think harder to come up with something equally pithy for figure skating.

Skate Crime?

Death Spiral?

Death Drop?

For a sport all dressed up in pretty sequins and international brotherhood, death did seem to come up quite a bit with them.

Fortunately, Bex was spared the trouble of composing her own skating-induced epitaph when the elevator doors opened on the third floor and revealed that most hated of all figures: two Xenia Trubin fans. These days, like the Erin Simpson fans, they were rather easy to spot. They were the ones with their fists clenched tightly by the their sides, ready to leap in and defend their chosen girl on a moment's notice, eyes darting anxiously, ears perked up to the extreme, and perennially on alert for the latest attack, wherever it may come from.

The Erin fans saw the Xenia fans.

The Xenia fans saw the Erin fans.

They locked eyes.

The boa-wearing champion's fans took a step farther back into the elevator, practically doing a duck and cover. Somewhere, Bex felt certain, the musical theme from *The Good, the Bad, and the Ugly* was playing.

Six pairs of nostrils flared.

Bex, at that moment, would have traded anything for a piece of tumbleweed she could roll out between them.

Finally, the first Xenia fan tossed her hair over one shoulder and haughtily informed her friend, "Let's wait for the next elevator. Something stinks in there."

It would have been an excellent closing line, had the elevator doors dramatically closed right then and there.

They didn't. So, for a moment, the standoff remained in limbo.

"Oh, yeah?" an Erin fan finally found her bearings to retort with questionable wit. But, by then, the doors had closed.

"Can you believe her?" Blond ponytail asked no one in particular.

Two of her minions nodded. One shook her head. All three clearly meant the same thing, though.

The elevator finally reached the lobby. Bex allowed everyone else to exit before her. Because, while her new friends had been loudly discussing the lack of class exhibited by certain skating fans but, really, what could you expect considering the skater they followed, and honestly didn't what goes around come around and breeding will tell and it takes one to know one, amen to that, Bex had finally done something she maybe should have done back in Sergei's room.

She looked at the phone number he'd given her.

Like she'd suspected, Sergei had scribbled the phone number on the back of a receipt. Bex absently unfolded it, noting that it was a yellow credit card copy from the hotel boutique and that it listed several purchases. A roll of hard candy (lemon-flavored), a packet of tissues (travel-sized), aspirin (extra-strength), and ibuprofen (ditto). And that the signature at the bottom of the charge read: Silvana Potenza.

Five

So. Time to review. Sergei Alemazov, coach of Xenia Trubin, the disputed winner of the ladies' world championship title, who claimed only a passing acquaintance with Silvana Potenza, dead as Francisco Franco, just happened to be walking around with a telephone number he'd scribbled down on a credit card receipt belonging to—What do you know?—the same, still-dead judge. A telephone number he claimed provided him with an alibi for the judge's time of death. Question: How often did Bex get to make two *Saturday Night Live* references in one thought? Answer: Lucky her, here came another one: *"How conveniiiiient."*

This was getting confusing. Bex didn't much like confusion. That's why she became a researcher in the first place. Find a fact, write it down. Writing the fact down made it true. No muss, no fuss, moving on to the next fact.

At least, it had worked that way in school.

But, then again, school wasn't real life.

And real life was, most certainly, not figure skating.

Naturally, upon spying Silvana Potenza's signature, Bex's first impulse was to turn right around, take the elevator back up to Sergei's hotel room, and demand an explanation for why he just happened to be in possession of a receipt belonging to a woman he claimed he barely knew. But, then, Bex remembered how even Sergei's eyelids seemed to be rippling with muscles. And then she remembered her initial concern about getting out of his room alive after accusing him of being at best a killer, at worst a fixer of results. And then she remembered her giddy euphoria at actually managing to do just that. And then she decided to hold on to that happy and alive feeling for a while longer.

Besides, as long as Bex had the receipt, the evidence was in no danger of disappearing. And, as long as she was already in the lobby, she might as well follow her original plan and check up on Sergei's phone records. Frankly, at this point, Bex was willing to do anything to stay out of the elevator and avoid another discussion of leather pants.

Bex approached the front desk clerk wearing her brightest smile and wielding her biggest bucket of chutzpah. Still smiling, she asked if she could see Sergei Alemazov's phone log.

"No," the clerk said, without even looking up. Darn. A perfectly good smile gone to waste.

Undaunted, Bex moved on to the chutzpah. She said, "Look, here's the situation: I'm with the organizing committee, and we've committed to picking up the tab for all the skaters and their coaches' phone calls. Unfortunately, we've been informed that certain people have been abusing the privilege, and we'd just like to check it out before we make any accusations."

"Guests phone records are confidential, ma'am."

Bex sighed. She dug in her pocket for her 24/7 ID. She asked the clerk, "Would you like to be on television?"

The woman looked up. Now, it was her turn to flash the dazzling smile. "What can I do for you, ma'am?"

Ten minutes later, Bex had a full printout of Sergei's bill to date. He'd made very few calls, obviously saving money since, despite Bex's lie, the local organizing committee was most certainly not picking up anyone's bill. They had no trouble matching the number he'd written on Silvana's receipt against a call Sergei had indeed made that morning. A call he made fifteen minutes *after* Silvana's established time of death.

Bex did the math. The skating arena was a five-minute walk from the official hotel. Even with another five minutes in the elevator, Sergei could have made it back from his killing spree in plenty of time to make the call and deliberately establish an alibi.

Furthermore, Silvana's cause of death, electrocution, indicated that the killer didn't even need to be on the premises at the exact moment when she died. After all, if Bex's theory was correct and the killer lured Silvana to the refrigeration room by calling her on her cell from the pay phone directly across the way, he or she presumably had plenty of time to pour the water underneath the rigged lightbulb and be at least a mile away by the time Silvana got there to pull the cord. Which meant that, in the end, Sergei's alibi didn't stack up to a hill of ice shavings.

Add to that the fact that just because the call came from Sergei's room didn't mean that Sergei was the one on the line—if he was smart enough to kill someone and set up a phony alibi, he was certainly smart enough to ask someone else to make the call for him to substantiate the alibi—and Bex didn't feel exactly flooded with confidence. She used a pay phone in the hotel lobby to dial the number he'd given her.

The line rang three times before a woman's voice came on the line.

"Stern, Morgan, and Chao, how may I direct your call?"

Bex opened her mouth, then closed it. Sergei describing his chatting companion as a friend had preconditioned Bex to expect a private individual, not a place of business.

"Uhm, hello," Bex stammered. "Please, I—where am I calling, please?"

"Stern, Morgan, and Chao," the woman repeated, less gracious this time. Bex could hear other lines ringing in the background and presumed the tone was supposed to imply that they were very, very busy here, and really didn't have time to talk to people who didn't even know where they were calling.

"Are you—is this—what kind of business are you?"

With a name like Stern, Morgan, and Chao, Bex was thinking delicatessen, bank, and fine antiques. And then she remembered her earlier internal chastisement of Gil's political incorrectness. And then she promised to give herself a stern talking to, followed by a changing of her ways. Just as soon as she got this murder thing settled.

"Stern, Morgan, and Chao is a law firm. How may I direct your call?"

A law firm? Fifteen minutes after the death of a woman who had the potential to destroy Sergei's entire career, he'd made a call to a law firm? Interesting. Bex was sure this new clue meant something. Unless, of course, it didn't.

But she currently had a bigger problem. She had no idea

how she, in fact, wanted her call directed. Sergei had given her the reception desk number and no name to go with it.

"Actually, I—I'm—a friend, this person I know, he called the office earlier today, at about 8:47 A.M. actually, and I was wondering if you knew who he asked for—"

"I'm sorry, ma'am, I only come into the office at nine. Prior to that, your friend would have reached an electronic directory."

"Is there any way to check—"

"No, ma'am, I suggest you ask your friend. Have a lovely day." *Click.*

Darn. Why couldn't Silvana have been killed an hour later? Some murderers just had no consideration for Bex's needs.

Well, that was that. Bex figured she had no choice now but to get back on that elevator, duck both the Erin and Xenia fans, and head back on up to Sergei's room to ask him about the receipt. She wondered if bringing a can of mace with her would do any good.

And then she had another thought. Bex looked at the printout of Sergei's expenses again. This time, instead of just skimming to find the number he'd given her, she instead looked for a series of short, local calls. Ones that would indicate a computer being logged on repeatedly. She found nothing that would confirm such a pattern, leaving Bex to assume that Sergei had told the truth and that he didn't travel with a laptop.

On the other hand, not traveling with a laptop didn't mean a total lack of Internet access. The hotel, for one, provided several computer terminals, complete with printers, for guest use. Not only could Sergei have sent an E-mail from there, but Silvana could have printed it out from the exact same location (which wouldn't explain the European-sized paper, but Bex couldn't have everything). If Bex knew her hotels and their fervent desire to squeeze guests' money out of the most basic transactions, both would have been charged for the privilege. And their payments—complete with day and time used—dutifully logged.

Time to pull out that smile again.

And the chutzpah.

As it turned out, though, she could have saved both.

The smile proved utterly unnecessary, as all Bex had to do was mention to the concierge that she needed to use a computer with an Internet connection, and he instantly directed her to a room left of the elevator banks. The woman on duty asked Bex's name and room number, and then handed her a clipboard to sign in on. The clipboard had a stack of pages on it, all with signatures and dates and times of those who'd come before her.

All Bex had to do then was pretend to drop the clipboard and, when she bent over to pick it up, quickly scan through the pages underneath. It could hardly be considered chutzpah. More like a weak *I Love Lucy* sketch.

For her trouble, she did see Sergei's name on the list several times, both before the ladies' competition and after.

Silvana Potenza's name didn't come up once.

Again, it was time for Bex to summarize what she knew.

Silvana was dead. Either by accident (the official version). By suicide (the Erin Simpson fans' version). Or by murder (the version Gil Cahill would prefer).

If it was an accident, then Silvana Potenza was obviously a very odd person with an even odder penchant for cold, wet rooms. If it was a suicide, then maybe Silvana really did fix the ladies' results and either couldn't live with herself or was afraid that the truth would be pried out of her in the course of an investigation. And if it was murder, then she was either killed by the Russians to keep from talking about the fix, or by the Americans as revenge for Erin's loss, or by the Canadians, Germans, Italians, Chinese, Japanese, Dutch, and British because they weren't invited to the party, or by the fans from either side, or by a random psycho with a penchant for odd women who liked to spend time in cold, wet rooms.

There. That was simple. Bex should have no problem straightening it all out in time for the live show on Sunday. Two days from now.

While sloshing the facts she already knew versus the ones she didn't around in her head like an enthusiastic mouth washer prior to the spitting stage, Bex decided that she had picked on the Russians enough for one morning, and it was now time to hear from the American contingent. The one that, after all, seemingly got the short end of the stick.

Short sticks tended to make people cranky, didn't they?

Killing cranky?

Fortunately, Bex reached her decision to switch targets right around the time she saw Erin Simpson and her mother Patty cross the hotel lobby. Well, all right, maybe actually seeing them came before the decision to question some Americans. But they were right there in front of her face, and Bex was a big believer in seizing the moment. Especially when it meant a chance to procrastinate getting back into the elevator and talking to Sergei again.

Both of the Simpson women, Erin dressed in blue jeans and a pink belly shirt that showed off her amazingly toned abs and utter lack of cleavage and Patty in a green skirt suit that wouldn't have seemed out of place at a PTA meeting, were in the company of a rather tall—definitely over six feet—lanky man dressed in khaki pants, a neatly pressed white shirt, and matching khaki tie, and sporting clean-cut, straw-blond hair the same shade as both of theirs. Despite his towering height, he moved with the grace of an athlete, not slouching so much as an inch as he rested one hand on Patty's elbow and the other atop Erin's shoulder and gently escorted them through the lobby, weaving them through the throng of fans that descended on Erin like a puff of smoke.

Bex waited for the mandatory autograph and picture-taking session to wear itself out, noting how gracious Erin was with each fan, asking their names, offering a friendly smile, and—in a wonderfully political touch—taking the time to compliment them on something personal, be it a cute barrette in their hair or the sparkliness of their pens. The girl was good. Very, very good. No wonder she inspired such excessive devotion. The fans in the elevator had looked ready to get into a fistfight for Erin. Would they have been willing to kill for her, too?

Finally, when the last autograph had been signed, Bex stepped forward. "Hi, Erin. Hello, Patty."

After a season of following them from continent to continent, Bex and the Simpsons were on a casual hello basis. Bex intended to milk it for all it was worth.

"Hi, Bex." Erin's smile stayed permanently in its place, and her mother, realizing that media was in the house, forced herself to do the same.

"Hello, Bex. How are you? Glad to be almost done?"

"Well, we still have the exhibition show on Sunday."

"Oh, of course, of course. I guess for us, with the competition being over, it feels like we're already on vacation.

It's probably different for television. You still have to put on a show no matter what, right?"

"Right. . . ." Bex turned her attention to the tall man in their midst. "Hi," she said, "I'm Bex Levy, the 24/7 researcher. I don't think we've met."

"Jasper Clarke." His height and the tight knot of tie at his neck had brought to mind Disney's *The Legend of Sleepy Hollow* and Ichabod Crane, and Bex had been expecting a high, reedy—okay, let's call a spade a spade, here—nerdy voice. What she heard instead was a deep and mellow baritone. If the center of a Milk Dud had a voice, this would be it.

"Oh," Bex said, "You're Erin's Web master."

He was a skating fan. But hardly a typical specimen. While female skating fans tended to fall into three categories—older women with free time on their hands to travel to competitions, middle-aged women dragging a reluctant spouse or child behind them, and perky teenagers on their way to becoming either of the above—the men tended to fall into a single classification: odd. Not only the Lolita factor, but how they dressed—as if, for them, fashion froze sometime in the 1970s. They usually crept about from place to place trying to blend into the woodwork until the competition actually started, at which point they commenced whooping and hollering, "Go for the gold! Go for the gold! Go for the gold!" from the moment their skater stepped onto the ice until she or he or they stepped off. Some carried around photo albums of their favorites, or chatted up the skaters' parents, or built Web sites and tried desperately to have them declared official.

Jasper Clarke seemed to fit the typical profile on the surface, but there was something different about him. Maybe it was his body language. He moved alongside Patty and Erin like an equal, not a supplicant. Maybe it was his laid-back manner. He didn't seem to be doing the usual dance of currying Erin's or Patty's favor, sniffing around like a mutt hoping for a stray crumb of approval to fall from the big table. Jasper Clarke looked utterly confident in his own skin, like he'd never beg anyone for anything. Or maybe it was simply the fact that tall, confident, athletic blond men with mellow voices were seriously Bex's type, and she thought he was adorable.

Yeah. That last one. That may have been it.

Of course, Bex reminded herself, she had no time for this digression right now. She was investigating a murder, and she had questions to ask and clues to piece together and a live show on Sunday. And besides, Jasper was old. He was like, ten years older than her, she bet.

So, in the end, all Bex said was, "Nice to meet you, Jasper. I hear the petition on your site is doing really well."

"We broke ten thousand signatures a half hour ago. We're very pleased."

"People are so nice and supportive of me," Erin chirped in, even though Bex didn't recall asking her.

Patty said, "Gil has already asked Erin if she will skate an extra number at the exhibition. He can't get her the gold medal spot, of course, that's the ISU's call, but he asked if Erin would skate to close out the show, after Xenia and after the finale, so our last image can be of her."

"Wow," Bex said, truly impressed. "That's pretty major."

"Well, everyone knows Erin should have won the gold. This just concludes the show the way it should have been in the first place."

Bex used every second of her high school drama class to try to sound nonchalant and casual as she asked, "It must be tough for you, with Silvana Potenza dead, to know that you'll never get the whole story about what happened."

Patty said, "Francis and Diana Howarth told the whole story on the air the night Erin lost. Everything else would just have been more lies."

"We'll be sending our petition to the ISU tonight," Jasper said. "That gives them two days to change the results."

"You really think they will?" Bex asked, thinking back to the passage in the rule book that said official results could never be overturned by anyone for any reason.

"What choice do they have? There's certainly enough evidence to launch an inquiry."

"Really?" Bex wondered if she'd missed something. "What evidence would that be?"

"Francis and Diana, for one thing," Patty snapped, her fondness for Bex diminishing like an ice cube melting in warm vodka. "They're skating experts; their testimony can't be ignored. And then there's the block voting. The entire Eastern bloc voted for Xenia. Tell me that's not an obvious bias. Erin would have won if Silvana Potenza hadn't sided with them."

Bex felt like she was in the middle of some never-ending scratch spin, having the same conversation over and over again. She considered pointing out the obvious flaws in their theory but, to be honest, she was sick of it.

"Actually," Bex said, "I did want to talk to you both about Silvana. You and Erin were at the rink practicing when she died, right? We're doing a special on her death, and I wanted to—"

"We'd love to do an interview," Patty said, "but now is not a good time. Erin needs to take a nap before tonight's practice."

"Well, when would be a good time to—"

"We'll call you," Patty said. She placed a protective arm around Erin and, guiding her with sheer body weight, like a bicycle, pointed her toward the elevator. "Jasper, we'll see you at the practice. It was nice seeing you, Bex. Let's talk more later."

And they were gone, leaving Bex with Jasper.

Still tall. Still cute.

He said, "Looks like we both got blown off."

Bex shrugged. "I'm a researcher; I'm used to it. I had a skater once give me the totally wrong elements for his program. On purpose. He thought it would be funny. So there we are live on the air, and Francis and Diana have all the wrong info. Francis says, "Now he's setting up for a triple Salchow," and the guy does a triple flip."

"You'd think that's a problem that could be avoided if your announcers actually looked up at the person on the ice, instead of at the cheat sheet."

"You'd think that," Bex agreed.

"But you would be wrong, I take it?"

"Oh, so very, very wrong."

"Sounds like a tough gig."

"Well, that's why they pay me the big bucks."

"I see." He was smiling at her. He had a nice smile. Unlike Erin's on-ice portrayal of Happiness, this one actually had some sincerity.

Bex said, "I'm guessing you must make the big bucks, too, doing Erin's site."

"Actually, I do it for free."

Of course. He may have been taller and smoother than the average fan bear, but, in the end, Jasper was just another fanatic, obsessed with an admittedly legal but still prepubescent-looking girl to the extent of spending his own money to follow her around the world and build Flash-based electronic shrines, all for the return thrill of having her mother blow him off in a hotel lobby. How disappointing.

Jasper said, "I'm retired. I've got nothing but time on my hands, and I love the Web."

"Retired? How old are you?"

"Forty two."

"Wow." As in *Wow, you look good for your age,* and *Wow, you're already retired,* and *Wow, how do I get me some of that action?*

"Like I said, the Internet has been very, very good to me."

"Wait, are you actually one of those real-life guys who got in at a good time and out at an even better one?"

"Yup." There went that smile again. "I started a software company fifteen years ago, sold it five years ago. And then there I was, newly retired, newly rich, no need for money, and nothing at all to do."

"So you decided to become a professional skating fan?"

"Something like that."

Intriguing. "And you've been working with Erin and Patty ever since?"

"Give or take."

"I bet you know them pretty well."

"More or less."

"Jasper," Bex asked, "Would you like to have lunch with me?"

"I'd be delighted."

He proved to be a man of multiple surprises. The first one came when Bex took his acceptance of her lunch invitation to mean what a skating event lunch invitation always meant. She turned right, confidently heading for the hotel restaurant. Jasper turned left, heading for the outside world.

He said, "The restaurant at the Cliff House is really excellent. Have you ever been?"

Bex gulped. Outside? Eat outside? *Go* outside? Was that even allowed? Since the day they'd arrived, the 24/7 crew had eaten their every meal either at the hotel restaurant or while sitting on the floor of the production trailer, scarfing takeout from the hotel restaurant. After two weeks, Bex had sampled every item on the menu and could with confidence report that the ideal dinner was honey-baked salmon with the side order of fries, steamed broccoli, carrot wedges, and lemon slices. She'd had it for breakfast, lunch, and dinner every day for the past four days. Any minute now, she expected to grow honey-baked gills.

Bex said, "I've kind of been busy, here. . . . "

"Well, that's a crime, then. Visiting San Francisco and not sampling at least some of the restaurants. You wouldn't do that in Paris, would you?"

Actually, she had. In Paris, she'd subsisted on hotel steak with a side order of spinach, and then crème bruûlé for dessert. Paris had been a fun, if fattening, time.

"Uh, no?" Bex answered his question with a question.

"Come on. I'll show you the town."

In all the mystery stories Bex had ever read, it seemed to her like the detective spent an awful lot of time narrating their travels. She couldn't pick up a whodunit without encountering pages-long descriptions of "and then I took this freeway to this freeway to this freeway, and then I got to this neighborhood and boy, wasn't it picturesque and filled with colorful locals full of charm and anecdotes."

As a reader, Bex had assumed the technique was nothing more than filler. After all, she'd been a student when she did the bulk of her reading, and at the time, Bex certainly knew all about papers with word count requirements and the padding inspired therein. Later, when she worked as a freelance writer and was lucky enough to snag an assignment that paid by the word, she got really good at using six when one would have done. However, now that she was a sleuth herself, Bex decided to give all those poor, maligned writers the benefit of the doubt and guess that the interminable itinerary listing was actually a sensible way of organizing their thoughts in a linear fashion, the better to make sense of the knotty puzzle before them.

Riding shotgun in Jasper Clarke's cool blue Ferrari (another way in which he diverged from the average skating fan; this was Bex's first Ferrari ride), she decided to give the strategy a try. She looked out the window. She noted that they seemed to be driving down Nineteenth Avenue. The street was . . . street colored. Concrete colored. Gray. The houses whose windows looked out onto the street-colored street all looked the same, like Monopoly houses painted shades ranging from a tasteful white with green shutters to, she kidded not, a hot-pink facade with neon-orange windows. There were several gas stations on the street. Also a few outdoor flower stands, bus stops, and, periodically, trolley car tracks. The trolley cars were green. The people on them were mostly Asian. All of whom, Bex reminded herself to think, were individuals, not a clichéd mass. She was confident that they worked in many different professional fields, and she bet some of them were probably not even that good at math.

There. That ought to be mea culpa enough for her earlier, inadvertent ethnic slight.

And anyway, now they had left Nineteenth Avenue and were driving through Golden Gate Park, which was pretty and green as parks were wont to be. Finally, they pulled out of the park and alongside the Pacific Ocean. It was blue and big and, presumably wet.

Well, that certainly was an instructive exercise.

Bex felt no closer to figuring out who killed Silvana Potenza than before she left the hotel, but at least her adjectives had gotten a heady workout.

Naturally, along the way, as she'd been narrating her internal travelogue, Bex had been acting the good guest and keeping up her end of the conversation with Jasper.

He'd started by asking Bex all about herself, her pretelevision career, how she'd come to work at 24/7, all of the usual pleasantries. Bex dutifully replied, hoping that her own openness would inspire reciprocity on his end.

It seemed to do the trick as, sitting down at their table at the Cliff House restaurant (description, just in case it really was programming her brain in the right, crime-solving direction: white tablecloths, brown plush chairs, crystal glasses, off-white china, sea-themed ambiance, big windows looking out over the ocean, and a jutting, black, slimy rock covered in barking sea lions), Jasper quite happily answered Bex's questions about his own past.

"So there I was, no job, lots of money, and utterly no idea what to do with myself. Sure, I did all the cliché, nouveau riche things. I traveled: I went skiing, I went to the Caribbean, I walked the Great Wall of China, and I took pictures of the place where the Berlin Wall used to be. Then, once all that was out of the way, I bought a house in Silicon Valley, decorated it with the most expensive things I could buy—even if I still can't tell a Ming vase from a Renaissance damask. I went out to dinner and I went out to bars and I have a closet full of clothes people tell me are quite fashionable. But want to guess what I did most?"

"Read *Silas Marner?*' Bex took a guess.

He smiled, getting the reference. "Nah. Fortunately, I had a business manager to take care of the hoarding and polishing for me. What I ended up doing, mostly, and tell me if this isn't the most pathetic thing you've ever heard—I watched a lot of TV."

"A man after my own heart!" The words burst out of Bex before she'd had the chance to fully calculate how they might be interpreted. She sincerely hoped he would interpret them the way she meant for them to be interpreted now, and not the way she might have meant them a half hour ago when she was still busily pondering his tallness and his blondness.

Luckily, he didn't even seem to notice she'd spoken. Jasper went on, "And I mean, I watched anything: sitcoms, dramas, documentaries, news shows, game shows, cooking shows. . . . One time, I even found myself watching—"

"Figure skating?"

"Yeah." Jasper shook his head, as if he couldn't quite still believe it himself. "I found myself watching figure skating."

"Football game canceled due to rain?"

"Actually, I just couldn't face another *Friends* rerun. My theory is, it's one thing when you catch yourself wondering how unemployed Monica and Rachel can afford an apartment that size in Manhattan—that's normal. You'd be odd if you didn't wonder. But, when you actually go on-line to see if cab licenses are transferable in the state of New York and thus could Pheobe really be legally driving her grandmother's hack—"

"That's a problem."

"I thought so, yes. At the rate I was going, my friends would either have needed to stage a *Friends* intervention, or I had to change the channel."

"To figure skating."

Jasper shrugged. "Look, it's not like I had anything against it or anything. I mean, I was a serious jock in college: basketball, swimming, rowing, skiing—I was on all the teams. And I respect athletes in any sport. I even have respect for the golf guys. I knew figure skaters worked hard and were amazing athletes. I just never cared to watch them do their stuff."

"So what changed your mind?"

"Erin," he said simply. The word hung over the table like Princess Leia's hologram in *Star Wars*. (Bex wasn't just a TV geek, she went to the movies occasionally.)

"She was that good?" Bex racked her brain to recall. "It sounds like you would have seen her at, what? Her first? Second worlds?"

"Her first. It was her first world championship. She was this tiny little thing in a bright yellow dress, her hair in a ponytail, the biggest smile on her face. So much excitement, so much energy. You know, of all the skaters, she was the only one who looked really thrilled to be there. She just lit up the arena when she came on. Even when she fell, she never stopped smiling."

Bex had seen the tape of the event Jasper described for a feature she helped compile on Erin. And Jasper wasn't just waxing in retrospective poetics. There really had been something special about Erin on that film. She just seemed so thrilled to be competing at her first worlds, making her mother so visibly proud, that her enthusiasm was contagious.

"She just enchanted me. And wait, wait, don't say it. I know what you're thinking: Do I also spend my nights trolling the web for kiddie porn?"

Well, she hadn't exactly been putting those words in that

order . . . but, yeah, his phrasing wasn't that far from Lolita, et al.

"I swear to any God anyone believes in, my fondness for Erin has no sexual component. Believe me, I've done a lot of soul searching in that regard."

At least he was self-aware. That was a good thing. Wasn't it?

"She just . . . I know, I know, check out the ego trip on this one . . . but, she just reminds me so much of me. When I was her age, I was just as enthusiastic about everything. I loved sports, loved to compete, loved to be the best, loved to win. Now that I've made it—whatever that means—people always ask me the secret of my success. And, you know, I've got to say it—I'm certain my sports background had everything to do with it. I like to win. And, more importantly, I really, really hate to lose."

He paused for a moment. Accepting their arriving lunch with a friendly smile at their waiter. And, in that moment, Bex saw a newspaper photo of Erin with a silver medal around her neck, and then a photo of Silvana Potenza's body being carried out of the refrigeration room.

Erin reminded Jasper Clarke an awful lot of himself. He related to Erin. He related to her a *lot*. And Jasper Clarke did not like to lose. And now, Silvana Potenza was dead. Maybe that watching the street while they drove along strategy had been good for her, after all, because suddenly, Bex was connecting an awful lot of dots.

She asked, "How did you and the Simpsons hook up?"

"I picked up the phone and called." In response to Bex's surprise, Jasper said, "You're a researcher. You know it's really not that hard to find anyone's number when you're motivated."

Yeah. Bex bet getting Silvana Potenza's cell was a piece of cake compared to reaching Erin.

"And Patty just welcomed you to the team?" Considering that in the almost two decades she'd been coaching her, Patty had refused any offers to send Erin to another choreographer, or even a jump or spin specialist for a day or two, Bex couldn't imagine her being Ms. Open Arms to a stranger on the phone.

"Patty? Are you kidding? But, she came around. When I showed her how useful I could be, building the Web site and everything, then she really came around."

"All three of you seem pretty tight now."

"Erin is a great, great kid. Now that I've gotten to know her, I admire her so much, even outside the skating. She's got an excellent mind. Competing isn't her only interest. She's a big reader. Whenever she goes to a new country to skate, she always tries to take in some museums, picks up a little of the language. I've even been teaching her how to code HTML. She's got a lot of interests. She's an awesome young woman."

Okay. This was getting creepy again. This guy could give the obsessed girls in the elevator adoration lessons. Which brought Bex to . . .

"Erin sure has a lot of devoted fans."

"She's very good with the public."

"Yes. She is. Jasper, do you think any of Erin's fans could have taken matters into their own hands? Do you think they might have been so incensed at her coming in second that they might have killed Silvana Potenza?"

It may not have seemed obvious to the untrained eye, but Bex was actually being very clever. Sure, it may have seemed like she was being clumsy and transparent, asking Erin's most obsessed fan if an obsessed fan could have committed murder for her. But, in reality, Bex was cleverly shifting the onus onto *other* fans, while, at the same time, gauging Jasper's reaction to the scenario. Really. She was being clever. Take her word for it.

"No." Jasper shook his head. He didn't even have to think about it. "No, I can't even imagine that being possible. Erin's fans are some of the sweetest people on earth."

His facial expression didn't change. He looked as calm and unruffled as before. This obviously meant that he was either innocent or a complete psychopath.

Gosh, but it was nice to narrow it down to only two options.

Bex asked, "Were you at the arena when Silvana died?"

"Actually, I was back at the hotel, writing code so that every time someone signs Erin's petition, they get an automatic thank-you note back."

"Oh."

"Why? Do you think I did it?"

Maybe, Bex thought.

"No!" She exclaimed, wondering if volume would make up for honesty.

"That's all right. You have to explore all your options; it's the only logical thing to do. If you like, I'd be happy to show you the E-mails that went out. They all have a time stamp."

"Can't that be faked?"

"Yes. But, only by someone who really knew what he was doing."

"Someone like you?"

"Guilty."

Bex pushed her plate of pasta away, half-eaten. Somehow, she wasn't in the mood to finish the shoelace-length beige strands of carbohydrates with their red chunks of tomato and sprinkles of green pesto sauce. (Bex figured if she kept piling on the details, maybe she'd have another breakthrough.) "You're awfully relaxed about all this, Jasper."

"That's because I have nothing to hide." He wiped his mouth with a square cloth napkin, leaving a smudged, brownish lip print, courtesy of his roast beef and mashed potato platter. "Or maybe it's because I'm a psychopath."

Who also did a little mind reading on the side, apparently. Great. Just what Bex needed.

"That's not funny," Bex snapped.

"I'm sorry." His apology was instantaneous and sounded much more sincere than her earlier denial had. "I truly am. You're right, this isn't funny in the slightest. I may not have been a fan of Silvana Potenza, but the woman is dead. And, what's even more frightening, her killer is walking around, thinking they got away with it."

"Who do you think did it?" Bex figured if she couldn't nail him as a suspect, she might as well take advantage and do a little picking inside a brain smart enough to get out of the stock market before it needed a Zamboni to wipe up after it.

"I think it's obvious: Cui bono?"

"Who benefits?" Bex translated.

"I'm impressed!" Jasper raised an eyebrow. "Not a lot of people your age are so quick with the Latin turn of phrase."

"I know a lot of useless stuff," Bex explained. "I went to Sarah Lawrence."

"A fine school. I'm a Stanford man, myself."

"So who do you think benefits from Silvana's death?"

"Well, the Russians, obviously. Now that she's dead, no one will ever be able to prove beyond a shadow of a doubt that Silvana fixed the vote. The ISU won't have grounds to strip Xenia of her gold medal."

"What about your petition?"

"Oh. That. I must admit, that's more to keep Erin's spirits up than anything else. I don't expect it to do much good. Under the best, best, best circumstances, they might decide to award Erin her own gold. But they'll never take Xenia's away from her. And I know my Erin; she's not a big fan of consolation prizes."

"So you think it would have been better for Erin if Silvana were still alive?"

"Absolutely! Silvana was the only one who could testify to robbing Erin. I think that would have been so important for her. She's been working so hard. She needs the validation."

"Xenia has been working pretty hard, too, these past ten years."

"Oh, Xenia." Jasper managed to dismiss the other woman's sweat and determination with the wave of a hand. "Xenia doesn't care about the skating. She only cares about the money."

Déjà elevator vu.

"Why does everyone keep saying that?"

"Because Xenia says it. She says it to anyone who asks. Read any of her interviews. She can't stop talking about the prize money and how happy she is that amateur skaters can win prize money now. That's why she's stayed in this long. It's not for the title, it's not for the love of it. It's so she can make some quick bucks."

"But what's wrong with that?" Bex pressed. "I mean, skating is her job. Why shouldn't she get paid for doing her job?"

Frankly, Bex had come up against the same issue herself. She'd lost count of the number of times 24/7 had been accused of putting a lousy skating broadcast on the air, with the last line of the angry letter or E-mail reading, "Of course, you're only in it for the money; 24/7 does anything for a buck. No one there is a *real!!!!* figure skating fan." Bex wondered what Catholic world was this where poverty equaled dedication? By that logic, no one should take a salary for doing any profession, lest they be accused of not being truly devoted to it. Gil wouldn't let her, but Bex was really itching to write back and ask if the poison-pen pals got paid for doing their own job, or did they volunteer for free, to demonstrate their love?

"Erin skates because she loves it. Patty, too. Think about it. When Erin was first starting out, long before prize money was even a possibility, think of all the money Patty gave up to coach her. I mean, Patty coaches for a living; that's the only livelihood she and Erin have ever had. She could have made a lot more giving lessons to other kids. Patty didn't make a cent coaching Erin. But, she did it because both she and Erin love their sport."

Bex asked, "Have you ever seen the musical *Gypsy*, Jasper?"

A twinkle of respect danced in his eyes, but he was, nevertheless, quick to defend. "It isn't like that. You've seen Erin on the ice. You've seen that smile of hers. Is that a kid being forced to skate against her will?"

"I don't know," Bex conceded. Mainly because all the skaters' smiles looked the same.

"Well, take my word for it. Erin is a happy camper."

"Unlike Xenia?"

"This whole fiasco has cost her a bundle. Xenia is getting up there in years. How much longer do you think she can skate? Her tendons must be ripped off the bone by now. Everyone knows she was just holding on to win a world title, figuring it would translate to big bucks on the professional circuit. Well, now she has her title, but the ultimate prize—the top spot with Francis and Diana's 'Harmony on Ice?'—they've offered it to Erin."

"Really?" Bex hadn't heard.

"Yeah. Patty got the call right before we ran into you. She's considering it as we speak. It's a very generous offer. To be honest, it's much higher than it probably would have been even if Erin had won. Without the controversy, I mean."

"Wow. So this is working out pretty well for your girl."

Jasper shook his head and, as if lecturing a child, patiently explained. "No. No, you haven't been listening to me. This isn't about the money for Erin. She could care less about that. It's the honor. It's the winning. It's the recognition of being the best. That was taken away from her. And now the poor kid can never, ever get it back. I'll level with you, Bex. I know it sounds harsh, but frankly the way I feel is: whoever killed Silvana should be charged with two offenses. The lesser one is the murder. It's what they did to poor Erin that's the real crime here."

Six

Bex worried. And not merely because she may have just finished having lunch with a cold-blooded killer. Or because, earlier, she'd been alone in a hotel room with a cold-blooded killer. Or even because she very possibly had no idea who the cold-blooded killer really was, which, in her well-read opinion, really raised the odds of said cold-blooded killer deciding to practice a bit more of his cold-blooded killing, this time in her direction.

No. What worried Bex most upon her return back to the official hotel was the fact that the cold-blooded killer's victim had been found with a printed out E-mail in her purse. An E-mail that could very well hold the key to what exactly happened to her and who exactly might have helped it happen. If Bex could only figure out where and when Silvana printed out the E-mail, it would go a long way toward answering several questions. For instance, if Silvana printed the E-mail out after the ladies' competition, it could hardly have influenced her judging decisions. On the other hand, if she'd printed it out before, then the possibility of a fix loomed much stronger.

But Bex could only pin down *when* Silvana did her printing if she could figure out *where* she'd done it. Most computers kept records of that sort of thing. Records that were very difficult to fix unless you were willing to screw up the entire system. And screwing up the entire system left tracks of its own. Bex already knew that Silvana never visited the hotel's media center for her printing needs. Which left several options. The most obvious was that the judge traveled with her own laptop and portable printer (which would also explain the European-sized paper). Personally, Bex found that to be too much of a hassle—simply being stopped by airport security and asked to take all the electronics out of her bag and plug them in to prove that no bomb was involved was daunting enough, much less the sheer weight of hefting several bulky pounds on her back and hip—but she did know people who swore by it.

So, obviously, her first course of action should be finding out if that was the case with Silvana. Since Bex doubted the woman would have carried it alongside the hard candy, empty tissue packet, and cell phone in her purse, odds were the printer wasn't down at the police station with the rest of her things.

Okay, then. So where was it? In fact, now that she was asking such a vital question, Bex felt obligated to ask: Where was all of Silvana's stuff? Had anyone thought to go into her hotel room and pack up her things for shipment back to Italy alongside her body?

Bex prided herself on being a nice person. She'd been a Girl Scout in the second grade (until her mother called it a paramilitary organization with cookies, and pulled the plug).

She'd volunteered as a grammar-school reading teacher while in high school. In college, she mentored several underclassmen. And she always told herself that she would donate to the United Way—as soon as she earned enough money. So, really, Bex was terribly, terribly nice; even if she did say so herself. And terribly nice people, in Bex's experience, did not wait to be asked to volunteer. They saw a need and stepped right in to fix it.

Bex picked up her metaphorical torch and prepared to go forth and be a hero.

Alas, the hotel staff did not quite see things her way.

"We can't let you into Mrs. Potenza's room, Ms. Levy," said the manager, who'd only agreed to see her because the front desk clerk and the concierge and the head of housekeeping couldn't take it anymore and had decided none of them got paid enough to listen to Bex's combination of logic and Good Samaritan arguments.

"But all I want to do is get her things together so we can return them to her family."

"I understand. However, without written permission from the next of kin—"

"They're all in Italy. And they don't speak English," Bex improvised. "And, well, you know, the time zone . . . " Bex gambled that if she didn't insert any verb, the manager would insert an appropriate one of his own.

Bex failed miserably.

Having struck out with pretty much the entire hotel chain of command, Bex threw all caution to the wind and decided to appeal to the highest authority she could: Rupert Newman, president of the ISU. He of the "Silvana Potenza's death was a tragic accident" press release.

Bex had spent a season in the same general vicinity as the man. She doubted he could pick her out of a police lineup if she stole his protocol. Nevertheless, she had no doubt he could recognize a 24/7 credential when he saw it. Besides, nowadays they were old friends; they'd practically bonded back in the refrigeration area over Silvana's accident-ravaged corpse.

She found him inside the ISU room, a converted ballroom on the hotel's balcony level. Since she was looking for printers, she noted that Rupert did have a travel-sized, personal one attached to his laptop. Complete with European-sized paper. And that another, larger printer stood in the far corner, attached to a computer currently being occupied by a chipmunk of a woman busily entering a long string of numbers into a spreadsheet. However, a quick peek at the computer connection told Bex that this particular machine wasn't connected to the Internet. Silvana couldn't have used it to print her E-mail unless she'd transferred it to a disc first.

Floppy discs, Bex made a mental note. Something else to search Silvana's room for.

Rupert Newman's desk—actually, a four-seat dining table obviously reassigned by the hotel for the occasion—was, nevertheless, the largest one in the room. It sat against the far wall, giving Rupert the ability to survey every activity taking place before him and in his name. He was a dapper little man, a former skater himself, once dubbed The Bug. Rupert Newman stood barely three inches over five feet and didn't so much walk as hop from place to place. Despite his miniature stature, however, and very much unlike the Russian delegation, he was an impeccably snappy dresser. His pocket handkerchief always matched his tie, and his suits never so much as hinted at the possibility of a wrinkle. Bex knew the man was going for class and grace, and she genuinely respected his efforts. Though, to her, he resembled nothing so much as a very tidily put-together doll. And, being the smart-ass that she was, Bex inevitably couldn't help wondering if he were anatomically correct.

Fortunately, all thoughts of Rupert being a child's doll were easily shaken from her head the moment he opened his mouth. Not that his language wasn't delightfully proper or his accent as charming and cultured as you would expect a British product of the public school system to be. The problem with Rupert was that early on in life he'd decided to make up for his lack of stature with a combination of ego and volume. Ten years earlier, he'd been fired from his commentating job with the BBC due to a tendency to yell all his remarks, most of which weren't even about the skater currently on the ice but rather about himself, his skating career, his past results, and what he thought his results should have been if only the judges had been more appreciative of his unique style and didn't spend so much time harping about how long it took him to skate his tiny strokes from one end of the rink to the other. However, for better or worse, his brief stint with the BBC had convinced Rupert that he understood the media far better than any ISU president who ever came before him, and he was always eager to prove this by telling everyone, from Bex up to Gil Cahill, how to do their jobs.

In fact, when he saw Bex's ID, the first words out of Rupert's mouth were, "Shouldn't you be at the arena, luv? After all, there's still the exhibition show to get on air come Sunday."

"Yes," Bex agreed. "That's why I'm here."

"Oh? Care for an interview, do you?"

"Sure." Bex leapt on his suggestion. "I mean, yes. Yes, I would."

"All right, then. Best start taking notes, then, wouldn't want to miss anything."

"Right," Bex pulled out her notebook and pen. "Ready," she said.

For the next ten minutes, Rupert Newman proceeded to wax poetic about what a fine championship this has been, how many records were set, how the technical level of skating was continuing to be raised alongside the artistic level, and how his fine management was responsible for it all. Bex scribbled furiously. The faster her pen went, the more Rupert seemed to want to talk. The more he talked, the more details Bex added to her pen-and-ink doodle of him.

Finally, he stopped to take a breath. And Bex took advantage of the lull to ask, "What about the Xenia Trubin/Erin Simpson controversy?"

She even stopped doodling to better comprehend his answer.

Rupert took a deep breath. This was obviously going to be a long one. He said, "Skating is no stranger to controversy. It is, after all, a subjective discipline. Why, I can't think of a single championship, local or world, that ended without at least one result being hotly debated for years thereafter. I'll give you an example: my last world championship. I finished fourth. We had school figures back then, you understand, and that counted for a large portion of your score. But I would be damned if everyone in the arena didn't believe I deserved third place. Probably even second if it weren't for the school figures. And, in fact, if there were no school figures then, and if I had been placed a mite higher in the short program, I would have won the whole thing."

And if my grandmother had gills, Bex thought, *she'd be a codfish.*

"So you understand, this is nothing new, luv. I am thrilled that our sport has so many dedicated and passionate fans."

"Erin Simpson's Web master is about to send you a petition with over ten thousand names on it, asking that the ISU award Erin Simpson a gold medal."

"Is that a fact? Yes, yes, I do believe I heard some such rumbles."

"What will your response be?"

"Well, I haven't received it yet, have I?"

"Pretend," Bex said, probably sharper than was wise. But, she couldn't help it. Her head hurt. And this guy was annoying her.

"Well, naturally, the ISU takes all valid input under consideration, but we cannot allow outsiders to dictate our inner workings," Rupert said without saying anything at all.

It took all of Bex's energy to keep herself from snapping, *Pretend harder.* Instead, she asked him, "Will Silvana Potenza's death affect your decision one way or the other?"

"Whatever do you mean?"

"What I *mean,*" Bex stressed the word, "is since the justification for awarding Erin the gold over Xenia is an accusation of foul play, wouldn't it make it harder to get to the bottom of things with your, chief witness—and defendant—dead?"

"Silvana Potenza was neither a witness nor, certainly, any sort of defendant. She was only one judge on a panel of nine. She voted one way. Four other judges agreed with her. I see no foul play. No foul play, at all. The only thing I see before me is two excellent performances by two wonderful, marvelous skaters. Their rivalry has made skating most exciting all season, and I look forward to many more seasons of such excitement to come."

"Not if they both turn pro." Bex had to admit, she said the last just to spite him. Skating lived and died by its superstars. Sure, the hard core would watch even a flight of pre-preliminary girls, they were that devoted. But the casual fan only tuned in when there was name recognition. The ISU knew that. It was why, a decade earlier, they'd broken down and allowed their skaters to start earning money for competing, performing, and coaching. Otherwise, as soon as a skater achieved any modicum of fame, they would inevitably turn pro and run to the ice shows, leaving the ISU without the big names they themselves had brought into being. It wasn't profitable for the ISU and so, as incentive, they allowed their skaters to make money, as long as they made money in venues the ISU approved and got a cut of. Francis and Diana Howarth's ice show most certainly didn't fit the bill. If Erin accepted their offer, the ISU would be left without a rivalry and without their biggest household name. Rupert knew it. He didn't need Bex telling him. She did it mostly to let some air out of his sails.

Rupert said, "Xenia Trubin has been in skating for a long time. I'm sure she's tired and, now that she's won the gold, I wouldn't be surprised if she did, in fact, retire. After all, the lass has nothing else to prove to anyone, does she? She is our oldest ever world champion. I suspect her record is destined to remain unbroken for a long, long time. As for Erin, though . . . no, I don't think our Erin will be turning pro for a good, long time. I know her well, and I know her mother even better. We skated at the same time, you know. It broke Patty's heart to retire without ever having been world champion. She won't let Erin suffer the same sort of disappointment."

"So you could say," Bex chose her words with care, still forming the thought even as the words tiptoed out of her mouth, "that it was a stroke of luck for the ISU that Erin didn't win gold, here. Otherwise, she might have achieved her life's goal, turned pro, and that was that."

Rupert stared at Bex with a combination of new respect and utter, utter disgust. "Well, yes, I suppose one could say that. But luck has nothing to do with anything. It was a competition, and the results speak for themselves."

"Yes," Bex agreed, though not with what he was actually saying. "They certainly do." And, to herself, all she could think of was Jasper Clarke asking, "Cui bono? Who benefits?"

But while she flashed back in Latin, out loud Bex asked, "Will there be any sort of memorial service for Silvana? A moment of silence before the exhibition maybe?"

"We hadn't thought of that," Rupert admitted. "We've been so busy. The media requests at this particular championship far exceeded our usual tally."

Well, that's what happens, Bex thought, *when the whole world is talking about a result this office doesn't find at all out of the ordinary.*

"Was Silvana in the States alone?" Bex asked, "Or did she have some family with her?"

"Silvana's husband rarely traveled with her. Skating was Silvana's passion, not his."

"That's too bad," Bex said. "I guess it must have been difficult for you then, having to be the one to get her things and send them on. But, I'm sure her family appreciated it."

"Her things?" Rupert asked, his voice actually lowering to indicate his lack of Napoleon confidence on this particular issue.

"Well, she was here on behalf of the ISU, so I just as-

sumed the ISU was taking care of all the arrangements and
everything. It's only proper, after all, isn't it?"
   A beat. And then: "Of course it is," Rupert's head bobbed
up and down. "Of course it is. It's the least we can do for her.
It's the only right thing to do." A pause. And then, "Bex, luv,
would you happen to know which room Silvana was staying
in?"

Naturally, Rupert himself did not go to collect Silvana's
things. He sent an underling. A lovely, young Swiss woman
who spoke English so flawlessly Bex would have never
guessed she wasn't local except for the fact that she spoke
English so darn flawlessly. And, equally naturally, Rupert
did not invite Bex to accompany her. Bex invited herself.
Natalie, not being American, was too well mannered to say
anything about it. This time, when Rupert himself called the
hotel manager and asked to be let into Silvana's room, there
was only the slightest pause on the other end of the phone,
after which Rupert reminded the manager how careful the
ISU had been about selecting his as the official competition
hotel and how careful they would be when choosing one for
the next event to be held in San Francisco. There was no
pause, then. Simply the information that a chambermaid
would be waiting outside of Silvana's room to let them in
ASAP.

Natalie went in first, but Bex was the one who promptly
commenced opening all the drawers and checking in the
closet before determining that neither laptop nor printer, not
even a lowly floppy disc, were currently on the premises.
   So either someone had removed them or Silvana never

had the accoutrements to begin with. In any case, Bex had learned all she could from the late judge's room.

She left Natalie to her conscientious, Swiss-like (Was that an ethnic slur? Was it an ethnic slur if you thought something positive about a people? Were the Swiss even an ethnic group, or were they a nationality?), tidy packing and headed out in search of a rogue printer.

And a killer who knew his way around cyberspace.

But first, Bex realized she had missed something very, very obvious. It was so obvious, she should have started with it instead of running around after Stace the cop/stand-up, Sergei the coach/suspect, Rupert the president/bore, and Jasper the fan/other suspect/lunch date. Before she did anything, Bex should have established a timeline for the morning Silvana died. After all, what better way was there to get to the bottom of "Sergei was with me at the practice"/"I wasn't with Xenia at the practice" than checking the one piece of evidence that, as far as she knew, had not been tampered with in any way. Following her search of Silvana's room, Bex headed to the production truck and the videotape Mark the cameraman/death messenger had been shooting prior to the body's discovery.

Naturally, that particular tape wasn't on the shelf in the corner of the truck dubbed Tape Storage. Why should it be? That would make Bex's job too easy and allow at least one thing to go her way. And no one wanted that. It would go to Bex's head and, next thing you knew, she'd feel free to slack, working only a seventeen-hour day instead of the required twenty-two.

An intern was manning the tape shelf. A gawky, local kid with a sprinkle of white-tipped pimples around his lips, who'd probably volunteered for the job with visions of Spielberg dancing in his head and, instead, found himself as far away from the action as humanly possible without actually being in another county. He sat now in a lightless crawl space, surrounded by shelves full of videotapes, all of which needed to be logged, color-coded with orange, green, yellow, and red sticky dots, and available whenever a producer burst in, wild-eyed and screaming that they needed a certain tape with a certain shot, and they needed it yesterday. After two weeks, the poor kid looked perennially on the edge of tears.

Bex saw no reason to upset his routine. It would probably just confuse him. She asked, "Who's got the tape from this morning's ladies' practice?"

He opened his logbook. Over his shoulder, Bex was impressed to note that despite his terror, he'd done an excellent job keeping track of what was shot when, by whom, and who'd checked the tape out most recently. Maybe the little guy had a future in the business, after all.

The intern gulped. The tears that usually merely coated his pupils now threatened to cross the line into actually hovering at the very precipice of his lower eyelid.

"Gil," he whispered with a horror most often reserved for the words *cancer, no survivors, really big snake that eats people whole and then spits out the bones,* and, well, *Gil.*

"Oh," Bex said, feeling her own eyes grow uncomfortably moist. The intern nodded understandingly and handed her a tissue.

A production truck is a twenty-wheeled monstrosity. In Bex's view, it possessed all the drawbacks of a big rig—very cramped space, impossibly complex mobility, eau de gasoline—without the cool stuff like a CB radio, tire flaps with naked girls on them, and trucker food. It was, however, the quickest way to set up a temporary television facility anywhere on the globe for very little money and even less comfort. Still, she had to admit, the 24/7 production managers were whizzes at their jobs. With only three trucks at their disposal, they'd managed to set one up for office space, one for editing and sound dubbing, and a third with the actual equipment to tape and broadcast the show.

It was the latter truck that Gil—after losing one too many battles with his rolling chair—had designated home base. He set up shop in the main, portable control room, a ten-by-five-foot rectangle of space, one wall covered in television monitors showing what every single camera was shooting at a given moment, and two rows of desks. The director, assistant director, audio guy, and technical director sat in the front row, actually putting the show together. Gil sat in the back row. His job was to throw pens, crumpled wads of paper, and an occasional stapler in the belief that such encouragement actually helped in the process of putting the show together.

However, when the show wasn't in the process of being put together, Gil sat in the front row, screening tapes the feature producer gave him to sign off on, and other video odds and ends.

When Bex walked into the production truck, Gil was pointing at one of the monitors, a playback machine showing the tape Mark had shot of the morning ladies' exhibition practice, and telling the operator sitting next to him, "Damn it, I told you I wanted a shot with Erin and the Russian girl skating in two different directions. I need it to open the Sunday show. Why the hell can't you find me that shot? How hard could it be?"

Pretty hard, Bex gambled, *if said shot didn't actually exist.*

"Pretty hard," the operator snapped, "since I keep telling you it doesn't exist."

Bex's mouth metaphorically dropped open. She'd never heard anyone speak to Gil like that. And then she remembered. The tape guys were union.

"You sure?" Gil asked.

"I ain't hiding your shot in my jockstrap, Cahill." Also, the tape operators were the same guys who did all of 24/7's football, basketball, and hockey shows. The guys were famous for being able to cue up and air an instant replay in the time between a ball/puck going in and the audience erupting in cheers. They were union, and they were good at their jobs. God himself wouldn't be stupid enough to fire one.

"Bex!" Gil thundered in her direction as there clearly was no appropriate answer to the tape operator's comment. "How's the research coming? We know yet who put Silvana on ice . . . so to speak?"

"Getting there," Bex reassured. She figured it wasn't a lie as long as she didn't specify where exactly "there" was.

"Better be, kiddo. 'Cause right now, for Sunday's show, I've got a couple of snooze-fest Russians who give interviews like they're out looking to capture moose and squirrel, and Erin Simpson grinning and telling me how much she friggin' loves her silver medal. I need something big, Bex. I need something I can tease at the top of the show that's going to pin butts to seats as sure as if I used this stapler, here."

The tape operator may have been a union guy with a job for life, but even he knew his life wouldn't be worth much if he forgot to duck when Gil started waving staplers around. There wasn't a person in the truck who didn't have at least one visible scar as a result of Gil using the office tool like a silver-spitting Uzi.

He ducked. Bex ducked. And, at the same time, she asked, "Are you done with that tape of the practice, Gil?

"Why? Silvana's killer on it?"

"Actually . . . possibly," (*hopefully*) "yes."

"Cool." Gil popped the tape out of the machine and tossed it to Bex. It's a good thing she was already ducking, because she needed to execute a base-worthy slide to catch it before it hit the floor. "Don't you go dropping the ball on me, Bex. I really get tired of hiring a new researcher every season."

Ɓⱸⱱ took her tape to the editing truck to screen. Fortunately, with the bulk of the event behind them, there were no more athlete up-close-and-personals to be cut. The only thing left were the exhibition opening montage, for which Gil had been looking for a shot of Erin and Xenia skating away from each other, and the piece on Silvana's death. But the bulk of the work had already been done on that particular segment. They had the shot of Silvana the night of the ladies' long program, looking unconcerned as the 24/7 camera zoomed in as tight as it could without actually hitting her on the forehead with the lens, and the shot of her body being carried out of the refrigeration room. Now all they needed was a shot of her killer to tie everything up. And Bex, as Gil so subtly reminded her, had better deliver.

She popped the tape into the machine, grateful that Mark had been the one scheduled to shoot that morning. Mark was a notoriously busy cameraman. He had a knack for being at the right place at the right time to get the best shot, whether it be Lian Reilly landing her one triple-triple of the day (footage they could use when Francis intoned, "Lian is one of only two women at this event boasting a triple-triple at this championship," since no way was she actually going to land one in competition), or Xenia Trubin psyching out her competition by glaring at them with such force she actually seemed capable of knocking them off their feet with vitriol alone. All season Mark had gotten Bex the shots she needed. She could only hope that their mutual luck would hold, and he'd captured something capable of blowing the whole Silvana murder thing wide open. Even if he—and, at the moment, Bex—didn't exactly know what that might be.

She rewound the tape to the beginning and punched Play.

Her first image was of Mark shooting straight down at the ice, white balancing his camera by shooting something devoid of color so that all his subsequent shots didn't come out a nauseating shade of blue green. After a minute of that, he panned up to display the still-empty ice surface. Lian Reilly hopped by the boards, doing jumping jacks to warm up and wearing her Team USA jacket over a hot-pink dress and matching gloves. The girl sure wore a lot of gloves. Almost like (hey, it was a thought) she didn't want to leave fingerprints or something. Next to her, coach Gary Gold sat in the front bleacher row, chatting amiably with Lian's mother. The happy coach and mommy scenario only emphasized how alone teammate Jordan Ares was. No mother—well, that wasn't new, Jordan was quite vocal about how happy she was to be legally emancipated and answering to no one, thank you very much. As far as Bex knew from looking at her records, no one had ever seen or talked to either Mr. or Mrs. Ares. What was more odd at the moment though, was that Jordan's coach, Igor Marchenko, was nowhere to be seen, either. He usually liked to be wherever Jordan was, if only to pry her foot out of her mouth ("The USFSA sucks,"

Jordan once opined at a press conference. "The money they give me wouldn't pay for a pair of skates, forget about serious training, but they want me to sit here and go on and on about how grateful I am for their support. Screw that").

Xenia wasn't in attendance, either. Neither was Sergei. Was this some Russian national holiday Bex didn't know about? An interesting development, considering Xenia swore that she and Sergei had been present.

Erin and Patty were there, though. Erin was the first one on the ice as soon as practice officially commenced, and she was, by far, the most dominating presence. It wasn't so much her physical presence, since Jordan was several inches taller and longer-limbed, to boot. It was more her sense of entitlement. She was the U.S. champion, the world silver medalist, and that meant she always had the right of way, no matter what. Hilariously, the attitude even carried over to her belongings. While both Lian and Jordan made do with squirreling out small personal places for themselves along the barrier, a couple of inches where they could put down their discarded skate guards, their boxes of tissues, their bottles of water, Erin practically claimed a suite for her very own. She took off her light-blue warm-up jacket—not Team USA like the other two, but "Erin Excitement!" (www.ErinExcitement.com)—and draped it over the prime barrier real estate closest to the entrance. Her skate guards were laid down a few inches to the left, next to her tissue box, while her water bottle stood almost a foot away, and, finally, there were her good luck talismans: the first gold medal she ever won (as a four-year-old at a basic skills competition), a hair ribbon Patty wore to win her final national title, and a Kewpie doll dressed in a green replica of Erin's costume from last season, its little shock of hair dyed blonde and painstakingly French-braided (a gift from a fan with quite a bit of free time on her hands). Erin, Bex knew from her research, couldn't practice unless those holy three items were standing, in order, at the barrier, protecting her from harm and the ill will of other skaters.

Erin, Bex didn't feel it was appropriate to add in the research notes, was very strange.

And Xenia, Bex noted as the first twenty minutes of the practice ticked by, was still nowhere to be seen.

Now granted, practicing for an exhibition wasn't as imperative as practicing for a major competition. Bex wouldn't have blamed Xenia if, after the two pressure-cooker weeks she'd had, culminating with the entire judging brouhaha, she'd want to slack a little bit. But, the fact was, if Xenia was looking to score a major pro contract, then setting the Sunday exhibition on fire wasn't just suggested, it was practically mandatory. And the other fact was, Xenia had claimed that she *was* at the practice. And why, lookie here, no Xenia. The camera didn't lie.

Bex continued watching the tape, getting a little glassy-eyed from the sight of three tiny women executing, with almost military precision, a series of skate, jump, landfall, stop by the barrier, blow nose, whisper to coach, look over shoulder to see what the competition was doing, whisper some more to coach, sip some water, blow on cold hands, skate away, try the same jump the competition just nailed, landfall, rinse/repeat ad nauseam. It was boring to watch, and, judging by the wincing and the thigh rubbing as each girl stood up, slower and slower after each successive fall, it was downright painful to actually do.

For herself, Bex had a pithy answer whenever someone, upon hearing that she was a figure skating researcher asked, "Oh, and do you skate yourself?"

"No," was always Bex's answer. "I really don't enjoy falling down."

Erin Simpson, however, seemed positively addicted to it. She was trying a triple loop-triple-loop-triple-loop, an excruciatingly difficult maneuver that, as far as Bex knew, had never been landed by anyone, woman or man. Bex guessed that Erin was determined to do something so fantastic in the exhibition that there would remain no doubt over who should have donned the championship crown. At the moment, though, the only thing Erin had to show for her trouble was a hip and thigh so red, Bex could make out the quickly swelling bruises even through the wet mesh of Erin's tan tights. She wondered how Patty the mother (not Patty the coach) could just sit there so calmly and watch her daughter struggle, near tears, and in obvious pain.

Apparently, she couldn't. Because about twenty-two minutes (Bex loved that the tape had a time stamp) into the practice, Patty whispered something to Erin and walked out of the arena. For a minute, Erin looked lost. She glanced over at Lian, flanked by both mother and coach, and then at Jordan, coachless but seemingly perfectly content, as if trying to decide which scenario fit her best. She bit her lip and looked toward the exit Patty had disappeared through. She then did a scan of the abandoned stands, searching for a familiar face and finding no one. Unexpectedly abandoned, Erin skated around the rink a few times, arms limply by her sides and not a triple jump in sight. She did a layback spin, then changed to a camel, dropping her free leg dejectedly before finishing the revolution.

Erin skated over to the edge of the barrier, grabbed her www.ErinExcitement.com jacket and skate guards, slipped them on, and, without looking back, clomped out the same exit her mother had taken. Both Lian and Jordan looked after her, surprised and curious but in the end much too self-centered to really care.

With Erin gone, the mood in the arena changed. She was no longer the undisputed star and center of attention, which left Jordan and Lian to duke it out for superiority. Jordan took the lead by laying out six gorgeous split-jumps, leaping effortlessly in the air and touching her toes, seeming to be everywhere at once. The handful of fans who'd stumbled out of bed to watch the practice rewarded her with a smattering of applause and a "You go, Jordan, you go, girl!" Lian's usually perky face puckered into a frown of definite nonperkiness. She glared at her mother and Gary, as if Jordan's showboating were their fault, and stomped over to the sleepy gentleman in charge of playing music over the arena's PA.

She handed him her tape and assumed her starting position at the center of the ice. Rink etiquette dictated that whoever's music was playing got right of way. Lian figured that should be enough to get her some undivided attention. Obeying the letter of the law, Jordan moved to the side. And then, in clear violation of the spirit, proceeded to do a jaw-dropping combination spin: flying-camel/change-camel/back-sit/ change-sit/layback/scratch-spin. The speed she got at the end made her look like the film had slipped the projector, it was so blurred. And it earned her another, even more enthusiastic round of applause.

Lian's frown turned to a scowl.

Fortunately, her music came on and, instinctively, she broke into a smile. It looked a great deal less sincere than the scowl had. Bex wondered if maybe, as a sort of anti-Erin, Lian should consider skating a routine whose theme was Unhappiness.

A generic female ballad bounced off the empty arena

walls. It could have been Celine Dion, it could have been Jewel, it could have been Madonna trying to sound plaintive. They all sounded the same to Bex, and she made a mental note to ask Lian who exactly she was skating to, prior to the exhibition broadcast.

Of course, sometimes asking skaters did tend to backfire. One skater had sworn he was skating to a piece by Liza Minnelli. After the show, they got seventeen letters telling them it was actually Judy Garland. Another skater, when asked the name of her long program music, had stared at Bex blankly and finally replied, "Irish."

"That's it? Just Irish? Does the song have a name?"

"I'm not sure."

"Who's the composer?"

"I'm not sure."

"Who's the performer?"

"It's Irish. I think it's Irish."

On the ice, Lian continued to emote her little pigtail off. While she was performing a spiral that, when long-limbed Jordan Ares did it looked stunning, and on petite doll Lian made it practically impossible to see her over the boards, Xenia Trubin finally made her grand entrance.

Talking to Igor Marchenko.

That was a most odd combination.

Granted, Marchenko was Russian. Or, actually Soviet. He'd competed for the Soviet team, even won a world bronze medal in men's singles, before defecting when still a teenager. He'd skated for the U.S., then retired to coaching at the same Connecticut Olympic Training Center that had so generously taken him in years earlier. Even after the collapse of the Berlin Wall and the Soviet Union, he remained virulently anti-Russian, even refusing to accompany his students when they competed there. He was the last man Bex would have expected to be buddy-buddy with the Russian team. And yet, he and Xenia appeared to be chatting very amiably.

Jordan saw Igor walk in and skated over to him. He said goodbye to Xenia and moved to confer with his student. With a stern jerk of the head, Igor indicated Lian and then pointed to the sound guy. Jordan dutifully picked up her own tape and skated over to stand in line for her chance to practice.

Xenia, for her part, did a few languid stretches, then sat down on a bench to tie her skates. If she was missing Sergei, she gave no indication. She didn't look either at the entrance or search the stands. As soon as her skates were tied, she stepped out onto the ice. And promptly bumped into Jordan. Neither woman fell, but both had to grab the barrier to steady themselves.

Xenia appeared to apologize.

Jordan appeared to accept it.

Neither one looked convincing.

Mark held his shot of the two until they'd skated too far apart in opposite directions to remain in the same frame. And, in that instant, Erin had apparently returned, because, all of a sudden, she was back on the ice, skating extra quickly as if to make up for the time lost.

She did one lap, weaving in and around Xenia, Jordan, and Lian, demanding her own way even though Jordan's music was actually the piece currently playing. She skated forward, then turned unexpectedly and did another lap backward. At the end of it, she skidded over to the barrier. And Patty was standing there, offering Erin her customary tissue and bottle of water.

Bex checked the camera's clock. Over a period of almost twenty minutes, Patty, Erin, Xenia, and Igor had been off the ice and out of sight. And Sergei—she fast-forwarded through the remainder of the tape—never showed at all. Xenia apparently gave up waiting for him and left ten minutes early.

Bex had to call Stace to make sure, but she already suspected that she would be right in her assumption. Patty, Erin, Xenia, Igor, and Sergei's unaccounted for twenty minutes were the same ones during which Silvana Potenza was killed.

Seven

And then there was still the little matter of Silvana
Potenza's receipt. No, ye of little faith, Bex hadn't forgotten
about it. She'd just been so busy with the E-mail and the
videotape and the suspects coming and going at the most in-
opportune time. . . . This detective work thing was really
hard. No wonder Stace dreamed of escaping to the low-
pressure land of show biz.

The fact was, Bex had been thinking about the receipt all
along. Just not consciously. But it had been percolating like
hot coffee, even as she did her geographic overview of San
Francisco and its surrounding beachfront property.

The time stamp on the little scrap of paper that was
signed by Silvana and yet somehow mysteriously material-
ized out of Sergei's pocket indicated that the purchases were
made at the hotel boutique, roughly a half hour before Silvana died.

Bex's next step was obvious.

Around the arena and across the lobby, to the hotel boutique she went.

Bₑₓ held several truths to be self-evident:

Gil was a lunatic. Television work was thankless. Skaters always think they should have been marked higher. And a hotel is a hotel is a hotel, the only difference being what language the staff chastises you in.

Now, she had a new one: All hotel boutiques are created equal.

Walking into this latest hotel boutique, Bex might as well have been in any city in any state in any Western (and ambitious Eastern) country. There was the stand with the newspapers. There was the rack of magazines and paperbacks. There was the cooler with sodas. Hello, candy counter, makeup shelf, and feminine hygiene products.

There was the clerk behind the cash register, reading a newspaper and looking warily over the tip of his nose at her, ready to scream "Shoplifter!" at the slightest provocation. The only difference was gender—this one was male and the disparate amount of hair on his head—this one had a wispy, gray ring circling a sunburned bald spot. The suspicious expression on their faces, though, was always the same.

"Hi!" Bex said brightly.

"Hello," he looked not at Bex's face, but at her pockets, lest loot be lurking.

"I have a question for you," Bex pulled the receipt out of her pocket, smoothed it out as best she could, and placed it gently on the counter. "You recognize this?"

He looked at her as if Bex were the stupidest person on the planet. In retrospect, she probably deserved it for asking something so obvious.

"Uhm, what I mean is," Bex stumbled over her own tongue, "Do you remember selling this stuff this morning?'"

He tore his eyes away from her potentially sticky fingers to peer at the list. He said, "Yeah, I remember. It was real early. Hate skating people staying in the hotel. Everybody gets up so damn early."

Bex didn't blame him. She asked, "The woman who bought all this—it was a woman, right?" After her dumb question of a moment earlier, the last thing Bex wanted was to have a "When you assume you make an ass out of you and me" moment.

"Yeah. A woman. Big, fur coat. When she yelled at the guy with her, it was like a fox snapping. All I could see was fur. And teeth."

Goodness, but Bex did love it when people volunteered information without her having to go fishing for it. She'd changed her mind. This detecting thing wasn't that hard after all.

"She was fighting with a man?"

"You calling me a liar?"

"No, no!" Bex wondered how she managed to insult people without trying, and yet her sarcasm often soared over the victim's head without so much as a nick. "Can you describe the man?"

"Tall."

Okay, that eliminated Rupert Newman, Tom Cruise, and that Mini-Me guy. Three down, every other man on the planet left to go.

"Anything else?"

"He talked funny."

Gil Cahill funny? Francis Howarth funny? Latka from Taxi *funny?*

"What do you mean funny? Was he speaking loudly? Using big words?"

"Accent."

Here lies Rebecca Levy, dumbest girl in the land of the free.

A tall man with an accent . . . "Did he have red hair?"

"Yes."

Duh, Bex, what might be a logical way for Sergei to get his hands on Silvana's receipt? Like, maybe he was with her when she bought her candies, etc. . . . ?

"You said she was yelling at him? Do you know about what?"

"Something."

"Can you be more specific?"

"She yelled, 'Don't you threaten me.' Yeah. 'Don't you threaten me,' that's what she said. Also, 'It's done. If the ISU asks, I'll tell them exactly what happened. I told you I would.' "

Bex had been to quite a few hotel boutiques. She'd never felt the urge to kiss the clerk before. She felt that urge now. She suppressed it.

"One more question."

"Yeah?"

"After Silvana paid for her things, which way did she go?"

"Where do they all go? Arena."

"Did the man go with her?"

"Yeah."

"Still yelling?"

"Never stopped yelling."

Time to review: Silvana Potenza and a threatening, tall, redheaded, Russian-accented Sergei exited the hotel boutique and headed toward the arena. A half hour later she was dead, and Sergei, despite Xenia's insistence to the contrary, never made it to the practice. Instead, he hurried back to the hotel and phoned a law firm, with whom he chatted for a good ten minutes. It did not take ten minutes to say, "Wrong number." Also, at some point after they left the hotel, the signed receipt for Silvana's merchandise ended up in Sergei's pocket, the law firm's number scribbled on its back.

Okay, the time for review was now over.

It was now time to talk to Sergei.

Again.

A knock on his hotel room door produced no answer. Neither did a second one. After a moment, Bex let out a breath she didn't even know she'd been holding and admitted to herself that she was relieved. Mathematically speaking, the odds of her getting out alive from a potential killer's room obviously decreased every time she confronted one. No need to push it.

A search of the competitors' lounge also came up empty, although Bex did catch a glimpse of Patty and Erin breaking bread (or a plate of salad, in Erin's case) alongside Jasper. When he spotted her across the room, he raised his arm and waved. Patty did the same, then promptly turned away and pretended to be fascinated by her breadstick, lest Bex decide to walk over and actually take Patty up on her promise of an interview with Erin.

Luckily for Patty, Bex had other matters on her mind. Sergei wasn't in his room, and he wasn't in the competitors' lounge.

There was only one other place he could be.

Bex headed for the parking lot.

Of course, he was there. Sergei, plus all the male members of the Russian figure skating team—three singles skaters, three pairs skaters, three ice dancers—two more Russian coaches, a federation flunkie, and—surprise, surprise—even Igor Marchenko. Only one thing could get all these men— two of whom hated each other since they first competed at the age of six, two of whom used to sleep together and now hated each other, and one who'd slept with all four of the above and so spread his hate around evenly—into a hotel parking lot in the middle of the most important championship of the season: a pickup soccer game.

And not just any game, mind you. As far as Bex could tell, this game was perennially ongoing, having started during the first Grand Prix competition in September and continuing wherever and whenever at least four of the combatants met. Bex had seen them play in a parking garage in Ontario, Canada, a schoolyard in Paris, France, and an open field in Beijing, China. Now, it was apparently a parking lot in San Francisco's turn to host this alternate world cup/celebrity death match spectacle. Bex wondered who was winning. And then, watching a skater who only two days ago gave Bex an interview swearing that his teammates were his very best friends in the world viciously head-butt that same teammate in an attempt to send him crashing into a parked car, Bex wondered if the score really mattered. Obviously, this was a game wherein he who inflicts the most pain, wins.

Due to his size, or maybe due to the fact that, as far as Bex knew, he held no particular grudge against anyone else, Sergei was playing goalie.

The goal was two cars, parked one space over from each other. A blue Toyota Corolla and a green station wagon. Neither one looked as if a soccer ball through the windshield would be welcome. But, then again, not a single player looked as if he really cared.

The match on the field was vicious, with players sliding and slamming and high-kicking with the same intensity they brought to their performances on the ice. Briefly, Bex wished that all the nay sayers who claimed that figure skaters weren't real athletes could take a gander at the sheer physicality of this supposedly friendly game. Sweat gleamed off muscles toned by decades of intense work, as the most complicated of forward/back/foot/knee/head/foot-again kicks were knocked off in single, fluid movements. There was no doubt about it: these were men who would have excelled in any sport they picked. They just happened to pick figure skating, and the viewing public was all the luckier for it.

But, then again, Bex was here to ferret out a killer, so maybe she shouldn't be passing out public service medals quite yet.

Sticking to what she could only guess were the designated outskirts of the parking lot turned playing field, Bex ducked her head between her shoulder blades and held her research binder to the side like a shield as she slowly and in fear for her life from an errant soccer ball inched toward Sergei. She stopped when she reached the far side of the Toyota and leaned over the hood, hissing, "Sergei!"

He turned his head briefly, noted who was hissing, then instantly turned his attention back to the game. Even though, as goalie, his job seemed to consist solely of stopping any ball that dared to fly in between the cars, Sergei insisted on hopping up and down, shifting from side to side like a manic aerobic instructor, his arms up and extended, fingers flexing, ready to catch even when the ball was all the way on the other end of the field.

"Hello!" He boomed in that Beatles-trained accent of his.

"I need to talk to you." Bex looked over her shoulder to check if anyone could overhear them. Luckily, in the middle of battle, no one could care less.

"Listening," he offered and craned his neck for a better view of the action, still hopping.

"It's kind of private."

"And I am rather busy at the moment."

Bex tried to turn her latest set of lemons into lemonade. She'd been afraid of confronting Sergei alone. They certainly weren't alone now. Besides, she doubted he would kill her in the middle of a soccer game. It might cause him to miss a goal.

She asked, "Why didn't you tell me you saw Silvana the morning she died?"

Anyone not watching closely might have missed the rhythm break in his hopping. But Bex happened to be watching very closely. And she knew an ex-skater like Sergei would never skip a beat unless he was somewhat rattled.

He didn't turn to look at her when he lied, "I did not see her."

"Really?"

"Really." Another hop. "Well, perhaps in the elevator or something like this. In the morning. I cannot remember everyone I may have seen in the elevator or in the corridor."

"The man in the hotel boutique says you came in with Silvana. He says you were yelling at her and threatening her when you found out she planned to testify in front of the ISU."

"It was not I." This time, he didn't even break stride. Like any professional athlete, he'd adjusted his rhythm to the situation.

"The clerk said it was a tall man who spoke with a Russian accent."

"Not I," Sergei repeated. "Perhaps the clerk is mistaken. Tall means different things for different people. And a Russian accent—are you certain that he did not hear a Polish accent? Or maybe Czech? They sound very much alike, do you not think?"

Boy, this guy was good. Bex almost would have believed it, except . . . "Silvana Potenza signed a credit card receipt for her purchases. You gave me that receipt when you handed me that phone number back in your hotel room."

The hopping finally stopped. He even tore his eyes away from the game long enough to look at Bex. He said, almost more to himself than to her, "I had forgotten."

"Forgotten what?"

"The phone number, she wrote it down on the back of her receipt. I had forgotten."

Actually, Bex was relieved to hear it. She would have hated it if Sergei had deliberately given her the incriminating slip of paper, meaning for her to figure something profound out, and she'd totally missed it.

"So you *did* see Silvana."

"Yes." He sounded like the last few drops out of an arid gardening hose.

"And you threatened her."

"I did *not* threaten Silvana." Sergei's hands fell by his sides, and he squinted into the distance, no longer following the game, but still avoiding Bex's eyes.

She said, "Look, Sergei, I know English isn't your first language, so let me define the word *threaten* for you. I don't think it comes up a lot as part of "Love Me Do.""

"Nor did the word, *patronize,* Miss Levy, but I recognize what it means, also."

Oooh, sarcasm. Well, good. Bex was comfortable with sarcasm. It made her feel on more solid ground, no matter what the language.

"Do you want to tell me what happened, or should I take the clerk's story and the receipt straight to the police?"

"Silvana gave me that receipt."

"Why? Were you going to reimburse her? Is that what all the shouting was about? Expense reports?"

"Do you want to talk?" Sergei snapped. "Or maybe attempt to listen?"

"Tell me something I can believe."

"Yes, I did see Silvana this morning."

"Tell me something I can believe that I don't already know."

He sighed, darted to the right when the ball appeared to be heading in his direction, then straightened up again when the game moved away into a huddle of flailing arms and legs.

"I was heading out for the practice, when I saw Silvana in the hotel boutique. I went in to address her."

"About what?"

"Xenia."

"Okay, one more time, Sergei, tell me something that isn't obvious."

"I asked Silvana a question: if ISU holds a hearing about Xenia and Erin and the gold medal like her Web site requests, will she answer to them?"

"What did she say?"

"She said that she would."

"Okay, Scooby Snack for honesty on that one."

Sergei looked at her queerly. Bex remembered too late

that Scooby-Doo didn't often come up in the Beatles oeuvre, either.

She followed up, "You didn't want Silvana to talk to the ISU?"

"I did! Absolutely, I did. Yes, I very much wanted Silvana to talk. Thursday night, I begged Silvana to answer the questions for the press. I begged her to tell them we did not cheat, Xenia won the competition fairly."

"Well, if you didn't cheat, why didn't she want to tell the press that?"

"Silvana, she is—she was a very difficult woman."

Bex believed it. In all her years of mystery reading, she had yet to stumble—literarily speaking—upon a corpse whom *someone* hadn't considered difficult. Being difficult, after all, was what most often landed one in their corpseish state.

"How was she difficult?"

"Her standards, they were very high. Even when she gave you a first-place ordinal, Silvana's marks would be always the lowest on the panel. She is very particular. I remember, when we still skated our compulsory figures in competition, Silvana, she would get down on her hands and knees and touch the tracings with her fingers."

"Silvana got down on her hands and knees?" That was a bit hard to imagine.

"Silvana, she was younger then. And also thinner."

"Ah."

"Yes. She has very strong code of ethics. She believes what she believes, and no one can change her mind."

"But wouldn't you think a woman like that would want her name cleared, then?"

"Silvana believed that to answer questions suggests that she is not certain in her position. She said to me, "If I dig—

dig—what is that word in English that sounds like dig, but means to answer?"

"Dignify?"

"Yes! Dignify! Yes, that is her word. She said to me, "If I dignify their questions, then I am suggesting they have rights to ask it in the first place. They have no evidence against me for any wrongdoing, and yet they arrest and try and judge me in the newspapers and on television. I will not speak in my defense to them, because there is nothing legitimate to defend."

"But she was willing to speak to the ISU?"

"Silvana was very proper. If her ISU asks her to speak, she will speak the truth. Silvana said to me, "The ISU, they have right to question me. Media does not.""

"And you swear she would have told them that she didn't cheat."

"I know she did not cheat."

"Still, it's awfully convenient for you and Xenia. Now, Silvana can't testify either way."

Sergei asked, "Did you call the number I gave you?"

"Yes. It's a law firm. But you didn't tell me the name of the person you spoke to, so they didn't know how to direct my call."

"His name is Eugene Varshavsky. He is a lawyer. He speaks Russian."

"A criminal lawyer."

"No." Sergei set his restless hands on his hips and actually turned to face Bex for the first time. "Why is it you think I would call a criminal lawyer?"

"Well, Silvana's murder does come to mind. . . ."

The hands went up in the air, exasperated. "How many times must I tell you this? I did not kill Silvana. I have no reason to kill Silvana. I need her to defend Xenia. I am a victim, too. Xenia and me. We are victims of American media."

Yeah, yeah, yeah, she'd heard this song before from his prize pupil.

Bex asked, "So what kind of lawyer is this Russian-speaking guy?"

"Libel." Sergei said definitively. Then added, "Maybe."

"Maybe?"

"Or slander. He is either a libel or slander lawyer. Silvana, she explained the difference to me. One is in speech, one is written. Though she also said television is like written."

Bex practically heard the pieces click into place in her head, like a joint cracking. "You were calling a libel lawyer because you wanted to sue on behalf of Xenia."

"Yes. Yes!" A light went on in Sergei's eyes, as if finally Bex had proven not nearly as obtuse as he'd previously feared. "Yes, that is exactly, precisely it. Silvana told me she would not speak to the press. That is why I was so angry with her in the boutique. Finally, she said to me, she said, "I will not speak to the press on your behalf. But they have no evidence to accuse you of cheating. Here is the name of a lawyer I know. He speaks Russian. He can help you. He can sue to make them stop saying those things about you and Xenia."

"And then Silvana wrote the number down. . . ."

"On her receipt, yes. I put it in my pocket, I did not look at it closely."

"The boutique clerk said you two left together, headed for the rink."

"Yes. That is so. But I turned around. I went back to the hotel and called the lawyer."

"And you didn't kill Silvana."

"No, Miss Levy," was the last thing he said before diving for a soccer ball flying in his direction. "I did not kill Silvana."

Bex was clueless. A woman without clues.

No. Scratch that. She had clues. She had two very big clues. She just couldn't make heads or tails of them.

Immediately after leaving Sergei to finish his soccer game, Bex redialed the number written on the back of Silvana's receipt and this time, with a name to request, was immediately transferred to a Russian-accented lawyer who confirmed Sergei's story. Which meant absolutely nothing.

Sergei's story could be one hundred percent true, and he still would have had time to call Silvana Potenza from the arena's pay phone, lure her to the refrigeration room, rig the electricity, and make it back to the hotel in time to talk libel and slander and all sorts of other lawyer things.

Except Bex couldn't prove any of it.

And then there was the incriminating E-mail. The one telling Silvana how to rank the skaters in the long program. The one signed Sergei Alemazov. The one Bex still couldn't prove had been sent by him. The one that could have been mailed and printed out any time, both before and after the long program.

Nevertheless, despite her general sense of failure and exhaustion (it was almost dinnertime, and Bex had begun her day at six A.M. after two weeks of equally long days), Bex was nevertheless convinced that the E-mail found in Silvana's purse was the key. If Bex could just prove when it was printed, she would be a long way toward knowing whether the document even could have influenced the judge's decision. After all, if Bex could prove the E-mail was printed after the event, it seemed unlikely that Silvana had been swayed. (Yes, yes, she could have read the E-mail on-line, voted the way it told her to, then printed it out later. But for what purpose? Because she knew she would be killed and wanted to leave some incriminating evidence in her purse? Hey . . . there was a new theory. Bex made a mental note to come back to it when she was really, totally out of ideas.) And if the E-mail was printed before the competition, well, then, Bex would be no closer to proving who, in fact, had sent it. After all, anyone could forge Sergei's name, and he, of all people, had the least motive to actually do so. But, at least she would have *some* information to go on.

And so, Bex's search for that elusive printer continued.

She tried staring at the E-mail, staring really, really hard, and trying to channel some sort of spirit out from between the neatly typed letters. Why couldn't this be an old-fashioned typewriter, she wondered. One that was fortuitously missing an *e* or had a T that didn't cross? Why did all computer printers have to look so uniform? If it weren't for the size difference between American and European paper, Bex would have absolutely nothing to go on.

And if it weren't for leaping to conclusions, Bex might have realized the obvious earlier.

Oh, damn.

Bex studied the E-mail again.

Oh, damn, what if she'd totally missed the boat, here? She'd made the assumption that Silvana's E-mail was printed on European paper because Bex had just spent the past few months wrestling with the stuff. But someone, well, normal, for lack of a better word, someone normal wouldn't have leapt to that conclusion at all. Someone normal would have thought the piece of paper was shorter than usual because its top or bottom had been chopped off.

Bex practically leapt in the air, except she was tired and her feet hurt and, as mentioned earlier, she really didn't enjoy the act of falling.

Instead, she simply asked herself an obvious, follow-up question: Why would someone deliberately chop off the top or bottom of a page they'd printed on?

Why, to remove all traces of a corporate logo, of course.

Bex grinned. A break! Finally, an actual break! All Bex had to do, Prince Charming and his Cinderella slipper style, was figure out which logo could have fit atop the E-mail copy, and she would be that much closer to figuring out where the original was printed.

And when.

And maybe even who sent it.

And why.

Eight

Bex tried the obvious, first.

She was sprawled on the bed in her hotel room, and so she got up, shuffled over to the desk with its leather-bound folder touting the wonders of San Francisco, and laid her copy of the E-mail against the hotel stationery. Yes, it seemed way, way too easy. But, if it turned out that after turning San Francisco upside down without the benefit of an earthquake to search for a holy grail of papyrus, the offending piece was in the hotel notebook and Bex hadn't bothered to check because it was too obvious, she would feel very, very stupid.

And so she checked. And, of course, it was too easy. The hotel crest was much larger than the space allocated at the top of the E-mail. If the guilty party had tried printing the E-mail on one of those sheets and attempted to avoid the logo, the message wouldn't have fit on a single sheet.

Oh, well. She tried.

Bex looked at the clock. It wasn't even ten yet, but she felt utterly dead. Even though she knew Gil would be on the phone bright and early tomorrow morning, demanding to know what Bex had unearthed for his precious exhibition show on Sunday, Bex, nevertheless, decided to give herself permission to hit the sack and do a Scarlett O'Hara imitation. "I'll think about it tomorrow." She figured the guilty stationery wasn't going anywhere, whereas she was about to do a nosedive into the frequently vacuumed carpet.

It was time for Bex to take a break from sleuthing and maybe—how's this for a wacky thought?—maybe even eat something.

She reached for the phone, intending to call room service.

It rang while her hand was resting on the receiver. Wow, this was a good hotel. Were they also calling to tell her what she wanted to order?

"Hello," she picked up the phone, cringing in anticipation of hearing Gil on the other end.

"Bex?"

Gil was not a woman. Ergo, this caller was not Gil. After the kind of day she'd had, that deduction was really stretching the depths of Bex's cognitive powers.

"This is Bex."

"Bex, this is Patty Simpson. You said you wanted to interview Erin. Tomorrow is going to be a very busy day for us, and Sunday, well, Sunday is impossible. So, if you could come over right now and get what you need, that would be great."

Bex covered her mouth with one hand and yawned. She rubbed her eyes and looked longingly at the room service menu.

She said, "I'll be right over."

Unlike every generic hotel room she'd ever seen, Erin and Patty Simpson's temporary home away from home looked like they'd brought in a personal decorator to cozy up the place. It wasn't just the travel suitcase standing on its side in the corner, with all of Erin's skating dresses hanging from individual hangers, organized from darkest color to lightest. It wasn't just the teak dresser covered with a ruffled, pink drop cloth to hold their face powder, lipsticks, eye shadows, curling irons, hair ribbons, and body glitter. It wasn't even the portable cooler stocked with Erin necessities like fortified sports drinks, fortified vitamins, and fortified protein bars. What really went above and beyond the call of duty for personalizing a hotel room were all the pictures. They were everywhere. Photos of Erin as a young smiling skater stuck along the mirror, photos of Patty and baby Erin in frames on the nightstands, two scrapbooks chockfull of newspaper clippings on the table, and a handful of Polaroids from the medal ceremony the night before.

This wasn't narcissism as a hobby. This was narcissism as a lifestyle choice.

Not—Bex, the politically correct and terribly nice person, reminded herself—that there was anything wrong with that.

Erin and Patty greeted her when she came to their door. Erin wore blue jeans that, even though obviously petite in size, still hung loosely about her waist, and a green, belly-baring shirt with the words Erin Excitement! glue-gunned in rhinestones across the chest. Her hair was loose around her shoulders. Finally freed from its French braid and ponytail, her scalp actually seemed to be smiling with relief. Patty, for her part, was still in her coaching outfit. She'd taken off her blazer, but she was still wearing a below-the-knee skirt and white turtleneck.

"Come in, Bex," Patty said and subtly directed her to one of two chairs in the room, the one next to the desk by the bay window. The one boxed into a corner. Patty took the other chair, facing Bex. It was as obvious a power play as Bex had ever been a part of. Thanks to Gil, she knew exactly what it meant when you were shoved into a corner. Erin, though, flopped down on the bed, legs bent at the knees and raised in the air, chin propped up on two fists.

Bex said, "Actually, Patty, Erin was the one I'm really interested in interviewing, so maybe you two could switch seats and—"

"Erin doesn't give interviews without me."

"How come?" Bex asked innocently, as if Patty's unbelievably fanatical, loony control over Erin was news to her. As if a few weeks ago, at the national championships, Bex hadn't been in the room when Patty threw a fit about Erin being interviewed for the broadcast in front of a pair of lit candles. They'd been put there to cast a complimentary light on all the skaters. Only Erin Simpson's mother had insisted on their being removed, lest it look like Erin was into—hand to God, no kidding—devil worship.

"Because," Patty said sweetly, "Erin and I are a team. People don't realize it when they watch skating and only see a single person or a pair on the ice at a time, but figure skating is very much a team sport. No one can succeed in skating alone. I know, in my case, it was a family effort. My father worked two jobs to pay for my skating, and my mother woke up every morning at five A.M. to drive me to the rink. She sewed all my costumes and she did my hair and makeup and she traveled with me to competitions, taking care of the hotel and the luggage and my meals so I didn't have to worry and could focus exclusively on my skating. My brothers and sisters, they pitched in, too, doing my chores and helping me with schoolwork. Every medal that I won, it didn't belong just to me, it belonged to the whole team. And it's the same way with Erin. You talk to her, you talk to me. That's just how things are."

Patty delivered her last few words in a tone even sweeter than she'd started. It were as if the air had suddenly turned into honey and was determinedly clogging Bex's pores and nostrils. But there was no mistaking the threat that came with the sugar.

Bex, as she was intended to, got the message. She decided it wasn't worth fighting about. For now.

Bex opened her notebook and, unlike with Rupert Newman, actually proceeded to take notes, so she could study them later. "Okay, then, let's just start: Erin, do you have a statement to make about Silvana Potenza's death?"

"It's a great tragedy," Erin recited by rote. "Though I know there have been questions about her objectivity as a judge, she was still a member of our extended skating family, and no one wants to see anything bad happen to family."

Right. . . . Now, do you have anything to say you haven't memorized like a trained monkey? Bex most certainly did not ask. Instead, she kept her face neutral and followed up with, "You were at the arena the morning she died. Did you see or hear anything suspicious?"

It was a question she hadn't been prepped for, and Erin scrunched up her face, looking from Bex to her mom, and back again. "I—what do you mean? What was there to see?"

"I don't know," Bex admitted. "But, we are doing a special on her death and, quite frankly, everyone keeps coming back to the same question: What in the world do you think Silvana was doing in the refrigeration area?"

"What gives you the idea that Erin would know anything about that?" Patty demanded, leaning closer to Bex.

"I was just asking, Patty." Bex had to shift in her chair and peer around Patty's shoulder to continue looking at Erin. "Any thoughts, Erin?"

The teen shrugged her shoulders. "I don't know."

It was amazing how much less articulate she got when the answers hadn't been scripted in advance. Bex wondered what the posters on her "Erin Excitement!" message boards, the ones who waxed poetic about how well-spoken Erin always was, thus indicating her keen intelligence, would think about this exchange.

"Did Silvana come in to watch the exhibition practice?" Bex asked. Mark's tape had only focused on the ice, so even though she heard the periodic, scattered applause, Bex had no idea who'd actually been in the audience.

"Maybe," Erin said. "I didn't see her, but she usually comes."

"When Erin is on the ice," Patty explained, "I try to encourage her to focus and not be distracted by the other people on the ice with her or in the stands. After all, you can't control what other people do, you can only control what you do, and that's, ultimately—"

"What you get marked on," Bex finished. "Yes, Patty, I know, I read the press kit." She wasn't usually so reckless with her subjects, but she was exhausted and hungry, and she'd spent seven months already watching "The Patty and Erin Road Show." Bex was in no mood for reruns, especially when the first run hadn't exactly sparkled.

Patty's spine stiffened, and she looked miffed. Did she really think that every time she dragged out that old chestnut, it somehow became brand-new again?

Bex told Patty, "I watched the tape of the practice session. About twenty minutes into it, you left. Where'd you go?"

Patty's head cocked to the side like that of an anthropo-morphic, lovable robot processing something uncom-putable. She was obviously used to answering questions meant for Erin, but one aimed directly at her seemed to set off a short circuit.

"It was very cold at the arena that morning. I don't think they'd really started running the heat yet, and, well, it's usu-ally close to impossible to warm an open area that large, anyway. . . . It was very cold, and poor Erin's nose was run-ning, which is the last thing we need, so I went to get a box of tissues from her bag in the dressing room."

Patty smiled, obviously pleased with her answer. She even looked Bex straight in the eye to demonstrate how open and honest and forthright she was being.

Except that . . .

"The dressing rooms are around the corner from the arena entrance. You were gone for almost a half hour. It takes a half hour to walk a few feet and back?"

"The tissues weren't in Erin's bag," Patty shrugged. "I had to come back to the hotel and get another box from our stash." Patty pointed to a stack of three boxes sitting on the dresser next to the overgrowth of cosmetics.

And it came to pass, from this day forward, Bex mused, the creation of what shall be known as the Great Tissue Alibi. It sounded as thin as . . . well . . . Bex refused to make a pun so obvious, but it was also pretty irrefutable. Bex had watched the tape. She'd seen Patty come back and hand the tissue to her daughter's cold-dripping nose. She wasn't lying about that.

So now Patty and Sergei were closer to being nudged off the suspect list, each with their not exactly off the hook but close enough alibis. On the other hand . . . Bex turned her attention to Erin who, apparently bored by her mother's reminiscences of practice sessions past, had turned her attention to the task of chewing her cuticles.

Even though Patty was sitting with her back to Erin, she'd somehow, mid conversation, sensed that her daughter was engaged in aesthetically inappropriate behavior. Without turning around or pausing, she reached behind her and managed to smack Erin's hand out of her mouth without breaking stride.

"Those fingers are going on camera tomorrow, remember, honey?"

Erin guiltily pressed the aforementioned fingers into the bedspread, one palm on top of the other. "I remember. I'll just put on nailpolish."

"We don't have the exact pink shade with us that matches the dress you wanted to wear for the exhibition. You know how bad two shades of the same color look next to each other."

"I could wear a different dress. I could wear the yellow."

"No, Erin, you can't."

"Why not?"

"You know Lian Reilly will be dragging out that horrible "Sunshine on My Shoulder" number, and she always wears yellow for it."

Well, this was certainly fascinating, Bex thought. In the next few minutes, she'd better either accuse someone of murder or risk falling asleep where she sat. It was one thing for a sleuth to tumble over unconscious when smacked by a gun barrel against the back of the skull. It was quite another to pass out because it was night-night time.

So, an accusin' they would go, before the sandman submitted his past-due notice.

Bex asked Erin, "What about you? Why did you leave the practice?"

From the looks on both Erin's and Patty's faces, Bex could guess that either this bit of news was quite a surprise for Mama Simpson, or that both were the best set of mother-daughter actresses since Vanessa Redgrave and Natasha Richardson (although their blonde coloring suggested that Patty and Erin might be more likely to appear at the movies in the form of Blythe Danner and Gwenyth Paltrow).

As soon as the words were out of Bex's mouth, the expression on Erin's face was silently screaming, *Ixnay on the Euvingluy,* while the one on her mother's was more of the *What the hell?* school.

Patty whipped around, facing Erin, her back to Bex.

"You left the practice session?" Her tone seemed more appropriate to asking, *You set the house on fire?* or at least *You've invaded Central Asia? Again?*

"Yes." Now that she knew there was no way to wriggle out of it, Erin appeared to have decided that the best defense was a blasé offense. Maybe if she pretended it was no big deal, her mother might start respirating at a regular rate, again. Either that, or Erin, the perfect child, was just being a typical bratty teen who knew the best way to get her mother's blood pressure up was to set her own reaction a few notches below snotty indifference.

If Bex were writing a graduate thesis on the varieties of family dynamics (and after some of the clans she'd met through skating, a project like that would practically write itself), she might have found this mother-daughter exchange absolutely fascinating. But Bex was looking to fish out a murderer here, and, in that case, she was a lot more interested in how the two women reacted to *her* questions than they did to their own.

Bex jumped in to ask, "So, anyway, Erin, why did you leave?"

"I'd like to hear the answer to that myself." Patty half-turned to tap her finger against Bex's notebook, indicating that she should write the next part down. "You have to understand, Bex, Erin never, ever leaves a practice. I find that once you plant in a skater's head the notion that they can just get off the ice any time they're tired or things aren't going well, it burrows into their subconscious, and it starts to affect their performances. Suddenly, if they take a fall in the middle of a competition and their brain is telling them that it's okay, they can get off, take a break and try again later, they lose all of their fighting spirit. They just give up. The next time you're watching a competition, check out the skaters that just deflate after a fall, the ones who stop trying and kind of skate through the rest of the event like a zombie. Odds are that their coaches allow them to get off the ice. I'd never do that to Erin. I'd never handicap her in such a way."

"Uh-huh . . ." Bex said, while visions of Erin shackled to the ice with a cast-iron chain while bleeding profusely from a gushing Uzi wound to the chest, danced through her head. "That's a very interesting philosophy, Patty. I'll suggest to Gil that we do a segment on it next season. But, in any case, Erin—three strikes and I start making up my own answers—why did you get off the ice this morning?"

Erin ducked her head, cheeks pinking to match the nail polish she apparently did not have. "I was looking for my mom."

"Why?" Bex and Patty asked in unison.

"Because," she looked close to tears. Genuine emotion or an Oscar moment? "My nose was running, okay? My nose was running and I didn't have any damn tissues and my music was about to be played and the last thing I wanted was to go into a scratch spin and have snot flying everyplace. That happened at Skate Canada practice when you wouldn't let me get off the ice, remember, Mom? It was disgusting. And Jordan Ares never let me forget it. After I finished the program, she skated up, and she was all, "Didn't know I should bring my umbrella to practice, ha ha." Lian Reilly practically peed in her pants, she laughed so hard. Her dumb mother did, too. And I looked over, and the judges, they were pretending they didn't hear her, but I could see they wanted to laugh. I was so embarrassed I wanted to die!"

"So you went to the dressing room to look for your mom and the tissues?"

"Yeah. Except she wasn't there."

Patty said, "I must have already gone back to the hotel for them."

"Whatever." Erin shrugged. "I mean, I figured that, but I didn't want to go through the hassle of taking off my skates and dragging them around with me while I went looking for you, so I just got a paper towel from the bathroom and blew my nose and got back on the ice."

Bex said, "The bathroom is right next door to the dressing room. You were gone from the arena almost as long as your mom, Erin. What took you so long to come back?"

"I—" Erin took a deep breath. "I sort of, I kind of . . . I had a fight."

"A fight!" Patty's tone was back to attacking Central Asia. "What in the world are you talking about? A fight? With whom?"

Erin bit her lip. "With Xenia Trubin—"

"Are you out of your mind?!" Not only had Erin apparently attacked Central Asia, but, judging by the fit Patty was throwing, she'd also lost the battle. "Did anyone see you? Was there press there? What were you thinking, Erin? Didn't I explain to you how carefully we had to play this? One word that sounds like sour grapes from you, and we lose all—all, do you understand?—of our sympathy factor. What in the world prompted you to—"

"She started it!" Erin defended.

Bex tried to think back to the practice tape she'd watched. Xenia arrived at the practice after both Patty and Erin had left it. But, just because she wasn't on the ice first thing in the morning didn't mean she wasn't at the arena. Taking care of other matters.

Bex asked, "What did Xenia say to you?"

"All sorts of trash-talking stuff!" Seeing that there wouldn't be much sympathy from her mother, Erin turned her attention to Bex as a sort of go-between. "She called me names, said I was a cheater and a liar. She said I was a lousy skater, I had no technique, and that the only times I ever beat her it was because the judges were cheating then, not now. She said if anyone fixed this competition it was you, Mom, you and Jasper with all his money, and she said you've been buying me medals since I was a kid, that everyone couldn't stop talking about how Jordan should have won nationals this year, not me, and that—"

"The little bitch!" Patty seethed. "I swear to God, if she mentions a word of that rumor to the press, I will have her up on charges so fast—"

The sarcastic part of Bex's sleep-deprived brain was this close to suggesting Patty ask Sergei for the name of his libel lawyer. The part that needed some vital information to present to Gil the next morning or else he would yell at her more than usual, however, asked Erin, "Where was Xenia when you ran into her?"

"She was right outside the dressing room."

With deliberate casualness, knowing that this was painfully important and thus desperate not to taint the evidence in any way, Bex asked, "You mean, where that pay phone is?"

She didn't add, *The pay phone from which Silvana got her last phone call, most likely luring her to the refrigeration room and subsequent death?*

"Yeah," Erin said. "They were all standing right around it, whispering."

"They?" Again Bex and Patty queried in unison.

Great, just what Bex always wanted, to end up on the same frequency as Patty Simpson.

"Who's they?" Bex managed to beat Patty to the question punch, reassuring herself that they hadn't been totally fused at the cerebral cortex just yet.

"Xenia," Erin counted out on her fingers. "And Sergei Alemazov, and also Jordan's coach, Igor Marchenko."

Bex needed a moment to absorb the information. Patty, apparently, didn't.

"I knew it!" Patty cried triumphantly. "I knew it! Oh, Erin, honey, this is wonderful. I wish you'd told me this before. Erin, Bex, this explains everything!"

Nine

Bex raised her hand, waving it in the air like a kid desperately trying to get her teacher's attention for a hall pass. "Hello? Patty? Over here? Focus. Good. Now. What the heck are you talking about? What explains everything?"

Because, all things being equal, Bex now felt more confused than ever. After everything she'd gone through to check out his alibi, including ducking the homicidal soccer ball, now Erin was claiming that Sergei Alemazov had been at the arena, after all? (To be fair, Xenia had told her the same thing, so now it was two against one.) And he'd been hanging out around the pay phone? With Xenia? And Marchenko? Was this some sort of *Murder on the Orient Express* ritual killing thing? A skating, satanic cult Bex had yet to be aware of?

Patty said, "Igor Marchenko is the key."

More confusion. Igor Marchenko? He was Jordan's

coach. He wasn't involved in the Xenia/Erin debacle. Why would he want to murder Silvana?

"Igor Marchenko," Patty explained, "was the go-between for the Russians and Silvana."

"And you know this how, Patty?"

"It's obvious. Marchenko is a Russian. It doesn't matter that he coaches an American girl. He's still a Russian, deep down."

"He defected," Bex said. "He hates the Russians. He won't even go there when one of his kids is competing."

"It's an act," Patty dismissed. "A cover."

"You're telling me that young Igor Marchenko defecting thirty years ago, abandoning his family and his life and his career, was just the first step in a plot to deprive Erin of a gold medal? Wow, talk about a deep, deep sleeper agent."

Erin actually giggled. Patty didn't seem to get the joke. Instead, she pressed on, "If Erin saw him talking to Xenia and Sergei, obviously he's in cahoots with them."

"Or he could just have been asking the time." Bex was convinced Patty was barking up the wrong coach. The key here was Sergei, not Marchenko.

"Sergei couldn't afford to be seen plotting with Silvana," Patty insisted. "It would have been too obvious when Erin didn't win that something fishy was up. So they used a go-between. And who better than Marchenko? Marchenko got to Silvana!"

"And what was in it for him?"

"Jordan, of course."

"Jordan?"

"Her bronze medal here. She didn't deserve it. Jordan is a mediocre skater at best, a sloppy one at worst. Everyone talks about her long limbs like that's a bonus. Honestly, she looks like an orangutan, all dangling arms and legs. When she turns in the air it's like she's moving in slow motion. Marchenko tries to hide her defects with that silly, flowing choreography. But he knows he's got nothing there to really work with."

"So . . . Marchenko got Silvana to give Jordan a bronze medal in exchange for Xenia getting first?"

"Not exactly. Jordan being third was Marchenko's reward for being the go-between. The initial deal was still between Sergei and Silvana."

"Okay. So Sergei told Silvana to put Xenia first, and she just . . . did? Why? I mean, what would motivate her to do that? What did Sergei give her in return?"

Patty guessed, "Money?"

Bex doubted it. A man who smuggled food out of the competitors' dining room and packed it in plastic bags for maximum freshness was not someone rolling in cash advances.

"Or maybe it was a two-part trade. Like, maybe Silvana put Xenia first in exchange for a Russian judge putting . . . putting . . . oh, I know! The Italian dance team! They were fifteenth last year and fifth this year! No one jumps that high in ice dancing. It just isn't done. Obviously, that's where the fix was. God, I'm so stupid. I should have seen it sooner."

Bex said, "The Italian dance team was fifteenth last year because the girl was skating on a sprained ankle. They fell in the original and the free dance. This year, she's fully recovered, and they didn't fall. They skated great. I think they have a new coach, too."

"And they had a judge in their pocket."

Okay. This conversation had reached its—if not logical, then at least annoying—conclusion. Bex'd had enough, and she doubted Patty could be swerved off her course at this late point. Besides, Bex'd gotten what she'd come for. Patty

and Erin's on-the-record explanations about why they'd
both left the practice arena. Plus Erin's fascinating tidbit
about Xenia, Sergei, Marchenko, and the phone. A tidbit
Bex found particularly interesting in light of the fact that
Erin had no way of knowing about the phone's significance.
And thus no reason to lie about it. Since she didn't know that
proximity to the phone could be considered incriminating,
she had no reason to deliberately point that finger in the
Russians' direction.

Unless, of course, Erin was the killer.

And she knew exactly what that phone had been used for.

Now that she was one herself, Bex decided that amateur
detectives in books had an unfair advantage over the real-
life variety. In real life, the last line uttered or written before
a paragraph break was always fraught with significance.
Even if the amateur sleuth didn't know it at the time, later,
as the facts began to accumulate, he or she could always
look back and exclaim, "Aha! The last thing the suspect said
before the scene change was, 'Of course, I never saw the
leprechaun.' But, now that I have found this swatch of green
cloth, the truth has become oh, so clear."

Bex couldn't do that. Unlike in books, her conversations,
by necessity, had beginnings, middles, and terribly mundane
ends. The last thing Erin said to Bex before she left the
Simpson hotel room, was, "Bye. See you around." The last
thing Patty said was, "Good-bye, Bex. We'll let Gil know
when Erin is available for her on-air interview."

The latter was a deliberate attempt to remind Bex of just
where she fell on the 24/7 food chain and what a great favor
the Simpsons had done by deigning to speak to lowly, little

her; but it was hardly the stuff puzzle-solving revelations were made of.

Bex returned to her room and fell into bed, still dressed, the makeup she'd put on that morning forming little clumps in the corners of her eyes, and desperately hoping for one of those movie-style revelatory dreams where everything meant something and, hopefully, a backward-speaking, dancing midget handed her a previously overlooked clue.

Before turning out the light, Bex looked at the bedside digital clock and noted that she had five hours of sleep available before needing to wake up at six A.M. for Gil's production meeting. She closed her eyes and begged for a coma.

Fifteen minutes later, just as Bex was rolling over to find a comfortable curl-up spot, her phone rang.

"This is your wake-up call, Miss Levy."

She peeled open her eyes and peered at the clock again. In the past fifteen minutes, someone had set it forward five hours.

Damn, but she hated when that happened.

Bex got up and prepared to face her day.

And, if the definition of facing her day could be semantically expanded to include sitting with eyes open/brain in sleeper mode for the first half-hour of Gil's seven a.m. production meeting, then, for a while there, Bex was doing a wonderful job of just that. Honestly, her mental state hardly mattered for that first half-hour. The problem with Gil's meetings (well, there were many problems, this just happened to be the currently relevant one) was that he insisted on every single staff member attending. Producers, directors, researchers, technicians, talent, production assistants, all were required to find a seat and sit in it until they were dutifully dismissed. Gil liked to say these meetings were like a football huddle prior to play. It made them all feel like a cohesive team willing to go the distance for each other. In reality, the only thing it made them feel was always tired and periodically bored. Because, on a production this big, there were a million different jobs that needed to be done by various experts. The cameramen and the director had to block out their shots for every routine. The feature producers needed to screen their pieces so that the line producer could plug those times into his rundown. The talent and researchers had to come up with a story line for the broadcast and hammer out their copy. The audio men needed to test their mikes. The executive producer needed to tell the production assistants which tapes from days past he wanted in the truck with him, and how to organize and code them.

But (and this was a big, big but), the talent didn't need to hear about the director's camera positions, the audio guys didn't need to know the story line, the production assistants had no input or interest in the rundown, and the cameramen, to a man, could care less about which features would be rolled in when. Alas, thanks to Gil and his delusions of football, they were all obligated to sit there and listen.

Right now, for instance, it was the technical people's turn to talk. That meant that Bex could safely tune out, stare at the wall, and pretend there were little toothpicks keeping her heavy eyelids upright. Across the conference table, Francis and Diana were amusing themselves by playing a game of tic-tac-toe on the hotel notepad. Each game took about thirty seconds, and it was easy to see who won what round based on which Howarth angrily ripped the page off its pad and crumpled it into a pointy ball. Plus, the winner inevitably stuck his tongue out at the loser. That was a good clue, too.

Finally, the technical portion of the meeting was over, and Gil turned his attention to the narrative of his show. On the one hand, Bex was happy, because finally here was something that concerned her. On the other hand, Bex was sad, because it meant she would finally have to listen, and that usually meant waking up. (On the third hand, she received another indicator of just how exhausted she was by the fact that, when it came to describing her emotions, the best Bex came up with was *happy* and *sad*. If they'd been dead, her college professors, especially those who once chastised Bex's excessive use of pretentious words like *supercilious* and *sanctimonious* rather than simply saying, *pain in the ass*, would be spinning in their graves.)

Gil beckoned a PA and handed him a stack of papers to pass out to everyone around the table. The sheets were copies of his two-page rundown, breaking the show down into timed segments, i.e., thirty seconds for the graphic opening titles, then a minute and a half for Francis and Diana's on-camera welcome to the folks at home, followed by a replay of Erin's long program from the previous night (five minutes, with marks and reactions), then back to Francis and Diana for another minute on the controversy, then go to the first exhibition, then . . .

Gil went on and on, reading them the rundown as if no one in the room had ever seen one before. He pointed out where they'd have their interview with Erin, where they'd stop to marvel about the scenic beauty of downtown San Francisco, and, finally . . .

"Right here, this is where we'll do our feature on the Silvana Potenza murder. Bex." Gil looked right at her. An IV of Brazilian coffee directly into her veins couldn't have woken Bex up any faster. "I haven't seen your write-up, yet. How's that coming?"

"Uhm . . ."

"Tick-tock, Bex. Time's running out. I'm not planning to cut to a black hole, here. When I say, 'Roll the Potenza feature,' there better be a Potenza feature to roll. We need our story. I already promised the network we'd have one. You doing the, *capice* thing, here?"

"Yes, Gil," Bex said, ducking her head so she didn't have to see the expectant way everyone around the table was watching her. "I am one with the *capice* thing."

In fact, Bex was *capiceing* all over the place. She knew what she needed to do. She knew why she needed to do it. She even knew where and by when. It was that pesky how (that odd *H* among the five *W*s), that was slowing what otherwise would have been warp-time progress.

She had to find out where Silvana's E-mail was printed, and her time for kidding around was running out. To that end, Bex left the production meeting and headed straight for the ISU room to check out their stationery.

She checked out their stationery. Like Cinderella's slipper on her stepsisters' feet (and OJ's bloody glove), it didn't fit.

Okay.

Now what?

Bex looked up from her failure. Through the doorway of the ISU room, she saw Igor Marchenko walking toward the front door.

Good enough.

"Igor!" Bex ran out of the ISU room calling the coach's name and waving her arms like a madwoman to get his attention. She caught him just as he got to the revolving glass hotel door and practically threw herself between it and him.

Igor, a man who presumably had seen quite a lot in his life, what with being a political refugee and all, did not look particularly disturbed by this madwoman/researcher/stalker person. Bex took this as practically an engraved invitation to debrief him.

"Hello!" She said.

"Hello." His Russian accent wasn't as noticeable as Xenia's, but there was no hiding his roots. And, Bex couldn't help wondering: Possible affiliation?

"I need to ask you a few questions. For research. Research questions."

"Yes?" Igor crossed his arms and surveyed Bex over both pointed elbows. Russian may have been his mother tongue but, at the moment, the only language radiating from the man was of the nonverbal, body variety. And it was very clearly saying, "Get on with it, young lady, and this had better be worth my while, or else I'm running over you like Soviet tanks over Prague."

She felt like he'd started a stopwatch. Unfortunately, Bex didn't know how much time she had before what passed for this man's good humor melted like an ice chip.

"Okay," Bex fired the start gun in her mind and prepared herself for a sweaty, verbal sprint. "Okay, right. Igor. I— yesterday, I interviewed Patty Simpson and Erin. About the whole Xenia winning the gold medal business. I—" Bex felt herself interrupting herself to digress, but she also couldn't help it. "By the way, what did you think of the results?"

Igor shrugged. "Skaters skate, judges judge. If we accept the results when we win, we must to accept them when we lose."

"So you think Xenia deserved to win?"

"Xenia did win."

Right. Like that was a fact Bex would ever be allowed to forget. She changed the subject. "What about Jordan? Were you happy with her results?"

"A bronze medal is very good start."

"Do you think she should have been higher? Like maybe ahead of Erin?" Bex really pressed now, figuring it might be her last chance to beat the clock. "I heard there were some people who thought Jordan should have beaten Erin at nationals."

Igor smiled. It seemed to both be covering his suppressed anger and also commenting ironically on the fact that Igor knew that Bex knew that he knew that he was suppressing. "Our sport, it is notoriously subjective. There are always different opinions. Jordan and Erin skate very, very differently. Different people like different skating."

Bex knew that Russians didn't have middle names. However, if Igor ever decided to go all-American and add one, Bex had the perfect moniker: cool. This guy was cool. Which was delightful for him, not so delightful for Bex. She'd never get anything useful out of Igor while he remained so unruffled and infuriatingly in control. Her only chance was to stab in the dark and try to ruffle him. Fast. He'd already taken one imperceptible step toward the glass doors. If he decided to beat it, Bex could hardly throw herself around his ankles.

And so she went ahead and stabbed. She told him, "Patty Simpson thinks you were the go-between for Xenia Trubin, Sergei Alemazov, and Silvana Potenza. She says Silvana arranged for Jordan to win the bronze here in exchange for your help in getting Xenia the gold."

Bex waited for Igor to percolate. Heck, she would have settled for boil. Simmer, even. What she got, instead, was, at best, a drip off an icicle.

Igor said, "The psychiatrists, do they not say that what we accuse others of, is actually our own wrongdoings?"

Well, if they did, Bex sure hoped they were clearer about it. She had to take a moment to untangle Igor's sentence and rearrange the clauses before she fully grasped what he was talking about. "You mean that Patty is accusing you of cheating, because—"

Igor only shrugged cryptically. And then he reminded, "You asked if people thought my Jordan should have beaten Erin at nationals."

"You're saying that Patty cheated? At nationals?"

"Erin won nationals. Xenia won worlds. Judges' decision is always final. Always."

"Can one judge really make that much of a difference, though?"

"In a five-four split?" Igor looked amused to be pointing out the obvious. "Yes, then, I would say one judge can make quite a bit of difference."

Bex wished everyone would stop speaking to her as if she were an idiot. She supposed a good way to nip that in the bud would probably be to stop acting like one. "So how did Patty do it, then? Did she bribe every single judge?"

"Why do you say bribe?" Igor waved his palm in the air, perhaps to indicate the sic- transit-Gloria of all things. Or maybe just to exercise his wrist. "Bribe is such a . . . such an . . . American . . . word. Why do you assume money? There are many, many ways to influence results, without bringing money to the table."

"Like what?" Bex asked eagerly. Her own instantly compiled list read: sex, threats, and/or a bomb wired to go off if a judge's marks dipped below 5.9.

"Talking," Igor said.

Bex blinked. "Talking?"

"Let us pretend you are a judge. A judge at the United States Nationals, for instance."

"Let's," Bex agreed.

"Good. Now. Your job as a judge at the United States Nationals, it is to . . . "

Bex realized he was waiting for her to fill in the blanks, and promptly jumped to attention. "Uhm . . . Your job is to pick the top three best skaters in each event."

"No," Igor said.

"No?"

"No. Your job is to pick the three skaters you think will perform best and win you medals at the upcoming world championship."

"Those aren't the same people?"

"Not necessarily. Let us say, for instance, you have the defending bronze medalist from last year's world championship. And, at the nationals, he or she has a bad day. A very bad day. Falls on everything, including taking her bows. Let us also say that, at the same nationals, is a skater who, for the past five years has always, always, always, frozen in competition. Always. Except, today, when she freezes, she still manages to perform better than last year's medalist. It is a miracle! It is also, probably, what you call a fluke. Now, I ask you: you are the judge whose job it is to pick competitors for the world championship. Who do you put in the top spot? The girl who ninety-five percent of the time skates well, but not today, or the girl who ninety-five percent of the time skates awful, but not today?"

"Oh," Bex said.

"Yes. Oh." Igor looked around, checking if anyone could hear them. From the look on his face, Bex couldn't be sure if he was trying to avoid, or in fact attract, eavesdroppers. "Patty Simpson, she grows up in American skating, no? She has many friends, many people she has known not just all of Erin's life, but most of her own. Patty is a smart woman, and she knows how to talk the right language. Let us pretend you are a judge at the United States Nationals."

"Let's. I'm on a roll."

"Let us say you have two skaters of almost equal ability. Both have excellent chances of winning you medals at the next world championship. And then, one day, as you are sitting in the arena, freezing cold, thinking about the money you are losing needing to take the weeks off from work to come volunteer as a judge in the middle of nowhere, your good friend Patty comes and sits down next to you, and she says: 'You know, that Jordan, she is not exactly what we here in America want to see in our champion, is she? She talks maybe not so pretty. She listens to no one, not even her parents. She is this . . . loose cannon. You never know what she will say and to who. You never know who she will insult. The girl is out of control. She will make us look bad. She does not know how to behave like the right kind of champion. Not like my Erin. My Erin always says the right thing. My Erin listens to her mother, and, of course, her mother, I, Patty, always listens to my federation. Oh, and Erin is a good skater, too."

"Oh," Bex said again.

"So, in my example, did Patty bribe a judge?" Igor asked. "Did she threaten? Did she even suggest that Erin should win?"

"Well, maybe not technically. But she did . . ."

"She did nothing wrong."

"Oh. Well, then." Bex asked, "Did you?"

Ten

"Did you?" The question hopped off Bex's tongue like a renegade frog off a favorite lily pad. She hadn't meant to just blurt it out like that. She'd meant to be crafty and sly and as cool as he was. But that didn't work out so well. And now the question was out there. Bex figured she might as well go with it. The naturalized native was getting restless. "Were you involved in getting Xenia the gold medal? Did you talk to Silvana and suggest . . ."

For the first time, Igor's face actually darkened. The icicle didn't so much drip, as crack. "I am a member of the *American*," he stressed the word, "team. Why would I ever, ever make a deal for a Russian girl to win?"

"I . . . I don't know. But Patty thought—"

"Patty! Patty Simpson is like all the rest. I skate for American team. I win my Olympic gold for American team. I spend my life coaching in America, making American champions. I have not returned to Russia, not seen my mother, my sister, since I was a boy. But, it does not matter. I am still a Russian to you. My loyalty is still in your question."

Oh, God. She'd been politically incorrect again. Damn karma.

"I didn't mean—"

"I know exactly what you mean. I barely know Xenia and Sergei, and here you have me in cahoots with them, against the Americans!"

Okay. Bex may have been squirming with embarrassment, but she hadn't dissolved into a puddle of goo so deep that she still couldn't pluck the lie out of his tirade.

"You barely know Xenia and Sergei?"

"We speak maybe two words every competition."

"Really?"

"Yes. Really. I do not talk to Russians. They are not my people."

"Then how come Erin Simpson says she saw you, Sergei, and Xenia deep in conversation the morning Silvana Potenza died?"

The icicle that had earlier broken off now hit the ground with a thump. Mr. Cool was gone. In his place was Mr. Deer in Headlights.

"Well?" Bex asked. "I have the tape of the practice, so I know you were all off the ice at the same time, then. Erin said you were standing by the pay phone across from the refrigeration room, speaking Russian."

A moment of silence.

A moment of silence during which Igor didn't deny it. He didn't deny it! Oh, my God, he actually wasn't denying it! Bex wondered if it was possible to pat oneself on the back, and whether doing so suggested more than an acceptable hint of arrogance.

Igor said, "That conversation, it had nothing to do with Xenia beating Erin."

"So what did it have to do with, then?"

"That is none of your business."

"True," Bex agreed. "But I bet it would be the police's business."

She knew that it was wrong, she knew that it was something a truly nice person should never really do, but when Bex said the word *police,* she hoped it triggered some sort of post traumatic stress in Igor, where he actually thought KGB, and cowered accordingly.

"You can tell the police, or you can tell me, and I'll decide whether it's worth going to them about."

Boy, she was brazen. Bex had no idea where all her bravado was coming from, but she certainly hoped it wouldn't wear off before Igor figured out she was full of it.

He looked around again. This time, Bex felt pretty certain he most certainly did not want them to be overheard.

"Sergei Alemazov, I have arranged for him to begin coaching at the Olympic Training Center in the next year. And he can bring Xenia to train with him. The ice where they are now, it is horrible. No place for a champion and her coach to work. But Sergei did not want the Russian federation to know of it until the matter was definitely settled. You know the problem they have been having with their federation. That is why we were keeping it a secret."

"You're sure that's all you were talking about? Your getting Sergei a job?"

"That is all," Marchenko said definitively, turning dramatically towards the revolving doors. "Anything else is just Patty Simpson nonsense."

With Igor out the door, Bex did a single sweep of the hotel lobby just in case another potential witness felt like falling into her lap. When such a miracle failed to occur twice in one morning, Bex hightailed it back to the ISU room, where, after much charm and a little lying, she managed to get her hands on a standard piece of Italian Skating Federation stationery, just in case Silvana's E-mail had been printed on that.

It wasn't.

Of course it wasn't.

Why should anything about this be easy? After all, if detecting were easy, how would Nero Wolfe earn the big bucks to live in that cool New York townhouse? Bex lived in New York. She knew how much real estate cost. Nero Wolfe had to be billing major, major cash for every case he solved. And probably dealing drugs on the side to keep up with the maintenance charges.

But, as she was wont to do, Bex digressed.

She walked out of the ISU room and plopped on the nearest plush lobby couch. The better to lay in wait for further prey.

It was also as good a place as any for her to finally stop procrastinating and at least begin writing that report Gil needed from her on the Silvana murder. What a shame that everything she knew to date was utterly circumstantial, unsubstantiated, and uncorroborated. (There Bex went with the big words again. She must have been feeling more awake now.)

Awake enough to notice something that previously she'd completely blanked on.

Bex looked at the piece of 24/7 stationery she'd pulled out to take her notes on. It had the network's logo at the top of the page. A 24, slash 7, all against the background of a supposedly spinning globe. "Everywhere, all the time" was the 24/7 motto. It was written in capital, block letters beneath the spinning globe.

Her stomach did a roller-coaster dive and lodged somewhere behind Bex's Adam's apple. She didn't dare think what she was thinking. She ordered herself to stop thinking what she was thinking. She chastised herself for thinking it. And then she thought it.

Bex reached into her pocket and pulled out the copy of Silvana's E-mail. She lined it up against the 24/7 stationery. The gray, fuzzy area on top, the one that indicated where a few inches of paper had been chopped off, matched the space taken up by the 24/7 logo. Perfectly.

Bex's stomach left her Adam's apple. It moved into her brain, where it swelled until she thought her ears would shoot off from the pressure.

Silvana Potenza's E-mail had been printed on 24/7 stationery.

And 24/7 stationery was located exclusively within the 24/7 printer.

The 24/7 printer stood in the 24/7 production truck.

Silvana Potenza's E-mail had been printed right underneath Bex's own nose.

Bex swallowed the information like a whole watermelon. And then she ran to the production truck.

Well, she tried to, anyway. She got up off the couch, hurriedly gathered up her things, and turned to face the direction of the doors, all in preparation for running.

But then, a split second before the *Run, Bex, run* message from her brain reached her feet and galvanized them into action, Bex's peripheral vision spotted Xenia walking the opposite way, toward the elevator. *Abort!* her brain shouted to her feet, and, before Bex knew it, it shoved her in Xenia's direction instead.

As a result, Bex did not run to the production truck. She ran to Xenia. Unfortunately, once she caught up with her, she wasn't sure what exactly she wanted to say. Her brain hadn't briefed her that far ahead.

"Hello!" Bex said, gambling that it was a safe and non-suspicious opening.

"Hello . . ." Xenia's narrowed gaze suggested that non-suspicious was the last impression Bex had managed to convey.

"How are you?"

Xenia said, "Erin Simpson is skating an extra exhibition number tomorrow, at the end of the show."

That, Bex understood, was skating for *I'm crappy, thanks for asking.* The last spot in the show was, by tradition, supposed to go to the gold medal winners.

"You sound really angry at Erin," Bex told Xenia, hoping that the language gap would at least take a small tinge off her stating the obvious.

Xenia's look suggested that it, in fact, did not.

Bex decided to try a new tack. She said, "You know, Xenia, you were right about the Western media being un-sympathetic toward you."

Xenia didn't reply. But it was obvious Bex had her attention.

"But it's not deliberate, not really. The Western media, especially the American media, they like to tell a story with a good guy and a bad guy. They like to make things simple for their audience." Bex figured she could skip, for now, the part where, as the 24/7 researcher, she played a major role in that dumbing down of the American TV viewer.

"So they decide that I am the bad and they decide that Erin is the good?"

"But it doesn't have to stay that way!"

Now, Xenia was definitely interested.

"The media loves, loves, I'm talking *loves,* to shove someone on a pedestal, then pull them down again. Today's good guy is tomorrow's bad guy, it's practically guaranteed. You can still persevere here, Xenia. All you have to do is be . . . be . . . you have to be more sympathetic."

Xenia stared at Bex queerly. "I have to be a good skater, that is all that I have to do."

"Boy, are you wrong. Xenia, a successful professional career isn't about being a good skater or how many titles you've won. That's almost the least of it. A successful professional career is all about getting the public to love you. And the way you get the public to love you is to give them a good story, a sympathetic story. Like if you've come back from a career—or even better—a life-threatening injury. Or if you're a poor orphan. Or even just poor. Xenia, I know how hard you've had to work, how the federation has been against you every step of the way, how they said you were too old and tried to sabotage you. You have a great story; you just have to tell it to the world. I can help you with that. I can tell your story. I can make you sympathetic. But only if you work with me. For instance, you have to try to be more gracious to Erin in public. Like, the morning that Silvana died, screaming at Erin outside the practice arena, you just can't do things like that, no matter how angry you—"

"I did not scream at Erin." Xenia wasn't so much defensive as confused.

"Erin said you did. She said you were standing there with Sergei and Igor Marchenko, and Erin walked by, and you attacked her."

"Erin Simpson is a liar. I never yell at her. I never even speak to her. Ask Sergei. Ask Igor. We three, no one speaks to her. What would be the reason for this?"

So Bex had her confirmation. Erin hadn't lied about seeing Xenia, Sergei, and Igor outside the refrigeration room
minutes before Silvana was lured to her death. Xenia wasn't
denying that they were there. Even as she challenged the rest
of Erin's narrative.

Bex asked, "What were the three of you talking about?"

"Nothing." The answer Heimliched out of Xenia's
mouth, and she looked away, refusing to meet Bex's eyes.

"You had to have been talking about something."

"Nothing. Igor, he just was congratulating me on my
win."

"That's all? Erin made it sound like you spoke for a
while."

"We talked about Russia. Igor is Russian. We talk about
him maybe visiting where we live soon, where we will go,
what we will do."

Bex knew Xenia was lying now. Igor never visited Russia; it was a fact. Xenia stressed, "We did not speak to Erin
Simpson, and Erin Simpson did not speak to us. She just to
walk by, and make a call on the telephone there."

Bex froze. "Erin made a call?"

"Yes."

"On the pay phone?"

"Yes."

"To whom?"

"I can not hear. She turn her back, like hiding. I not hear
anything. Maybe whisper."

"How long was she on the phone?"

"Not long. Maybe minute or two. She look in a big hurry,
looking over shoulder, like scared someone coming. Probably scared Patty will come out and see Erin off the ice. Patty
see Erin off the ice, Patty is ready to kill."

Bex shivered involuntarily. And wondered if homicide could be genetic.

Contrary to the impression Bex generally gave out, the 24/7 production truck wasn't only the place where Gil railed at his employees while waging battle with the perennial, insubordinate, downhill slope of the floor. On certain occasions, the production truck could actually be a place of certain, sleep-deprived, punchy merriment.

At this particular event, it all started with the information wall.

Since the 24/7 staff was so large, and since all of them worked on such wildly different schedules (not that any of them worked less than the bare-minimum eighteen-hour day, but they didn't all begin and end at the same time), the information wall was set up as the place they could turn to at any time to pick up the latest information and bulletins. The PAs took legal-sized manila envelopes and taped them to the wall, like large, hanging pockets. Each envelope was labeled to indicate its contents: Directions to the Arena, ISU Communications, Judge's Draw, Ladies' Results, Men's Results, Pairs Results, and Dance Results. Except that, on this show, the PA in charge had made a mistake, and written instead: Pears Results. It was a boo-boo no self-respecting joker could pass up.

The next day, a new envelope went up on the wall, labeled "Peaches Results."

It was joined less that twenty-four hours later by an envelope labeled: "Picasso's Draw," an abstract crayon doodling hanging out to drive home the point.

Next, up went: "Quick Draw McGraw."

Then, "Draw Binky and get accepted to art school!"

It probably was only funny to the sleep-deprived and skating-overloaded. So naturally, the staff of 24/7, Gil included, found it absolutely hilarious.

Usually, upon returning to the truck, Bex always made a point of stopping to check out the latest witticism. But not this time. This time, she had a date with a 24/7 printer, and an entire contingent of *People* magazine's fifty most eligible bachelors couldn't have intercepted her.

During Bex's dash across the parking lot, she'd tried to make some sense of the fact that Silvana's E-mail had been printed in the trailer. It wasn't so much that they never got visitors. As the host broadcaster (meaning they'd paid the most money for rights, and so got the best camera and announce positions, plus actual control of the event), 24/7 had visitors coming and going all the time. Everyone from desperate skaters (at Skate Canada, the Latvian ladies champion had come running in hysterical, begging for a strip of powerful gaffer's tape to seal up a nasty tear in her dress) to desperate fellow broadcasters (some foreign broadcaster inevitably forgot that American paper wasn't standardized to European and Asian versions and had to come asking to use their three-hole puncher) usually made an appearance by the time the show was over. So a judge wandering in asking for one favor or another wouldn't have been so odd.

Except that the 24/7 printer wasn't just standing there waiting for anyone to use it. The printer was attached to a single computer, one that required a password to print. Everyone on staff had their own password, so it wasn't difficult to access. But a judge coming in from the outside would have needed to depend on the kindness of strangers. Which meant someone at 24/7 had, if not read the E-mail in detail, at least seen it, and might be able to offer Bex a few key details as to Silvana's state of mind and general reaction to the missive.

You didn't have to be a snoopy British spinster with dozens of cozy best-sellers to her name, to know that was serious clue material.

Bex sat down at the computer and flipped it on, looking for the archive directory. She scanned the log of documents printed, noting that, during the competition, only two single-page items had been printed. That wasn't unusual. Most of the things that got printed were detailed results or complicated rundowns. Except for her own updated skater bios and jump sheets, Bex couldn't really think of who else might have a reason to print just one page at a time.

She checked the dates. One of the potential Silvana E-mails was printed the morning of the ladies' long program. Perfect time to influence Silvana. Perfect evidence that she had, in fact, been swayed.

Bex looked up who'd printed it.

Gilbert Cahill, Executive Producer.

Oh, how very, very wonderful.

Bex looked over her shoulder. Gil was sitting in his corner office, typing something on his laptop and cursing his chair. Bex steeled her nerve. She walked over to him.

She lost her nerve, and pretended to be fascinated reading the fire escape instructions on the wall. She gave herself a pep talk. It failed. She forced herself to yell his name. "Gil!"

So now it was too late to back out. Bex often needed to play mind games with her own good sense to force it into doing stuff. It probably wasn't good for her health. But then neither was unemployment and its subsequent follow-up, starvation.

"What is it, Bex?"

"I . . . I was about to print my Silvana Potenza report for you, but then this notice came up, saying that the print queue still had a document you'd tried to print out Thursday morning. I was wondering, did you ever get that document, or is it stuck in the memory somewhere?"

Bex also wondered if the word *bullshit* was writing itself in bloody beads of sweat on her forehead. To anyone actually paying attention, her story was really, really unlikely. But then again, Gil had a really, really weak grasp of how computers worked, as evidenced by his yelling and calling it stupid every time he accidentally deleted something he actually needed.

"What document?"

"I don't know," Bex said very honestly and very hopefully. "But you tried printing it on Thursday morning and it says it was one page long, and—"

"Oh, that. Right, I remember. My wife flew in Thursday night to spend the weekend in the city. I printed her flight info. I got it, don't need it anymore. You can go ahead and delete or whatever you have to do to print your thing. I need that report, Bex, and I need it soon."

"Got it, Gil," Bex said, believing him. For one thing, she'd seen the lovely Mrs. Cahill around recently, and for another, Gil was too bombastic to lie. The man said the first thing that came to his mind the first time he thought it. Subtle, he wasn't. Or sly.

Which left the only other single-page E-mail in the log. The one printed Thursday night, the night *after* the ladies' long program. Which meant that, if Silvana was swayed to vote a certain way, it was unlikely this E-mail was responsible.

Still, Silvana had printed it out for a reason. Maybe she

needed it for evidence against Sergei. And someone at 24/7 had helped her do it.

Bex punched a series of keys, waited patiently, and finally got the name of the person who'd printed the E-mail.

Francis Howarth, Announcer.

Eleven

It was time to review.

Ahem: The copy of the E-mail found in Silvana Potenza's purse was an exact match for a piece of 24/7 letterhead, its logo cleverly sliced off to obscure its origin. The 24/7 letterhead was loaded exclusively into a single 24/7 printer. The single 24/7 printer was located exclusively in the 24/7 production truck. It wasn't portable. It weighed nearly a hundred pounds. It was highly unlikely someone decided to spontaneously take it for a walk, dragging the cord like a makeshift leash. In the instance of that actually happening, someone would have noticed. And definitely mentioned it. Ergo, one had to assume that Silvana Potenza's original E-mail was printed in the 24/7 production truck. And since Silvana couldn't access the printer alone, she obviously had help. From, it appeared, Francis Howarth (or, oh yeah, someone who knew his password).

Bex listed the facts in a little column in her head. Then

she reviewed them again, top to bottom. She rearranged them in a circle, to show how one fact flowed smoothly into the other. And she reviewed them a second time. And one more time, just for the heck of it. She figured the gods who send lighting bolts down upon the heads of the conceited had to forgive her this once. It was the first time in days she'd had any facts at all, much less potentially relevant ones. Of course, their usefulness was yet to be determined. And for the determining, Bex needed to talk to Francis Howarth. Soon.

But first, there was one more fact she needed to confirm.

After all, Bex was on a roll.

"Gary!" Bex found Lian Reilley's coach at the arena. He was coaching his top male skater, who'd won a silver medal earlier in the week and was also scheduled to perform in the exhibition. Bex came up to lean by Gary at the barrier. Suddenly, standing so close to him, Bex changed her exclamation point to a question mark, and added a layer of formality. "Mr. Gold?"

Because, even though Gary was about the same age as Igor Marchenko, whom Bex had called by his first name, and actually younger than Rupert Newman, to whom Bex had so boldly done the same, the fact was, U.S. coach Gary Gold was by far the most formal man in skating.

He was always impeccably groomed. If Bex didn't know better, she'd think he kept a damp comb in his pocket and continuously whipped it out to keep every follicle of his hair and mustache in perfect order. And, while other coaches wore suits and ties to the rink, especially for major competition, Gary's were the only ones looking tailored and perennially freshly pressed (his colleagues made do with hanging

their clothes in the shower to steam out any wrinkles in-
curred by a fortnight of cramped travel). And God only
knew what calamity might strike the human race if Gary
ever appeared without a matching pocket handkerchief.

But it wasn't just his wardrobe that defined Gary Gold's
otherworldly air. Or his exact, precise, *I have a degree in
English Literature from Stanford and don't you dare forget
it* diction. (Gary not only never used contractions and always pronounced every necessary vowel in every word; Bex
also sometimes thought he pronounced a few that weren't
originally there in the first place.) There was also that pesky
and disturbing lack of facial expression.

The man didn't have one. Perhaps forty years on ice had
frozen it. This was no colorful exaggeration, but video-
documented fact. The man's face truly never moved. Bex
could say this with impunity because one night, after spending exactly thirteen hours straight in the edit room, and high
on MSG from the dozen open, half-eaten cartons of Chinese
food perfuming the air, Bex and the feature producer had
popped a tape of Gary standing by the barrier during one of
Lian's performances up on their biggest monitor and
watched it in super slow motion.

There he was, whispering to Lian minutes before her
name was called: no expression.

Lian landing her opening jump: no expression.

Lian missing her combination: no expression.

Lian pulling it together to skate an overall great program
and win her first medal on the senior level: no expression.

Well, maybe he blinked once and/or his chin jerked just
a little toward the heavens. But it may also have just been
the tape skipping a frame.

Although, to be truly descriptive, one had to admit that
the man didn't really have *no* expression. After all, he'd

have to be Claude Raines in *The Invisible Man* for that. The fact is, what Gary Gold had was, in fact, a single expression. One that could best be described by the phrase: *Ewww, what stinks?*

Or, in Garyese: *Goodness gracious, what is that vile odor defiling my nostrils?*

It was exactly the look that Gary gave Bex when she sidled up to him at the barrier. But she decided not to take it personally. She presumed he'd react exactly the same way to Ed McMahon delivering a Publisher's Clearinghouse check to his doorstep. And he'd probably correct his grammar, too.

"Hello, Mr. Gold," Bex said. "Do you have a minute to answer a few questions for me?"

"Unfortunately," Gary indicated his student, "I am in the middle of something."

"I'll be quick."

"Young lady, Mr. Sherry's parents are paying me a fair amount of money to instruct their son. I hardly think it ethical to charge them for a period during which I was not focusing my whole attention on his progress."

"I just want to know about Sergei Alemazov coming to teach at the OTC with you."

Gary Gold's expression may not have changed, but he did unethically tear his eyes away from young Mr. Sherry to look at Bex. "I beg your pardon?"

"Igor Marchenko said he'd arranged for Sergei to join the staff. He said it was all set."

"I assure you, my dear, you are mistaken. No new instructor may join the staff without approval from the Olympic Training Center's board, of which I am a member. No such proposal has been put before us. And, if it were, I would have voted it down immediately."

"Why?"

"Because. It was insidious enough when Soviet skaters were subsidized by their own government. While my parents worked two jobs each to pay for my skating, my competitors were receiving it all for free from their government without sacrificing so much as an ounce of their Olympic-eligible status. That fortunately all ended with the collapse of the Soviet Union. But now it seems that American taxpayers wish to step in where the Soviets left off. Our OTC is subsidized with federal money, and yet these ex-Soviet athletes are being let in by the planeload. We give them free ice, free room and board, we even allow their coaches to offer lessons to our pupils. We take earnings out of American coaches' pockets and hand them over to the Russians. Frankly, Miss Levy, as long as there is even a single American instructor toiling seven-day weeks to make ends meet for his family, or even one young American skater struggling to pay the bills, I am never, ever going to agree to let Russians into our training center. If Igor's precious Sergei Alemazov wants in on the American charity pie, he shall have to look for it elsewhere."

It was the longest speech Bex had ever heard Gary deliver. And damn if he didn't do it without changing his expression.

Which was okay, because Bex's face had enough expression for both of them. It said, "Well, what do you know, Igor was lying about the topic of his early morning chat with Sergei. I wonder what else he's lying about?"

Of all the people Bex worked with at 24/7, she supposed, if pressed, she would have to say she knew Francis and Diana Howarth the best. Not that they were friends or anything. Bex couldn't imagine Francis and Diana, who lived on New

York's Upper East Side in a duplex over Central Park, and talked about sitting on committees to support the symphony/ballet/museums and eradicate diseases from ALS to zoster (which was actually a fancy word for chicken pox; Bex looked it up because she was weird that way) could ever consider someone like her a friend. After all, most of the time, the Howarths weren't even sure Bex wasn't their personal assistant. Why else would they send her for coffee, and to make photocopies, and to, "Do me a favor, Bex, Francis forgot his tuxedo shirt back at the hotel. Would you be a dear, scurry over and fetch it?"

"But . . . uh . . . Diana, the broadcast is about to start."

"You'd best hurry then, hadn't you?"

However, friends or not, Francis, Diana, and Bex did spend a lot of time together. As soon as America's sweethearts arrived at their latest location (usually days after the grunt crew, Bex included, decamped), they called her up, expressed dismay that she should already sound so tired when the competition hadn't even begun yet, and then off all three of them would go to the rink to watch the practices. Because it wasn't only judges who came to the practices to get an idea of who was doing what with which consistency, and how they might mark them accordingly. Announcers came, too: to stock up on their pithy, extemporaneous comments.

For three to five days, depending on the length and importance of the competition, Bex, Francis, and Diana sat shivering in the stands, Bex huddled in her 24/7 (one size fits all as long as you're a pro football player) down jacket, Diana elegantly sipping hot toddies from a thermos colorcoordinated daily to her outfit, and Francis wearing a furry, mink Russian hat with earflaps he'd purchased from a street vendor in Moscow back when *entrepreneur* was still a Soviet dirty word. They sat, and they watched practice group after practice group, skater after skater, ranging from jumping beans to artists to technicians to people who obviously won their country's national championship by virtue of being the only citizens to own ice skates. They watched athletic talent so breathtaking it made you doubt you even belonged to the same species as them, and they watched the painful results of paying for your partner and your lessons and your costumes and, thus, your spot in a world championship.

As every skater stepped onto center ice to perform a run-through of their program with music, Bex would pull out her bio and jump sheet, urging Francis and Diana to do the same, and they would click through each element as it was done, note whether or not it was completed (so that, during the broadcast, in case of a fall, Diana could exclaim, "I don't know what happened! He/She/They were nailing them in practice all week!"). At the end, they'd have a brief meeting about what they wanted to say about this particular skater when they got on air, how to introduce them, which element to tell viewers at home to look out for, and which aspect of their personal story to highlight. If any of them made a particularly pithy comment, Diana would diligently write it down and, later, she and Francis would divvy up the cleverness.

Of course, based on how both behaved the night of the ladies' long program, most of the time Bex felt like she was just talking to herself. The only time Francis or Diana ever actually followed the narrative course she'd charted for them was when the other seemed determined to do the opposite. Still all three of them diligently went through the charade of preparation.

And, in the middle of the charade, while the ice was

being cleaned, or while the skaters were warming up, or while one boy whom Francis called "as exciting as watching paint dry," was on the ice, the Howarths and Bex just chatted. One day Francis and Diana might regale her with tales from their amateur days, when everyone competed outside, and a stiff wind could be either your biggest friend or greatest enemy. They talked about being the first Westerners to travel to some Iron Curtain towns and of getting a private tour of India's Taj Mahal. On other days, they might decide to talk about their first tour, and how they put it together on a wing and a prayer, not realizing how much work and extra expense was involved in physically transporting not only an entire chorus line of people (which they budgeted for), but also multiple costumes and sets (which they hadn't) and how as a result, despite playing to packed houses all over the world, their debut season was a huge financial failure. And sometimes, Francis and Diana merely kicked back and gossiped about everyone they knew. Who was sleeping with whom, who was cheating on whom, who was about to dump their coach, and whose partner was secretly trying out with others. They were witty, they were knowledgeable, and, in their own way, they were quite charming.

Which was why Bex was having a hard time picturing the Howarths as killers.

But the fact remained; they'd been somehow involved with Silvana. They'd printed the E-mail urging her to cheat. And now she was dead. Someone knew something. And, seeing as Bex still knew nothing, the Howarths were a logical place to turn.

She went to their hotel room, hoping that privacy might compel them to reveal secrets not conducive to a public space. She found that, unlike the Simpsons' attempt to personalize everything in sight, the Howarths, having been on the road for over forty years, had long ago given up on such touches. They'd unpacked their garment bags, hung up the outfits likely to wrinkle, put toothbrushes in the bathroom, and called it a day. They didn't even go sightseeing anymore. Bex doubted there was a sight on earth they hadn't seen yet.

When she found them in their room, both were wearing robes, his in dark blue, hers in dark green. Diana wore no makeup, and her hair was pulled off her cold-cream-gleaming face with a terrycloth headband. Francis hadn't shaved. Neither the hair on his chin nor the tufts that periodically sprouted from his ears and were diligently clipped back on show days had been tended to. Suddenly, the two most formidable people Bex had ever met looked terribly old.

Bex, who had been lobbing accusations back and forth like a week's worth of *People's Court* episodes, couldn't think of what to say. Or at least how to begin.

And so, she just showed Francis and Diana the E-mail.

And waited to see their reactions.

Which she got. As soon as both finished fumbling around and found their glasses.

Still, Francis needed to hold the sheet at arm's length to read it properly, while Diana squinted and pressed her face closer to the paper. Once they'd both gotten the gist of it, though, they exchanged glances.

Nervous glances, as far as Bex could read.

Diana straightened up, and Francis lowered his arm.

"Where did you get this E-mail, Bex?" Diana asked.

"It's a copy. The original was in Silvana Potenza's purse."

"Why, this is extraordinary!" Francis exclaimed. "What a find! This proves everything. The fix was in. Silvana was ordered to place Xenia first. Erin Simpson is the true winner. Bex, do you know what you've done?"

"Not exactly," Bex said, realizing she'd inadvertently answered two questions with one uncertainly. "There's a problem. This E-mail was printed out after the competition ended."

"Oh, no. No, Bex, you're wrong. Look at the time and date, right up here." Francis indicated the top of the E-mail. "It says the morning before. Sergei told Silvana how to vote the morning before."

"That just shows when the E-mail was written, not when it was read. There's a fancy computer way of finding out when something was opened, but we don't have access to that. Besides, to open an E-mail, Silvana needed access to a computer, and she didn't travel with a laptop or use the hotel's media center. I couldn't find any evidence of her ever reading any E-mail while she was here. So I had to go with the next best thing and try to figure out where and when she'd printed it. And I did. It was printed in the 24/7 production truck. The evening after the competition. By you, Francis."

After winning their second Olympic gold medal, Francis and Diana played starring roles in a big-budget Hollywood movie about a lovely Ice Capades star and the lowly chorus boy who loves her. The movie tanked, and both Howarths got nearly unanimous negative reviews.

Bex could finally see why.

They sucked at this acting thing.

Upon digesting Bex's accusation, both opened their eyes very wide and, in near unison, pressed their hands to their chests. The better to express deep surprise.

"What?"

"No!"

"We didn't—"

"How could we—"

"What makes you think—"

"I barely know how to operate the infernal machine!"

Bex said, "I know you did it. I have proof. Proof that you both are somehow connected to her death."

Francis blurted out, "Well, we certainly didn't mean to get her killed!"

As soon as the words were out of his mouth, Diana whipped her head around, and Bex braced herself for a harangue extraordinaire. But before Diana even finished the gesture, she suddenly looked as tired as Bex felt. She sighed and said, "He's telling the truth. We had no idea how horribly this all would end."

Was this a confession? Bex wished she had more experience with these things. All she knew at the moment, though, was that this might have been a confession, but it was far from an explanation. Ergo, Bex was still most confused.

She said, "But what I don't understand is, why did Silvana ask you to print her the E-mail in the first place? Did she need it for evidence? Was she going to turn Sergei in to the ISU?"

"No. Because Sergei didn't write that E-mail," Francis said.

"He didn't?"

"No. In fact, it's not even an E-mail."

Oh, good, now Bex was completely lost. If it turned out the E-mail wasn't even an E-mail, then who knew what else she'd misinterpreted along the way?

"What is it then?"

"It's a . . . it's a . . . What's the word?" Francis struggled.

"A dummy," Diana put in. For the first time since meeting them, Bex actually believed Diana was trying to help her husband out, instead of cleverly hurling an invective at him. "It's a phony. It was made to look like an E-mail, but it's not really one. It's painted, like a forgery. We didn't get it off the Internet. It was on a disc. We just put it in and printed."

"Okay," Bex said, "Here comes a dose of the obvious: Why?"

"Because. It would help prove Erin was the rightful winner."

"Was she?"

They shrugged in near unison.

"It was very close," Francis said.

"It could have gone either way," Diana agreed.

"That's not what you said on the air."

Diana said, "Erin Simpson is a lovely skater."

Francis said, "And a marvelous ambassador for our sport. Every time she appears on TV, the enrollment at local rinks just swells."

"Great. She's a Madison Avenue dream. May her endorsements be plentiful. But, was she cheated out of a gold medal here or what?"

Diana said, "She's been working so hard for so long. Patty, too."

Francis said, "This was supposed to be her year."

"Okay," Bex said. "Either start making sense, or I'm leaving here and going straight to the police. You can explain all this to them. Good-bye and good luck."

"Wait, Bex," Diana was using the same tone she usually wheedled to send her scurrying for Francis's lost shirt. Only this time, there was a trace of fear to it. "What we did, it may have been wrong, but it wasn't criminal. There's no reason to get the police involved."

"How about a corpse? Is that a good reason to get the police involved? Silvana is still dead, whether you meant for it to happen or not."

"We didn't even know Silvana would be involved. It was a random draw; no one knew how she would vote."

"You're over here," Bex raised her left arm. Then, she raised her right arm, and held them as far apart as possible. "And making sense is over here. Try harder, folks."

Diana said, "Both Francis and I thought Erin would be a lovely addition to our tour next fall. We've been needing some new blood for a long time. Some of the people currently in the cast, well, they won't be seeing thirty again. It's hard to draw a younger audience with skaters who won before most of them were born. We needed someone younger, more energetic, a bigger name with the younger generation. Erin Simpson is the brightest star to come along in a while."

"And she's been skating so well this season," Francis flipped on his announcer voice, as if that was supposed to impress Bex. "We felt certain the world title would finally be hers this year. Especially with the event being held in the States."

"We wanted very much for her to win."

"We needed her to win. It would make her a much bigger draw."

"So when she didn't—" Bex felt like a kid learning to ride her bike. It was time for dad to let go of the backseat. She was ready to soar on her own—"You two decided to stir up a little controversy, get her name in the papers. After all, getting cheated out of a medal will get you even more press than simply winning one. Am I right?"

"You," Francis sighed, "are right."

"So you made up the whole thing? About the results being wrong, I mean?"

"Well, no. Like I said, it really could have gone either way. If only Silvana—"

"So you just picked Silvana at random. You had no more evidence that she'd cheated than you had on anyone else."

"She was the only Western judge to vote for Xenia over Erin. That was . . . odd."

"But certainly defensible."

"If you like that Russian arm flailing sort of thing," Diana conceded, "then yes."

"So you dragged this poor woman's name through the mud, not to mention Xenia and Sergei's and the integrity of the entire sport, all in the name of building up Erin Simpson's name recognition and putting a few more butts in the seats the next time your tour comes to town?"

"You must admit, Bex," Diana rationalized, "this has been a media bonanza not just for us, but for the sport as a whole. Ratings have never been higher. 24/7 must be thrilled with the numbers they've gotten for this championship."

"And that's good for everyone," Francis pointed out. "Even you, Bex. The more skating shows 24/7 chooses to put on, the more work for you. It's a win-win."

"Except that Silvana is dead."

"We had nothing to do with that!" they said in unison.

"You printed that E-mail making her and Sergei look guilty. Were you going to release it to the press? Offer it as proof? Or did you plan all along for it to be found on her body?"

"Bex!" Finally, Diana's shock looked real. "Do you honestly think we killed her?"

"Why not? Isn't that the next step? For the good of the sport, I mean? After all, Silvana alive could always blow your whole game by testifying that she never cheated and Xenia was the rightful winner, no question. How big of a damper would that burst of honesty have put on Erin and your precious tour? Enough people might have believed it eventually, and then what? All that hard work of yours down the drain. No, with Silvana dead, it would be much easier to keep up the fiction. Especially when this E-mail was found on her body!"

"Would you please stop saying that?" Diana begged. "Body, body, body . . . It's so unseemly. And you're making it sound like we personally created the E-mail to frame her."

"You mean you didn't?"

"Of course not. Francis types with two fingers and I'm still working on mastering the fax machine we have at home. I'm ages away from getting on the World Wide Web and all its sundry oddities. For goodness' sake, Bex, we only printed out the blasted thing, we certainly didn't create it. It wasn't even our idea."

"So who's idea was it? Who created and gave you the E-mail to print out?"

"It was that fellow, the one who follows Erin and Patty around like a love-struck manservant. Jasper Clarke, is that his name?"

Twelve

*S*o, *I Had Lunch With a Judge-Killer.*

As a memoir title, it had a very pithy ring. As something that actually happened to her, the memory made Bex want to vomit up said lunch and everything she'd ingested since then.

She double-checked with Francis. "Jasper Clarke asked you to print out the original of this E-mail?"

"He came up to us after the competition on Thursday night and handed us the disc. We printed it out in the production trailer and gave it back to him. That was the last we saw of it. I don't know how it ended up in Silvana's purse."

"Did you have this planned all along? I mean, from before the competition started?"

"Of course not!"

"How could we?"

"We didn't know going in it would come to this. Erin had

beaten Xenia soundly all year long. We were expecting more of the same."

"How were we to know the Russian girl would finally put it all together?"

"We couldn't have planned something like this."

"We just took advantage of the opportunity handed us."

"Apparently," Bex said, "you weren't the only ones. Jasper had to have worked pretty fast to dummy up that E-mail like that. When he first gave it to you, did you know what you were printing out? Well, even if you didn't in the beginning, you must have, when you saw it."

At least the Howarths were decent enough to look sheepish. Diana said, "We knew. We thought . . . we thought it could only help us. Well, help Erin, and, along the way, us. I thought he would leak it to the press and even if no one could prove anything, it would still guarantee us a few more days of press. By then, hopefully, we'd have Erin signed for the tour."

"Has she, by the way?" Bex asked. "Has Erin signed? I know you made her an offer."

Had Jasper told her that? Bex wasn't sure. The only thing she was sure of was that now she really couldn't be sure of anything he'd told her.

"Not yet," Francis said. "Patty is ready, but Erin seems to be dragging her feet. She says she wants to stay eligible. A horrible idea in my opinion. Strike while the iron is hot, that's my motto. She'll never be able to top this. If she does win a world championship finally, everyone will just shrug and say, well, she deserved to win last year. And, if she doesn't, people will begin to believe she never deserved to this year, either."

"She didn't win this year, Francis. Remember? She didn't win, and apparently she didn't even deserve to."

"It was very close."

"It could have gone either way."

Bex would have rolled her eyes, but she figured one more time and they'd freeze that way. Instead, she pointed out, "You do realize that you're responsible for all of this."

"Us?"

"I told you, Bex, we had nothing to do with Silvana's death."

"You put the whole thing into motion! If you hadn't started the uproar over Erin's scores, Jasper would never have gotten the idea to do what he did. Or, even if he had the idea, he certainly wouldn't have had the opportunity. He had you two print out that E-mail so that he could kill Silvana and plant it on her body."

"We didn't know."

"We really didn't."

"Bex," Diana asked with genuine trepidation, "what are you going to do now?"

What she wanted to do was confront Jasper immediately.

What she did not want to do was end up on the tail end of a sentence that began, "Jasper Clarke, cold-blooded killer of international figure skating judge Silvana Potenza and others . . ."

Considering the risk she'd taken by confronting Sergei alone in his hotel room (though now, of course, she knew there'd been no risk greater than death by stale bagel), Bex figured she'd exhausted her death-defying luck for the week. This time, she should probably chat up her latest suspect in a public place. The problem was, whenever Jasper showed up in a public place, he was inevitably attached to

Patty and/or Erin. And Bex wasn't quite ready to take on all
three of them as an athletic, blond, six-legged set.

Bex needed a clever idea for separating the Siamese
triplets.

A clever idea.

Yeah. That's what she needed.

Where were they selling those, these days? The Gap?

Momentarily stymied, Bex decided to set *clever* on the
back burner and become one with the obvious. Even though
she currently had a pretty good idea of who'd turned Silvana
Potenza's lights off, Bex still hated being lied to. And even
if it had nothing to do with the murder at hand, somebody,
either Igor Marchenko or Gary Gold, was still lying to her.

Bex picked up the phone, and called the Olympic Training Center. She asked if there were any plans for Sergei Alemazov to begin teaching there. After being asked to repeat
his name twice, spell it once, and spending five long minutes on hold, Bex was informed, "Not to my knowledge,
ma'am. You have a nice day now."

Bex said, "Hmmm."

And went to find Marchenko.

Igor said, "This is all Gary Gold's fault."

"Your lying to me is Gary Gold's fault?"

"I did not lie."

"I asked what you and Sergei were talking about the
morning Erin Simpson saw you outside the refrigeration
room. You said you were telling him he had a job at the
training center. Gary said there was no job, and the center
confirmed. I know English isn't your first language, but I
don't think this was a translation problem. Do yes and no
sound that alike in Russian?"

Igor told Bex, "You are a very rude, young woman."

"I am very tired, very cranky, and I know I'm right. Now, let's try it again: What were you and Sergei talking about that morning?"

"A job. For him. At the training center."

"So Gary Gold is the one who's lying?"

"Gary Gold is a bastard."

"Fascinating," Bex said. "Irrelevant. But fascinating, nonetheless."

"Gary is the killer."

"Excuse me?"

"I had it all arranged for Sergei, and then Gary . . . he must have voted against it."

"Probably. He told me he didn't want Russians coming to the center and taking money away from American coaches."

"American coaches who are called Gary Gold! Gary is jealous, you understand. He knows Russian coaches are one hundred percent better than he. The only students he gets now are girls I have no time for. You go to Mrs. Reilly. You ask her how much she would pay and how many thank-yous she would cry for me to coach Lian. Gary knows this. He knows he is number two, and if Sergei comes, Gary then is number three. He says he loves America? Gary loves Gary, no one else. He still talks how I take his place as number one American skater when I defected. He is still angry, still bitter. He uses Sergei to punish me. This is Gary. This is skating life."

"This is skating life." Igor's phrase danced circles in Bex's brain like a ladybug trying to get off the ground. This was skating life. Where people held grudges for twenty years. Where increasing the gate for your show was worth destroying an innocent's reputation. Where murder was a small price to pay for gold.

Bex really needed to talk to Jasper.

And, after spending an hour trying to come up with some clever way to get him alone, a chance glance at the day's practice schedule allowed Bex to formulate something obvious.

She headed across the parking lot to the arena. Erin was practicing. Which meant that Patty was coaching, rink-side, with the lucky troll dolls and assorted other accoutrements. And Jasper, Bex bet, was watching from the sidelines. Close enough to see everything, but far away enough not to be heard.

He was, in fact, sitting in the stands, about six rows above Patty's head. Perfect.

Bex approached in what she hoped would be perceived as a nonchalant manner. Jasper looked up, recognized her, apparently bought the nonchalance facade, and smiled. *He did have such a nice smile.* Bex quickly told herself to think murderous thoughts to keep it at bay.

She sat down next to him, following Jasper's gaze in time to catch Erin getting ready to practice her "bonus" number. The one she would do at the end of the show, after even the gold medalists had skated. A few feet away from her, Xenia glared with more ire than Khrushchev once reserved for his poor shoe and the United Nations table it was hammering. The reason for such rancor could be the break in exhibition protocol. Or it could be because Erin had chosen to skate to the gag-inducing "Thanks for the Memories." By Bob Hope, yet.

Jasper asked, "How's life in the research biz, Bex?"

He'd given her an opening. Bex hadn't planned to go that way, but didn't they say the great ones improvised? (Or was it that the great ones always had a meticulous plan? Either way, Bex figured she was about to find out.)

She said, "Actually, I could use a bit of your help with that."

"Shoot." He was talking to Bex, but he hadn't taken his eyes off Erin. Bex couldn't blame him. A teen who looked like a fifth grader attempting to glide gracefully to the off-tune warble of geriatric *was* a sight to see.

"I'm putting together my final report on the medal controversy. Do you have the latest for me? How's the petition coming?"

"Fabulous. We presented it to the ISU this morning. Rupert will be announcing their decision right before the conclusion of the exhibition tomorrow."

"They've already come to a decision? Without a hearing?"

"Well, this event is over in twenty-four hours. And no one wants it to drag on. The public needs closure. So we can all move on."

"Right, a fair hearing with a chance for both the persecution and defense to prepare their case *would* be such a drag." Bex tried to swallow her bitterness, but almost ended up gagging on it. Why did it seem like, in the end, she was the only one who cared that an actual person, not just a judge, was dead, here?

"Look, Bex." Jasper managed to tear his eyes away from Erin and Bob long enough to bat those baby blues in Bex's direction. Was she supposed to melt or swoon? "I know how this looks and sounds, but the fact is, Rupert is in a really tough spot. With Silvana dead, it's pretty obvious no one will ever know the whole story about what happened. However, once the specter of impropriety has been raised, the ISU needs to deal with it in some way."

"So what's the decision?"

"Erin will be awarded a gold medal. They'll do a cere-

ALINA ADAMS

mony at the end of the exhibition, as soon as she finishes her
bonus number."

"And they'll strip Xenia of her title?" Bex gasped and involuntarily looked at the Russian girl on the ice. She looked
mad now. Bex could only shudder at how angry she was capable of really getting.

"No. In addition to. A second gold medal will be awarded,
and they'll go into the record books as co-champions."

"Because the ISU doesn't know what really happened?"

"Because they'll never know. The whole truth died with
Silvana. This seemed like the fairest way to settle things."

"Wow," Bex said. "This is pretty precedent-setting.
Thanks for the heads up, Jasper, I'll let Gil know so we can
be ready with a camera crew to film the festivities." Gil
would honestly be ecstatic. It was a hell of a way to end a
show.

"No problem. You're my favorite researcher, you know."

Yeah, yeah, yeah . . . she already fell for this once. Good
thing Bex was so much older and wiser now. And that
Jasper's eyes didn't look nearly as blue without an ocean
crashing on the other side of the window.

"But what if there was some evidence?"

"What do you mean?"

"What if the ISU could find some definitive evidence of
cheating on Silvana's part?"

"Oh. Well. Then I suppose they could nullify the initial
result and give the clear win to Erin. Silvana was the only
judge keeping her from the gold, after all."

"Jasper," Bex lowered her voice. "I want to show you
something."

"What's up, Bex?" He wiggled his eyebrows at her seri-
ousness. The gesture reminded Bex of Erin's on-ice Happiness persona.

She slipped one hand into her jacket pocket. "This is top secret, now. You've got to promise to keep it quiet. If I don't give Gil an exclusive, he'll kill me. And then he'll fire me."

"Scout's honor. You have my word."

Bex pulled out the E-mail. She said, "This was found on Silvana's body."

She watched Jasper closely as he opened and absorbed the E-mail. And, she had to admit; the surprise on his face might have been interpreted as true shock at seeing the document for the first time, rather than as the unexpected recognition.

"I . . . " Jasper sputtered. "Where did you . . . How did you . . . Where did this come from?"

"The police. They gave me a copy."

"This is Silvana's vote list. From Xenia all the way down to the girl in twenty-fourth place. This is it exactly, no deviations."

Wow, Bex thought sarcastically, *you must be a heck of a skating fan, Jasper, if you can recognize every judge's ranking, down to the very last place. Either that, or you dummied up the list yourself based on the protocol, so you know it's accurate.*

"Do you think this would be enough to make Rupert's case for him?"

"Are you kidding? This is incredible! Bex, how can I ever thank you?"

"Well . . . " She took back the E-mail, folding it neatly and slipping it back into her pocket. "I suppose you could start by explaining how this E-mail ended up in Silvana's purse."

He cocked his head. "What do you mean, Bex? How would I know that? I assume she printed it out and kept it as a reference . . ."

"No. She didn't. At least, not before the competition. See, Jasper, I've talked to Francis and Diana. And I know them pretty well. I know when they're lying. And I know when they're telling the truth."

This, by the way, was untrue. Bex was lucky if she could guess when they'd had enough of each other seconds before fists started flying so she could get between them and play referee.

But Jasper seemed to buy the lie. And the implication.

Still, he put up a noble fight. "Francis and Diana? Howarth? What do they have to do with any of this?"

Bex said, "I showed them the E-mail."

"Oh." Jasper's pinkie began to twitch. Probably an old Silicon Valley/backspace injury: "What did they . . . what did they have to say?"

"Well, Diana said they were both pretty much computer illiterate."

"Oh, well, I'm not surprised." For a moment, Jasper thought he was back in his element, talking about those silly non–Web savvy people. "At their age, I wouldn't expect—"

"Which is why they couldn't have possibly printed this E-mail off the Internet."

"Why should they have?"

"Because the 24/7 printer says they did."

"Were they . . . were they friends with Silvana?"

"Barely knew the woman."

"I'm afraid you've lost me then, Bex."

"I don't think so." She stared right into his eyes. Then remembered that, in the animal kingdom, that sort of thing was interpreted as a threat and led to clawing and biting and all sorts of other unpleasant bloodletting, and maybe it wasn't such a good idea to engage in said behavior with a man who'd already proven himself capable of premeditated murder. So, instead of his eyes, Bex stared right into the top button of Jasper's shirt. Yeah. That would show him.

Not to mention make it difficult to see his face. Which was why Bex had no idea what it looked like when he told her, "I really don't understand what you're getting at."

"I think you do."

"No, I don't."

"I really think that you do."

"No. No, I really don't."

God, but it never went on for this long on *Murder, She Wrote*. Did all murderers need an impending commercial to speed up their confessions?

"I know that you dummied up this E-mail and gave it to Francis and Diana to print out," Bex finally blurted, mostly to cut her own tension. She had no idea how Jasper was handling his.

Now, Bex looked at his face.

He'd paled a bit. And that look of confidence had been replaced by one of uncertainty. It wasn't a confession, exactly, but it sure did boost Bex's self-esteem.

"Would you care to reply to what I just said?" she inquired politely. Now that it looked like she was back in control, Bex felt more inclined to let her arguably delightful sense of humor come flowing out.

"I don't know what to say.' Jasper exhaled.

"Just for the heck of it, how about starting by confirming what I just revealed. You did dummy up this E-mail and give it to the Howarths, yes?"

Bex wouldn't have thought the man had more to exhale, but, apparently, he did. The air came whistling out his nose, sucking his shoulders toward the gum and spilled soda sticky floor, curving his spine, and plopping both hands impotently in his lap.

"Yes. . . ." It was mumbled, it was quiet, but it was definitely confirmation. He looked over his shoulder, too, like yeah, right, that might distract Bex from the task at hand. She hadn't fallen for that *Look! Over there!* trick in weeks!

"But, why get the Howarths involved? The more people that know . . ."

"I didn't bring a printer with me. I never need one. Everything I do for Erin is on-line. And I didn't want to use the one in the hotel. They keep records, you know."

Yes, Bex knew. Boy, did she know. She pressed on, "So then you took the E-mail from them and planted it on Silvana's body after you killed her?"

"What?" Having lost all that air, his cry came out more like a gasp, but this time, Bex heard it loud and clear. "No! No, of course not! I didn't kill Silvana."

"So . . . someone else killed her, and you just planted the E-mail?"

"I didn't plant any E-mail."

This was not going the way Bex had intended. She decided to go back to what she knew for a fact. "But you did create it. Probably on some kind of desktop publishing system. I've got to admit, you did a great job. You had me thinking it was the real thing for the longest time."

"Yes, yes. I created it. But I have no idea how Silvana got her hands on it."

"Well, personally, I don't think Silvana ever had her hands on it. I think it was slipped into her purse after she was already dead, so that someone like me could find it and turn it over to Rupert at the ISU and, ipso presto, Erin has her proof and her gold medal."

"Ipso presto?" Jasper asked.

"You know what I mean. Don't change the subject."

"I'm not. I'm just trying to make you understand that I

had nothing to do with Silvana's death. I honestly don't know how she got that E-mail in her purse. I'm just the middleman, here; you have to believe me. Yes, I created it, and yes, I went to Francis and Diana about printing it. I thought they'd be a safe bet, because they wanted Erin to be the gold medalist as much as we all did. And yes, I met them later, and I got the printout."

"Were you the one who thought to cut off the 24/7 logo on top?"

"Actually, no. Francis did that. He's odd, Bex, but he's not an idiot."

"Right. Sorry. Go on."

"Yeah, so, anyway. I got the printout from them. And I gave it to . . ." he lowered his voice now, despite the music blaring through the arena. "Patty."

"Patty?" Now it was Bex's turn to inhale down to her ankles. "Patty was in on this?"

"Are you kidding? It was her idea! As soon as Francis and Diana said what they did on the air about Erin deserving to win . . . she decided to do it, right away. Honestly, I think she'd probably been planning this for a long time. She was just waiting for the opportunity, and I think she knew it would never be better than this. Right away, she said to me, 'Can you do this?' And I said, 'Sure.' It wasn't that complicated technically. I just took the shell of another E-mail on the same system, changed the header and text, added—"

"Yes, yes, I already told you, you did a great job. What do you want, a cookie?"

"I want you to believe me."

"That Patty was involved?"

"That this was Patty's baby from the get-go. After I got the printout from Francis and Diana, I gave it to Patty, and that was the last time I saw it. I swear."

Bex nodded. And then she said only two words. "Prove it."

"I can."

"I'm listening."

"The disk. The original disk I created the E-mail on. I gave it to the Howarths, they gave it back to me, and I gave it to Patty along with the E-mail. She probably still has it. All we have to do is find the disk, and I can prove to you that Patty is the one you're looking for here, not me."

Thirteen

"Who you calling 'we,' Computer Boy?"

"Well," Jasper said, "Naturally, when I say 'we,' I mean . . . you."

"I see." Bex nodded her head thoughtfully. "What I don't see, however, is how my going to Patty and asking for the disk with the original E-mail on it lets you off the hook."

"Technically, I suppose it doesn't. I guess Patty and I could have been in it together."

"Correct me if I'm wrong, but didn't you just confess to being in it together?"

"I confessed to making the E-mail for her, not to killing Silvana. If you think that the person who gave her the E-mail is also the one who killed her, then I know that wasn't me."

"You think it was Patty?"

"No. I can't imagine Patty . . . " Jasper trailed off and looked for a moment at mother and daughter. Erin was standing at the barrier. Patty had leaned over to whisper something in her ear. Their two heads were so close together, it was impossible to tell where one set of blonde bangs ended and another began. Jasper said, "She wouldn't do that to Erin. That kind of tabloid notoriety would kill Erin's career. Heck, she wouldn't do it to herself."

"So if you don't think Patty did it, why are you so eager to incriminate her?"

"I am eager to prove to you that I wasn't alone in the E-mail scheme. If you go to Patty, she can show you the disk, and then she can tell you what she did with the E-mail I gave her. I bet what happened is, Patty gave Silvana the E-mail, Silvana put it in her purse, and she just happened to have it with her when she was killed."

"By whom, a random, lurking, ice skating serial killer?" Bex wondered how long it would be before Jasper suggested that skating's equivalent of a butler, the referee, did it. "And anyway, why would Patty give Silvana the E-mail? I thought the plan was to leak it to the press. What good would Silvana having it do? Was she supposed to look at it and go, 'Oh, I guess I was influenced in my vote after all; I think I'll go turn myself in'?"

"Maybe Patty thought showing Silvana the E-mail would keep her quiet? Maybe she made Silvana a deal: If Silvana kept quiet, Patty wouldn't show the E-mail to the press. After all, if no one spoke, nothing could ever be proven. People would continue to think what they wanted to think, but there would be no official censure. Maybe Patty only threatened to show the E-mail if Silvana actually gave testimony. Sure, Silvana could say she didn't cheat, but the E-mail would cast doubt on her word. The ISU might even decide to believe it, and Silvana would risk losing her position. Patty's way, no one gets hurt."

It was a very reasonable proposition. Bex could see why Jasper must have gotten all that start-up capital for his dot.com. He was an excellent speaker, very persuasive. The way he laid everything out, so calm and so confidently convinced of his own position, he made it very hard to disagree without feeling like a candidate for the funny farm.

However, Bex worked in television. Where not only did they spin reality any way they felt like, they also sometimes created it out of utterly thin air. With the solid ground perennially shifting under her feet, Bex felt like a candidate for the funny farm all the time. So, be gone you Wicked Witch of the West, you have no power here.

She told Jasper, "No. That's not who Silvana was. She didn't jump in to defend herself right away, even before there was an E-mail to be blackmailed with, because she had principles. She even fought with Sergei Alemazov about it, because she wouldn't lower herself to answering such ridiculous charges to the press. This isn't someone who'd just take a blackmail note, slip it in her purse, and go off on her merry way to the refrigeration room."

"Sergei Alemazov fought with her? So maybe he—"

"He has an alibi."

"Well, so does Patty! She was right here at the practice rink with Erin that morning. I came by to pick them up at the end of the session, and they were both right here."

"Not the whole time. Both Patty and Erin got off the ice for a bit during the practice." Bex realized, "But you didn't know that. Because you weren't here watching. You only came to pick them up. Jasper, where were you the morning Silvana was killed?"

He answered instantly, "In my hotel room. Sleeping. I'm a big fan, but come on, if I kept skaters' hours, I'd be dead before the end of the competition."

"So you don't have an alibi, either."

"Ask Patty," he insisted stubbornly. "She'll tell you I gave her the disk and the only copy of the E-mail, and then she'll tell you what she did with it and how it ended up in Silvana's purse. Ask Patty. She'll clear this whole thing up, I promise."

Patty said, "Jasper Clarke is a liar."

Oh, yes, that cleared everything up perfectly.

Bex caught skating's most famous mother alone in her hotel room. She'd asked Jasper to keep Erin occupied for a bit so the girl wouldn't have to hear what her mother and Web master had been up to, and Jasper gratefully rose to the task, inviting Erin to step into his hotel room to look at some new pictures he was considering putting up on the site. Patty promised she'd join them in a minute, as soon as she checked her phone messages, and Bex took advantage of the once-in-a-blue-moon separation to corner her. She told her what Jasper had said and asked to see the disk.

That's when the liar part came up.

"You mean you don't have the disk?"

"What disk?" Patty threw her hands up in the air, fingers wiggling as if playing an upside down piano. "I don't know what that Jasper is talking about. You know, I was warned about him. When he first came around, everyone said, 'Don't let him get so close. After all, you don't know any-thing about him. He could be some weirdo, some sicko.' But he seemed all right. And he really has been so helpful. No one realizes that skating is about so much more than just the skater. I mean, yes, in the end, the skater is the one on the ice who needs to deliver. But, leading up to that, there's the coach, the choreographer, the costume designer, someone to do the music, the dance coach, the media training . . . And all those people are just the hired hands. What about the person who has to drive Erin to the rink every morning and to dance lessons every afternoon and to the costume fittings and the skate sharpening? What about the one who watches her diet and sees that she gets enough sleep and keeps track of her schedule and all of the interviews and personal appearances, and then there's the fan mail and the official Web site. . . . Growing up, I didn't realize how fortunate I was, having a mother and a father and two older brothers and even a grandmother who renewed her driver's license so she could help out. I didn't have that kind of support system for Erin. My mother was so disappointed with how my career ended, she just didn't have the heart to go through it again; I was on my own. And I won't lie to you, it was hard. That's why, when Jasper showed up and offered to help . . ."

Bex said, "Well, right now he's claiming he helped you perpetrate a fraud."

"He's lying."

"Yes, I believe you've already mentioned that." ' '

"You don't believe me?"

"I've heard a lot of stories the last few days. And most of them have turned out to be crocks of the first, second, and third degree."

"Why would I lie?"

"Because you killed Silvana, and that's considered a crime in some bizarre jurisdictions?"

"Be serious. Why would I kill Silvana? I needed that woman. I needed her to admit that she cheated her vote and Erin was the real world champion."

"But Jasper says she didn't cheat. That you two were the ones who cheated by making it look like she had."

"Jasper is a liar."

"Patty, it may be acceptable in skating to do the same routine over and over again. In conversation, it's called redundant."

"You think you're pretty smart, don't you, Bex?"

Well, yes, as a matter of fact she did. But she'd been raised to believe it was in bad taste to just blurt it out like that. Instead, Bex shrugged. "I did okay in school."

"School," Patty snorted. "Yes, I remember hearing that a lot when I was competing: '*But don't you want to go to school Patty, get a real education?*' I did fine getting tutored. I thought I was smart enough. But people kept nagging me, telling me that I'd regret it the rest of my life if I missed out on the college experience. So, what the hell, when I finished competing, I thought I'd give it a try and enrolled in Stanford. Turned out school, Miss Smarty Pants, wasn't all that. I didn't learn anything there I needed. I didn't finish, and I'm not sorry. School doesn't make you smart. Living makes you smart, and I've done plenty of it both before and after school. So don't you go patronizing me. I know more than you think I do."

"That was exactly my point," Bex said smugly. And, for the record, Bex knew more than Patty thought, too. For instance, Bex knew that Patty didn't just quit Stanford for no reason. She quit because she obviously couldn't do the work (her grades were below C level), and, oh, yeah, she was pregnant with Erin. "I do think you know more than you're telling me. I think you know all about this E-mail of Jasper's."

"You're really getting on my nerves, Bex."

"Jasper made an accusation. I have to follow up."

"Fine," Patty snapped. "You think I have this E-mail on disk? Go ahead, be my guest, look for it." She went to the dresser, opened a drawer, and pulled out a computer carrying case. She unzipped it, revealing a laptop and, in the side pocket, a handful of multicolored discs.

Bex knew the defiant gesture was probably supposed to shame her into leaving quietly. But Bex never did anything quietly, and she suspected now would be the wrong time to start.

Bex powered up the computer and systematically went through every file on each of Patty's disks. She found travel itineraries, costume and music notes, text for the "Erin Excitement" on-line journal, downloaded E-mails from fans, Patty's coaching schedule and billing system. She found all sorts of things. Just no E-mail.

"Happy?" Patty asked.

"Not really," Bex admitted.

"Get out."

Bex did. And Patty followed. As soon as Bex was out of the room, Patty tore down the hallway in the opposite direction. She banged on Jasper's door.

"Erin!"

Her daughter peeked out. "Hi, Mom."

"Let's go. We're leaving."

"But I thought you wanted to talk to Jasper about the pictures."

"Later." Patty grabbed Erin by the arm and dragged her down the hall, managing to somehow glare both at Jasper to her right and Bex to her left, simultaneously. She told Jasper, "I will definitely talk to you later."

And then she disappeared behind her own door.

Bex walked over to Jasper. She said, "It didn't go well."

He sighed. "I knew she'd be angry. She probably thinks I betrayed her. Did you explain that I only told you about her having the disk to protect her and Erin? I wanted Patty to tell you the truth about what she did with the E-mail so you wouldn't think she was involved in something worse. Did you explain that to her, Bex?"

Was that how Jasper remembered their conversation? Because that certainly wasn't how Bex remembered it. Her recollection leaned more toward: *I'm trying to save my own butt, so go bother Patty, why don't you?* Sure, Jasper had said a few words in Patty's defense, but only after he'd made sure to cover his own hide backward and forward. Bex wondered if he'd spent the last hour coming up with this rationalization so that he could sleep easier, or so that he'd have something to defend himself to Patty with. In either case, it didn't matter.

"Patty," Bex told him, "denied the whole thing."

"You mean about killing Silvana?"

"I mean about knowing anything about any E-mail."

"She's lying! She's probably scared of what this will mean to Erin, and so she's lying."

"Well, one of you definitely is."

"And you think it's me?"

To be honest, Bex really wished that she did. She would love to turn Jasper and his E-mail confession over to the police and let them deal with it. But, the fact was, she kinda, sorta, baby blue eyes and all, believed him.

Well, there was that, and the fact that he'd only made his confession to her, so she really had nothing but Francis and Diana's word, and who knew how they might change their story and God knew they were famous for turning on a toe pick so, really, she had nothing. Nothing the police would be interested in, anyway. And, until she got something solid, Bex was stuck. Both with the police and in her report for Gil. She figured she might as well stick with Jasper for now, since, at the moment, he was the only one telling her anything instead of just denying everything.

Bex said, "I don't know what to think. Patty let me look at all of her disks, and there was no E-mail to be found."

"So?"

"So. That kind of puts a little dink your story, doesn't it?"

"Not really. Patty probably just erased it."

"Maybe," Bex conceded. "But what good is that to us? We need to catch her with it red handed to actually have a shot at proving anything."

Jasper shook his head. "Bex, Patty may have been smart enough to erase the file, but I doubt she was smart enough to delete it."

Bex stared at Jasper. "What?"

"Most people don't realize this, but when you erase a file, you don't actually erase it forever. It's still there on the disk, until it's overwritten. And since Patty just deleted it a few days ago at most, I doubt she's had a chance to overwrite it."

"You mean it's still there."

"In computer-speak, yes."

"And you could retrieve it?"

"Probably."

Bex said, "I wish I'd asked Patty if I could take the disks back to the production truck to look them over, instead of doing it right there in her room. Then I could have just held on to them a little longer or something."

"Yeah," Jasper said. "Now we'll have to steal them out of her room, I guess."

It may have been, like she told Patty, redundant, but nevertheless, Bex went ahead and asked Jasper, "What do you mean 'we,' Computer Boy?"

"Once again, Bex . . ." Was she mistaken, or did he actually look like he was enjoying this somewhat? "I suppose I mean you."

"Okay. And how do you propose I do that?"

"Well, since you know where Patty keeps the disks, I suppose just going in and taking them would be the straight-forward approach."

"Uh-huh." Bex's head bobbed *yes,* while her tone screamed *no.* "Taking them. From where she keeps them. In a computer bag. In a drawer. Of the dresser. In her hotel room. Which is locked. With a card key. Which only she and Erin have."

Jasper said, "Don't get Erin involved in this."

And suddenly, he didn't look to be having any fun at all. Bex, on the other hand, perked right up at the sudden change in mood. Because, when Jasper got serious, Bex got a thought: Jasper had been so quick to point the finger at Patty as his accomplice. But Patty wasn't the only one with access to those discs and that computer. And she certainly wasn't the only one with a motive to print the E-mail and/or kill Silvana.

Bex had assumed that Jasper was protecting himself by dumping everything on Patty. But, as they'd learned from her fruitless snooping around after Sergei and Xenia and Igor and Gary, Bex had most certainly been wrong before.

She asked Jasper, as casually as she'd once approached him in the arena, "Why not?"

"Because she's just a kid."

"She's a legal adult."

"Which, in skating, counts for absolutely nothing. Come on, Bex, you know how these kids live. Their lives are totally orchestrated by someone else. They're pampered and they're taken care of so that they never have to make a simple decision or think about anything other than skating. Patty still picks out Erin's clothes. She tells her what to order in a restaurant. She braids her hair and she writes out her answers for interview questions in advance. Erin may be over the legal age of consent, but, emotionally, she's a little kid."

"Little kids," Bex pointed out, "often act first and ponder the consequences later."

"My God, are you now putting Erin on the suspect list?"

"She was off the ice when Silvana was killed. And I have a witness who saw her using the phone. The same phone someone called Silvana from, right before she died."

"Is this witness reliable? How do you know they weren't using the phone themselves and didn't just finger Erin to cover it up?"

"I don't."

"There, you see?"

"I'm just trying to cover all the angles."

"Erin would never, in a million years do something like that. Patty didn't even tell her about the E-mail, because she knew Erin would never go along. She's a sweet girl, and she works very hard, but she also wants to win fair."

"But maybe she thought it was fair. Maybe she really believed what Francis and Diana said on the air; she deserved to win. I mean, come on, a kid trains all her life for one moment, and then she skates great, but she doesn't win. Except everyone says she should have. How easy is it to convince yourself that the public is right and the judges were wrong? Skaters do it all the time. 'I drew the wrong panel,' they say. Or: 'They're making me wait my turn.' Or: 'They didn't want one country to win all the medals, so they deliberately marked me down.' Or: 'I skated too early and they were holding back marks.' There are a million excuses, and we've heard all of them. What happens, though, when it isn't only you saying it to yourself to keep your spirits up? What happens when it's the couple considered the ultimate skating experts who are saying it, and they're saying it loudly? If the

Howarths say you should have won, then you should have won. If the Howarths say there was a fix, then there must have been a fix. Unfortunately, there's no proof. Well, if a smart person makes their own luck, why can't they make their own proof, too?"

"You're just making it up now. You have no proof that Erin was involved in any way in this, and I'm telling you she wasn't."

And Bex was listening. She just wasn't believing.

Bex realized that before she attempted breaking into Patty's room and grabbing a handful of floppy disks, she needed to talk to Erin.

Their only other face-to-face had been the team tag with Patty, and Bex doubted either one was going to be straight with the other listening. So Bex needed to talk to Erin alone.

But first, she needed to do the impossible and actually *get* Erin alone.

Fourteen

Bex's 1.0 version of a clever plan to get Erin alone, away from Patty and Jasper, was simply waiting. She reasoned Patty had to be champing at the bit to blast Jasper for telling Bex about the E-mail, and she would come tearing out of her room any minute, banging on his door and demanding an explanation. Bex figured all she had to do was lurk in the hallway for a bit, and she would see the scenario played out, giving her ample opportunity to both chat up Erin and gain access to the Simpson hotel room.

So she lurked.

Only to discover that it was harder than the horror movies would lead you to believe.

For one thing, lurking was very tiring. She couldn't just sit down in a hotel hallway; it would look too suspicious. So, instead, Bex paced up and down from the elevator, covering the area to the cul-de-sac where Patty and Jasper's doors faced each other, and back again. Lugging her overstuffed research binder every step of the way. About ten minutes into the exercise, she started to sweat. Twenty minutes, and she could feel both her pinkie toes chafing against shoes that had suddenly grown a size too small. Half an hour, and her neck stiffened up from constantly swiveling to check out every door opening and every floorboard creaking.

Another thing Bex discovered was that lurking proved rather dull after the first few minutes of *Ooh, look at me, I'm a Charlie's Angel.* A hotel hallway wasn't exactly a bustling metropolis of things to look at. There were the tiny numbers above the elevator doors, lighting up and counting down, then up again. There were the prints on the walls, all standard-issue masters, already faded from constant exposure to the sun. There was the pattern on the carpet, brown diamonds in an interlocking pattern, surrounded by scuffed and over-shampooed generic green. And then there was the periodic maid coming out of a recently cleaned room or a food service delivery person with a silver-domed tray. After an hour, Bex got tired of looking at them. They, however, did not feel the same way about her.

Apparently someone on the staff found Bex interesting enough to alert the management, because, on her umpteenth trip down the hall, Bex was greeted by a smiling yet unquestionably firm fellow in a hotel maroon blazer, wearing a little plastic tag on his lapel that identified him as Joseph from Security. And Joseph from Security wanted to know what exactly it was that Bex thought she was doing.

Luckily, an hour's worth of pacing in painful shoes with nothing to look at had given Bex plenty of time to come up with an answer to just such a query.

"I'm waiting for a friend," Bex announced brightly. "We

were supposed to meet, but I guess he forgot the time. I'm sure he'll be here any moment, though."

"I see. And which room is your friend staying in, miss?"

Bex pointed to Jasper's door. "Right there. Jasper Clarke is his name."

She was feeling pretty good. After all, the best cover story meant sticking as closely to the facts as possible. If Joseph checked out her story, he would find that Mr. Jasper Clarke was indeed registered in said room.

"Have you tried knocking on the door?"

"Of course, I have. He's not in there."

"Let us try again, shall we?"

Uh-oh. Bex hadn't counted on that possibility. After all, weren't they worried about disturbing their guests or anything, here? On the other hand, she'd claimed the man wasn't in, so who was there to disturb?

Good going, Bex.

Joseph strode up to the door and, with a look that might have been heading smirkward at Bex, knocked confidently on the door. "Mr. Clarke?"

"One minute . . ." Jasper shuffled to the door. "Who is it?"

"Hotel Security, sir. There's someone out here to see you." Jasper opened the door. Joseph told him, "This young lady says she is waiting for you to meet her."

"Jasper!" Bex improvised on the spot, wincing at how phony her voice sounded, but reasoning that Joseph had never heard her under nonpressure circumstances, so what did he know? "You're here! I knocked on the door, but no one answered. Were you taking a nap, maybe? Or a shower?"

Jasper looked from Bex to Joseph, obviously weighing

the consequences of getting her into trouble against the trouble she could still cause him.

Self-preservation apparently won over the momentary thrill of watching her get knocked down a few pegs, and Jasper said, "Yes. I was."

Bex fought the urge to ask him, "What? Napping in the shower?" But wisely decided that this was not the arena in which to flaunt her idea of wit. Instead, she took her satisfaction in seeing how disappointed Joseph looked not to be getting the chance to drag her downtown, or, in this case, probably down to the lobby. She gave him her brightest smile and said, "Thank you so much for your help. Who knows how long I may have been standing here if you hadn't come along and rescued me?"

Bex could see that Joseph really wanted to grunt. But, instead, he mirrored Bex's brightest smile with his own, gave a polite little bow, and shuffled off toward the elevator.

Jasper waited until the doors closed and their floor number overhead dimmed, before asking Bex, "And what was that all about?"

"I was just staking out Patty's room," Bex half-lied. "Waiting for her to leave so I could search for the disk."

"Oh. Well, I doubt she will. Erin is performing tomorrow. They always stay in the night before to pick out clothes and do her hair and nails and such."

Bex thought fast. "In that case, maybe you could call her or something and get her out of the room for a bit? This really is our last chance. I'm in the booth all day tomorrow for the show. It's not like I could just excuse myself from the arena. I have to keep Francis and Diana under control. Besides, we need our info before the broadcast starts. At least I do. I've got to close the books on Silvana before we're off the air at four P.M. After that, I've got no more reason to be snooping. Not to mention I'm booked on a seven P.M plane back to New York."

Jasper said, "Patty has been calling me all afternoon. She's ready to chew my head off, and I don't blame her. She trusts me. Well, she used to anyway. This has been a huge, huge betrayal for her. She doesn't trust people very easily, and once you've blown it with her, you don't get a second chance. I'll be lucky if she ever lets me watch Erin on television again, much less have anything to do with them."

"All the more reason to clear the air, then. Tell Patty what you told me, that you only confessed about the E-mail because you were trying to protect her. I bet she'll understand. And she'll certainly be impressed by how you went to the mat to protect Erin. I can testify to that."

"Oh, yes, I'm sure Patty will be thrilled to hear from you again."

"We need that disk, Jasper. It's the only thing capable of proving you didn't act alone in Silvana's murder."

"Good Lord, Bex, how many times do I have to tell you? I had nothing to do with that, and neither did Patty or Erin."

"I believe you. I do. But, seeing as how you were ready to commit fraud and all with the phony E-mail, I suspect the police might like a little more evidence that you are capable of telling the truth on occasion."

"Oh, so what, now you want me to believe that you are doing all this to help *me?*"

"No," Bex said honestly. "I am doing it to get a great story to give to Gil so I won't lose my job and/or look like an idiot. However, I would very much prefer it if the great story I gave him were accurate and complete. Right now, I have the E-mail and Francis and Diana's testimony that you told them to print it out. You claim Patty was in on it, too? Fine, let's prove it."

Jasper hesitated. "She really denied everything?"

"Everything."

"Not just killing Silvana? She denied everything, everything?"

"She claimed she didn't know what you were talking about. She said you were a liar, and you couldn't be trusted."

"I didn't expect that," Jasper confessed.

"Then help me get the disk and find the original forgery. Once we confront her with it, I bet Patty will break down and tell us how the E-mail got into Silvana's purse, and you'll both be cleared of the murder charges."

Personally, Bex doubted it. In her scenario, their undeleting the original E-mail template and confronting her with it would lead to a confession of murder on either Patty or Jasper's part. Bex honestly didn't care which one broke first at this point, as long as she had something to show Gil, and, oh, yes, the police, too.

"I can't do it," Jasper said. "Patty is still too angry, I bet. If I confront her now, she'll just blow up; she won't listen to me. I'll lose all the rapport I've worked so hard to build up with her these past few years. I can't. It isn't the right time now. Maybe tomorrow morning. She'll be calmer tomorrow morning. You understand, don't you, Bex?"

Bex understood that Jasper didn't want to talk to Patty. She also understood that she *needed* Jasper to talk to Patty, as a confrontation with him was the only scenario Bex could imagine capable of separating Patty from her child/Siamese twin. Ergo, Bex needed to *make* Jasper talk to Patty. And not tomorrow morning. Tonight.

She moved her lurking down to the lobby. It was less suspicious to sit there, on one of the comfy couches, and watch, eagle-eyed, everyone coming and going. For two weeks, gaggles of fans had been doing just that. They were there now, segregated into groups based on whom they were stalking, and glaring at the opposing camps as they flipped through their stacks of pictures and scrapbooks, wondering which one they'd be asking their heroes to autograph this time around. How, Bex mused, had Jasper Clarke managed to jump the fence from just a gawker in the lobby (after all, running a skater Website was no big deal; at least a third of those assembled maintained cyber shrines to their favorites) to an official member of Team Simpson? What had he offered Patty that no one else could match? After all, she'd told Bex how badly she needed help. She would have presumably accepted it from anyone. So why Jasper?

A collective gasp from the ponytailed group of girls dressed in "Erin Excitement!" T-shirts clued Bex in that their national champion had appeared. The girls sprang up in unison, rushing past Bex toward the elevator banks, enveloping Erin in a chattering, pen-wielding swarm of what Bex might have called Mini-Mes, except that Erin was the tiniest figure in the bunch.

She greeted them all graciously, even calling a few of the girls by name, sweetly smiling for photos and signing anything thrust at her with apparent good cheer. She answered questions like, "How often do you practice a day?" and "Will you be touring this summer?" and the newest, "Isn't it horrible about what the judges did to you?" as if this were the first time she'd heard them. Bex had to hand it to Patty: she'd done an excellent job preparing her daughter for the role of star.

Of course, Patty's fine parenting wasn't what Bex wanted to talk to her about as she took advantage of her telling Erin, "I'll just check if the restaurant has a table available," and walking away for a moment to make like the uber-fans, and pounce.

Bex sidled up to Patty as she was waiting by the hostess's desk. When Patty saw her, she deliberately turned away, as if Bex weren't there. That was okay, though. Bex could walk around the other way.

"What do you want?" Patty demanded. "More stupid accusations?"

"Actually, yes. I talked to Jasper again. He's changed his story."

"You mean he's decided to tell the truth? How novel."

"Now he's saying you told him you were going to kill Silvana and plant the E-mail on her for the police to find and expose."

At that, Patty jumped high enough to complete a quadruple jump. Well, not really, her head merely jerked like someone had smacked her on the chin. But it felt quadruple high to Bex. She did love getting a reaction.

Patty grabbed Bex's arm and pulled her into a corner where they were less likely to be overheard by the dining public.

"Are you out of your mind?"

"I'm just telling you what Jasper said. He said you told him you were going to kill Silvana, but he didn't take you seriously. Now he isn't so sure."

"That goddamn son of a bitch!" Patty looked frantically around her, as if expecting Jasper to materialize through the sheer force of her bile. Bex didn't doubt that, if he did somehow materialize, Patty would happily pierce his carotid artery with the little gold skate pin clipped to her scarf. This was actually good. It was exactly what Bex had planned on.

Seizing the moment to direct all that wonderful anger, Bex told Patty, "Yes, he told me that a couple of minutes ago, up in his room. It's such a major accusation, I figured you'd want to respond, so I came right down and found—"

"Jasper is in his room?"

"Yes. But I think he wants to be alone. While I was there, his phone rang a couple of times, but he didn't want to answer it."

Bex figured if that little detail didn't confirm the veracity of her story, nothing would.

She'd barely gotten the last word out before Patty pivoted on her heel, displaying lovely grace indicative of the world-class athlete she'd once been, and stormed out of the restaurant, Bex hot on her heels.

She passed by Erin and her adoring throng and, in a surprisingly calm voice, indicative of the practice she'd had suppressing her anger in public places, told her daughter, "Erin, honey, I just remembered, I completely forgot to discuss with Jasper about how we're going to cover the ceremony tomorrow for the site. We really need to get the details ironed out so we can handle the press. I'm going to pop up to his room and go over the game plan. When you're finished here, why don't you go back up to the room and order room service?"

"Do you want me to order you something too, Mom?"

"No," Patty smoothed down a lock of Erin's hair that, as far Bex could tell, wasn't standing up. "I may be a while."

And she left Erin inside the safe bosom of her fans.

Bex counted to ten. And then she told the fans to scram.

And then she asked, "Hey, Erin, you want to have dinner with me?"

"Uhm." Erin shrugged. This making a decision on your own for the first time like, ever, was obviously a stumper. "Okay. Sure."

"Great." Bex seized Erin's shoulder, guiding her in a manner she hoped was reminiscent of Patty's firm, maternal hand. "Let's order room service up in my room. It'll really give us a chance to talk."

Once ensconced upstairs, neither Bex nor Erin needed to look at the room service menu before calling down and placing their orders. Both had made the "feed me" call enough times to know exactly what serving they wanted. Besides, to keep her size negative number figure, Erin probably only nibbled spinach leaves and bread crumbs. If the latter didn't have too many carbs.

"So," Bex plopped down on her bed next to a lotus-sitting and somewhat bored-looking Erin. "Are you excited about the ceremony tomorrow?"

"It'll be great to get a gold medal. I always said, if I ever win a gold medal at worlds, I'll give it to my grandma."

"Your grandma?" Bex had been so sure Erin was going to go with the cliché and say "Mom," that she had to hit rewind in her brain just to make sure she'd heard right. "Is she here with you, too?"

"Oh, no, she doesn't travel with us. She never comes to my competitions, even when they're local."

"Is she sick?" Bex asked.

"No. She just doesn't like it. She did it all with my mom. She's the one who got my mom into skating. They didn't know anything when they started. My mom was just this little girl who really, really liked to skate on this pond their town had in the winter. Grandma didn't think much about it; she figured all kids were as good as my mom. But then this coach saw her, and she told my grandma Mom could be a champion. Grandma had to learn everything about skating from scratch, like how the testing worked, and the competitions. When they started, she didn't even know what region

they'd be competing out of! Grandma totally dedicated herself to Mom, Mom says. Then, when Mom didn't become
world champion, Grandma just . . . it made her very sad. It
was her dream, she worked as hard as Mom did, harder
even, I guess, and Mom couldn't do it for her. That's why
I'll give her my medal. I think it will make her happy.
Maybe she'll even come and watch me skate. Now that it's,
you know, all okay, again."

Bex asked, "Are the other medalists going to be there?
Are they doing the whole thing again, with anthems and
everything, or is it just a ceremony for you?"

"Well, they invited Xenia, but she refused to come. And
Jordan is nuts. Nobody knows what Jordan will do till she
does it, not even Mr. Marchenko. So, I think it will be just
me."

"You sound kind of sad about it."

"I'm not sad. I'm getting a gold medal. A gold medal is
great." She said it with the same conviction she'd used only
a few days ago to wax poetic about her silver lining.

Their food came. Erin had a chicken breast salad. Bex
had the salmon. As always.

"Erin," Bex said, "I have a question for you. You know
when you said you saw Xenia and Sergei and Igor hanging
out by the phone outside the arena the morning Silvana
died?"

"Uh-huh," Erin moved her chicken breast and a few wal-
nuts to the side, then chewed some greens. So much for protein.

"Well, I asked Xenia about it."

"Did she say I lied?"

"Why would she say that?"

"Oh, I don't know. She's pretty mad at me right now.

She's probably saying all sorts of mean things about me to people. She thinks this is all my fault."

"Actually, she said she did see you."

"Oh." Erin stabbed a spinach leaf, rubbed it against a piece of chicken breast, then ate it. All the yumminess of meat without the pesky calories, Bex guessed.

"But she claims she didn't yell at you, like you said."

"Well, maybe she didn't yell at me exactly. She more like, you know, glared."

"You told your mom and me Xenia yelled at you."

"It was an analogy." Erin's head suddenly popped up, and she explained, "You know how, on the SATs, they have this section called analogy? This is to this as this is to that. I love those, they're like a crossword puzzle mixed with a jigsaw. I wish the whole test was analogies, instead of those logic problems: If Bob is taller than Bill, and Bill is taller than Fred, and Fred has blue eyes, which one of them is the professional basketball player? It's so stupid. Like you ever need to do stuff like that in real life."

Frankly, Bex agreed with her, but she asked, "You're taking the SAT?"

"I already did. Last summer, when I had some time off from the tour."

"So you can go to college?"

"Maybe. I don't know. Someday. I mean, you're supposed to, right? It's just something you're supposed to do, like brush your teeth and look both ways before you cross the street."

"Your mother doesn't seem to think much of it. She gave me quite a lecture about higher education and how nobody needs it."

"Oh. Yeah. Mom kind of goes back and forth. I mean, she went to college because she wanted to have a normal life after skating. When skating didn't work out for her the way she thought it would, she figured she'd just go to school and be normal and be happy. It was hard for her, though. She was so much older than the other freshmen, she was like, twenty-four. And going to class after being tutored all her life, I guess that was hard, too. But it couldn't have been all bad. I mean, she met my dad and everything. It was really tough for her before, being on the road all the time, never really meeting anyone. In school, she got to have a real boyfriend. That was cool. You know, having someone who cares about you not because you're a skater or you're on TV, but because you're just you."

Something about the wistful tone in Erin's voice prompted Bex to suspect that they had jumped off the Patty train and were making a stop in Erin-ville.

Bex asked, "Sounds like that's something you'd really like to have."

Erin shrugged. "Maybe. Someday."

She'd finished segregating her meal into food groups and now poked at the chicken breast with her fork, eyes downcast, hair falling down on either side of her face so that Bex couldn't see her eyes. Her hunched shoulders and generally slumped body language radiated defeat and vulnerability. So, naturally, Bex took advantage of it.

And she also took a guess. Bex asked Erin, "Is that what you were doing on the phone when Xenia saw you? Talking to a boyfriend?"

Erin's head popped up. "What phone?"

"Xenia said she saw you on the phone, the one right outside the refrigeration room, the morning Silvana was killed. Is that why you got off the ice? To make that call?"

"I . . . Are you going to tell my mom?"

"So you were on the phone?"

"Yeah, okay, I was. But, please don't tell my mom. She doesn't like anything to disturb my skating, and if she knew I was . . . Please, Bex."

"I guess you and your boyfriend don't get a lot of chances to talk."

"Try like practically never. The other day, when my mom went to get my tissues, and then she was gone for a while, I figured she went back to the hotel to get them, so I thought I'd take a few minutes and . . . but I did tell you the truth about Xenia and Sergei and Mr. Marchenko. They were standing around, whispering Russian and stuff."

"I know. They all confirmed it."

"Oh. So did they kill Silvana, then?"

"I'm not sure. The only one who could have done it was Sergei. Both Xenia and Igor were on the ice by the time she died. And Sergei has an alibi. He was on the phone back in his hotel room. I don't think he would have had enough time to make it back to make that call, if he really had killed Silvana."

"He could have had someone in his room make the call for him."

"I thought of that. I just can't prove it." Bex grinned. "You're pretty good at this. Want my job?"

"Oh, no," Erin shook her head. "Oh, no, no. I couldn't spend my whole life in skating."

The irony was getting a little too thick for Bex's taste. Besides, she couldn't bet on Patty chewing Jasper's head off forever. The woman would eventually be free to roam the hotel halls again, and that was the last thing Bex wanted. There was a part two to this master plan of hers, and Bex knew she'd better get to it. Especially now that Erin had given her such a convenient in.

Bex said, "You know what? I have an idea. Since you and

your boyfriend hardly get a chance to talk, why don't you call him from here? Your mother will never know, then."

Erin hesitated. "Uhm, no offense, Bex, but, I kind of don't want to talk to him with, you know, someone else around. The stuff we say, it's sort of personal."

Oh, God, this was going to be even easier than Bex had thought. It's like the kid was working off a script and feeding Bex every line she needed to hear.

"That's okay. I won't hang around, I'll give you guys your privacy. I know what that's like." Bex practically leapt off the bed to show her sincerity.

And, at the same time, she managed to accidentally-on-purpose knock off the bed Erin's jacket, which was lying on top of the plastic credential she wore around her neck on a string. The credential was marked C for competitor, and ensured that Erin had access to all the backstage areas of the arena. It was also a very handy place to keep her hotel pass card. All the skaters did it. Since they never left their rooms without their credentials, it also ensured that they never left their rooms without their keys.

Bex showed Erin the phone and told her to take as much time as she wanted. And, when her back was turned to dial, Bex slipped the pass card out of Erin's credential. She waved bye-bye and closed her own hotel room door behind her, heading for Patty's, in search of the undeleted E-mail.

Fifteen

Prior to commencing with the breaking and entering, Bex first pressed her ear against Jasper's door, all the while sincerely hoping Joseph from Security was nowhere around. She heard angry, raised voices on the other side. Not just Patty's, but Jasper's, as well. Good, at least Jasper was giving as good as he got and maybe, just maybe, they'd work this whole mess out by themselves, without Bex having to do any more work.

Yes. That's very, very likely Bex. At least it didn't sound like said argument was going to wind down any time soon.

She headed toward Patty's room. She slid in the pass card. It worked like a charm. Frankly, Bex had an easier time opening this door than she usually did her own. After a year of traveling the globe, Bex could say with great certainly that hotel cards, as a rule, hated her, and, more often than not, showed her the little blinking red light instead of the little blinking green light when it came time to opening her own door. Especially late at night. And when she really needed to go to the bathroom.

Bex opened Patty's door with great caution, just in case the woman currently screaming at Jasper was actually not Ms. Simpson, but yet another female he'd pissed off. Heck, for all Bex knew, Jasper designated one day a week exclusively for arguments, and then just had them all in a row, first Bex, then Patty, then the mystery woman behind door number 921.

Hey, it could happen.

Although, in this particular case, it didn't.

Patty's room was apparently empty. Bex stepped inside. She headed straight for the dresser, opened the top drawer and pulled out the laptop. She slid open the compartment full of floppy disks and spread all six of them out in front of her. At this point, she stopped.

Six disks.

Six disks of every color. Patty must have bought the rainbow set.

There was a problem, though. Bex didn't know which stripe of said rainbow might be hiding her pot of gold.

She supposed she could take all six and scan through them at leisure back in her room. But, Patty was no fool. She might not notice one disk missing, but she would certainly miss them all being gone. Bex needed to know what color disk she was looking for, and she needed to know before she left Patty's room—because who could guess when she'd ever be back.

Of course, as far as Bex knew, only three people could possibly point her in the right direction: Patty, Erin . . . and Jasper.

Bex decided that the devil she did know, at this point, was safer than the devil who would probably rip her hair out by the roots. And so she did something that, in retrospect, might very possibly prove to be her biggest misstep.

She dialed Jasper Clarke's room.

She heard his phone ringing in stereo, both on the other end of her receiver and down the hall. It rang three times. Four times. Five.

Bex was about to hang up when she got an angry, "What?"

Bex could hear, in the background, Patty screaming at him to "Hang up the fucking phone. I'm talking to you!"

Bex talked fast. "Jasper, it's me, Bex."

"What the—"

"Listen, I'm in Patty's room, trying to get the disk. I had to send her to you; it was the only way I could get her away from Erin. Uhm, yeah, sorry about that."

He didn't say anything. This was good. The last thing Bex needed was for him to blow her cover. She talked even faster. "I know you can't really talk with Patty there, but I need to know what color the disk was."

"Oh. Yeah. I . . . it was—"

"No, no, don't tell me the color out loud. She might get suspicious. Just let me run this by you, and when I hit the right one, you can say, yes, okay?"

"Okay . . . " He sounded exhausted. Bex knew how talking to Patty could do that. "Okay. So, is it the yellow one?"

No answer. Bex realized she hadn't told him to say no to the wrong one, just yes to the right one. Some spy she'd be.

"Is it the red one? The green one? The blue—"

"Yes."

"Yes? Yes, it's the blue one?"

"Yes. And, uhm, listen, I have someone here right now, but I have a feeling she'll be leaving soon." Jasper did his best to sound casual, even as he stressed the last two words.

"Got it," Bex said, "I'll be out of here in a second."

"Yes," he repeated. "Bye."

"Bye." Bex hung up the phone and grabbed the blue disk, sliding it into the pocket of her binder. She was in the process of putting the rest of the disks away in the laptop bag, when Bex heard the unmistakable sound of a key card being slipped into the lock.

At the moment, Bex was holding onto Erin's key card.

Ergo, it was not Erin at the door.

Now, granted, it could have been the maid. Because everyone knew that maids often just came in without knocking and introducing themselves. And they were famous for trying to clean in the evenings, when most people were probably in their rooms.

Double ergo, it was most likely not the maid.

Bex continued the process of putting the rest of the disks away in the laptop bag. Or, rather, she swept them all in with one hand, and, figuring there wasn't enough time to slip the laptop back into the dresser all the way across the room, grabbed its bag by the black leather handle, and jumped into the bathroom, hiding behind the double shower curtain.

From her damp hiding place (someone had showered recently and condensation from the ceiling happily dripped down on Bex's head like a private monsoon), Bex heard the hotel room door open. She heard Patty call, "Erin?"

She tried to recall if she'd remembered to turn off the light during her mad dash to the bathroom. She assumed that, with her luck and general ineptitude, she most likely had not.

"Erin?" Patty knocked on the bathroom door.

Bex held her breath. And tried to remember if, in *Psycho*, the shower curtain was only see-through one-way, or both?

ALINA ADAMS

But, getting no answer, Patty didn't even bother going into the bathroom.

Now all Bex needed was for her not to bother with deciding to hop onto the ol' laptop for some surfing the Web before bedtime, and she was all set.

Well, and, while she was making wishes, Bex figured she should probably also add that she didn't want Patty to get naked and decide to take a shower. Somehow, she suspected that scenario wouldn't end well for anyone. What with the screaming and the nakedness . . .

Luckily, Patty was neither in a showering nor a surfing mood. She called Erin's name one more time and, getting no answer, huffed rather loudly and walked out the door.

Or, at least, Bex heard the door open and close.

Which didn't necessarily mean that Patty went out. She could, for all Bex knew, be standing in the doorway, opening and closing the door to her heart's content. It would be a pretty stupid thing to do, but Bex had done quite enough leaping to conclusions lately.

Still, she needed to leave the shower at some point, if for no other reason than because the water was now sliding down her hair to the back of her neck, and it felt icky.

And so she pulled aside the curtain. So far so good.

She peeked out the bathroom door. No Patty.

She returned the laptop to its drawer. She looked out through the peephole. Still no Patty.

She counted to ten slowly, waited until she'd heard the elevator go ding, suggesting that Patty would have time to get off the floor, and, at long last, opened the hotel room door. Bex stuck her head out. She looked left. She looked right. She exhaled.

Nobody. And then she scurried up the back stairs to her own room.

Erin was off the phone when Bex returned. She was sitting on one of the chairs by the window, leafing through the spare research binder Bex always brought along to give to Francis when he inevitably lost the one she'd previously given him.

Bex gulped and winced simultaneously. This was not good.

The research binders were intended solely for the eyes of 24/7's cast and crew. As a result, Bex tended to get a little . . . creative . . . with some of her notes. They amused the talent and tech people. Heck, even Gil was known to chuckle once or twice at her witticism.

For instance, in summarizing the defending world bronze medalists' free dance, Bex had written, "The middle part is a tribute to all who've died due to religious persecution through the ages, hence the lift where Gregor picks up Anna and displays her crotch to the free world."

About a skater from Taiwan, she wrote, "Wei-Lee often leaves the ice with his eyes downcast, as if searching for something minuscule. Many have suggested it just might be his artistic mark." And so on. It wasn't an opus Bex really wanted Erin to read.

But, to Bex's relief, Erin simply closed the binder and said, "Wow, you really do a lot of work, don't you? Getting everyone's programs and stats like that."

Finally! Validation!

"It's not so bad," Bex said and/or lied.

"Did you go to school to learn how to do this?"

"Not really."

"Oh. So, what did you go to school to learn, then?"

A question often asked by Bex's parents . . .

She said, "I'm weird. I went to school because I like

learning, not so much because I wanted to learn anything in particular. Does that make any sense?"

"Totally," Erin said, sounding utterly unconvinced.

"Yeah," Bex said, thinking how much Erin sounded like Bex's parents. Supportive, yet very, very confused.

"How did your call go?" Bex deliberately pointed to the phone, gambling that Erin would instinctively turn her head to look in that direction. At the same time, Bex slipped a hand into her pocket to finger the room card she'd stolen from the girl earlier.

Like a good little Pavlovian skater, Erin did as Bex expected and briefly turned her head in the direction of the phone.

"It was great, thanks so much, Bex."

"No problem," Bex said. And pulled the keycard out of her pocket, dropping it subtly and smoothly on the floor next to her bed. "Oh!" Bex exclaimed like an actor who should only be heard in silent movies. "Look. Is this your key card, Erin? 'Cause I've got mine."

Erin walked around the bed. "I dunno." She checked her credential, lying next to her jacket. "Yeah, I guess so. I guess I dropped it. How weird."

"Weird," Bex agreed.

"Well," Erin said. "Thanks."

Bex said, "I think I saw your mom looking for you. You know, when I was outside. I saw her walking around. So I guessed. I didn't talk to her or anything."

The last thing she needed was the following exchange: Erin: "Hi, Mom, Bex Levy said you were looking for me." Patty: "I didn't tell Bex Levy I was looking for you. How did she know? She must have been hiding in our hotel bathroom."

Okay, so it was a stretch, but Bex still didn't need to risk it.

Erin said, "I better go. Thanks again, Bex."

"Double no prob." Bex walked Erin to the door. And, as soon as she'd closed it behind her, she hightailed it to the phone, hitting Redial.

Erin may have been cute and blonde and in possession of one of those "Who, me, would I lie?" faces, but Bex still liked to check every story out for herself.

She hit Redial and listened to the droning ring of Erin Simpson's boyfriend's phone. She heard a click after the fourth ring. A mechanized voice came on.

"This is a recording. If you are calling from a rotary phone, please stay on the line and someone will be with your shortly. Otherwise, enter you ID code and begin . . ."

Well, well, well. How interesting. Erin Simpson was having a long-distance love affair with a recording. . . . Bex continued to listen. When directed, she pushed the appropriate buttons. And, by the time she'd hung up, Bex had a much better grasp of the entire situation.

What, Bex wondered, was the world coming to, when you couldn't even trust a perky blonde to tell you the truth? And why, she continued to wonder in that overeducated way that she had, was nothing about this story even remotely straightforward? Would it kill at least one person not to be playing games with her?

Then again, the late Silvana Potenza was allegedly a straight shooter. And look where that got her.

Bex knocked on Jasper's door. Before he opened it, she expected him to look like a lightweight boxer who'd accidentally wandered into the ring with a heavyweight—or a runaway gaggle of circus bears. With rabies. And in a bad mood. Bex was thinking scratches on his face, hair turned gray, maybe a rip along his sleeve, like Captain Kirk after a wrestling match. Reality proved most disappointing.

Jasper looked as together as he ever had. About the only suggestion that he and Patty had been hurling invectives at each other was his unnaturally flushed cheeks. But he could have also gotten those from twenty minutes on the treadmill.

He was, however, rattled enough from his evening encounter to snap, "You know, a warning might have been nice, Bex."

"I was having a spontaneous moment."

"Don't do that anymore."

He grabbed her arm and yanked Bex inside the room. "Did you get the disk?"

"What did Patty say to you?"

"What do you think she said to me? I've blown her whole scheme. She was livid. She thought she could trust me, and I let her down. Patty does not respond well to being let down, FYI. Oh, and, by the way, thank you so much for claiming I told you Patty stated her intention to kill Silvana. That was very helpful in my trying to calm her down."

"I needed to get her out of her room and away from Erin. By the way, hello? It worked. I have the disk, right here."

"She told me not to bother coming to the exhibition tomorrow. She told me if she so much as saw me in the audience, she'd call Security. And she's pulling her endorsement of the Web site. 'Erin Excitement' won't be official anymore."

"Well, can't you have, I don't know, some unofficial excitement?"

"Oh, please. You want me to be just another fan with his little on-line shrine? That's for serious losers."

As opposed, Bex thought, to grown men who followed a teenager around the world for the privilege of getting to host her on-line journal, full of musings like, "It's not the size of the dreamer, it's the size of the dream," and "To me, skating is like flying, only without the wings."

"Patty will never let me speak to Erin, again," Jasper said. "How the hell could you do this to me, Bex?"

"Hey, you're the one so eager to turn the spotlight on Patty to protect yourself. Really noble behavior there, Jas."

"All I wanted was to straighten this whole thing out. I certainly never told you I heard Patty threaten to kill Silvana. If anything, I told you Patty would never do such a thing."

"To protect Erin's image."

"Well, and she's not a killer."

"But she is a perpetrator of fraud?"

Jasper reminded, "Erin deserved to win."

"Right. I think you've mentioned that already."

"Let me see the disk." Jasper stuck out his arm. Bex handed it over. And, for a split second, she had an image of him throwing it to the floor, smashing it with his heel and chortling, "Ha-ha-ha," or whatever passed for an evil laugh in Silicon Valley.

But, the fact was, Bex only knew about the disk because Jasper told her. Wouldn't it have been easier just to keep his mouth shut, rather than to manipulate Bex into stealing it so he could destroy it?

In any case, there were no "Ha-ha-has" to be heard. Jasper simply took the disk, sat down at his laptop, and popped it in. Afterward, he proceeded to type several keys, some of them more than once, while squinting.

Bex stood over his shoulder and hovered.

He seemed to hate it. At least, the muscles at the back of

his neck started pumping like overly frisky worms, and twice he looked over his shoulder, glaring at Bex as if sheer heat could push her back a few feet.

Bex refused to budge. Not that she had any clue what he was doing, but if Jasper was working to sabotage her, she at least wanted to be able to say she'd watched his every move.

Bex asked, "Did Patty say anything, you know, interesting?"

"You mean, incriminating?"

"I mean anything we can use to get to the bottom of this and see that you three are left alone and the right person is punished and put away."

"I.e., incriminating."

"Oh, for God's sake, what did she say?"

Jasper tapped another key and got a very long directory made up mostly of consonants. It was either a bunch of computerese or a listing of the Yugoslavian team members.

"She said I'd ruined everything. Once word gets out about the forged E-mail, Rupert will probably change his mind about awarding Erin the second gold medal."

"Well, yes. I'd expect that would be the least of it."

"She also wanted me to tell you that I made it all up, about the E-mail, that is."

"Really? And did she tell you what your reason would have been for doing so?"

"Patty thought I should tell you that I made up the story about Patty and the forged E-mail because I was covering for Francis and Diana really being the ones who did it. She thought that if I pointed out how the truth would hurt 24/7, you would back off."

"Not a bad plan," Bex conceded. "Frankly, if you and Patty stuck to that story, and even if I didn't believe it, even if I wrote everything up and handed it in to Gil, he'd probably have sat on the news anyway, for the same reasons."

"Right. That was Patty's backup plan."

And this was a woman who hadn't been able to handle the coursework at Stanford? Bex was impressed. Maybe Ms. Simpson was right. Maybe life experience counted for a heck of a lot more than book learning.

On the other hand, book learning, i.e., logic, was all Bex had to fall back on. She asked Jasper, "So that leaves me with only one question, then: Why aren't you saying that you lied and dumping the blame on Francis and Diana?"

Jasper hesitated. He sat back in his chair, hands in his lap, and stared up the ceiling. He said, "I thought about it. I really did. Frankly, Bex, I want to get to the bottom of this. I know that E-mail was faked, and I know that I gave it to Patty. What I don't know is how it ended up on Silvana's dead body. Sure, Patty's way, by lying or blaming Francis and Diana, we could sweep everything under the rug. But I don't want to do that."

"Because you think Patty killed Silvana?"

"No! Absolutely not. I keep telling you, Patty couldn't have done it. She loves Erin too much. And so do I. I care about that kid. And I am not going to let her spend the rest of her life under a cloud of suspicion. Because here's a fact I'm pretty certain of: That E-mail isn't going to stay buried forever, even if you or Gil decide not to do anything about it. The original is still at the police station, right? So they'll eventually send it to Silvana's family. And they'll see it, and maybe they'll believe that she was a cheater and they'll try to sweep it under the rug. Or maybe they won't. Or maybe her husband won't know what it means, but one of her skating friends will. And they'll decide to sweep it under the rug. Or they won't. There are too many variables, here, Bex, and neither Patty nor I can spend the next twenty years running around trying to guess who has the E-mail and how we can explain it to them. No, it's better to face this head-on. We get to the bottom of this now, and we don't have to worry about it coming up to bite Erin when she least expects it. I'm doing this for Erin. And for Patty, too."

"Judging by the screaming I heard when I called, I suspect Patty isn't utterly convinced of your benevolence."

"She'll come around. Once we get this whole thing settled and we know who killed Silvana, Patty will see that I was protecting her." Jasper leaned back over the computer. Bex leaned in over his shoulder, watching intently.

He clicked a few more buttons. The machine buzzed, hummed, then went silent. Jasper nodded his head approvingly. The screen went blank.

"What the heck—"

But Bex never got the chance to finish her thought.

Because there, on the screen in front of her, it was.

The E-mail. In all of its manufactured glory.

"This is fantastic!" Bex shouted.

Jasper didn't look convinced. Bex wondered if he was experiencing the computer equivalent of buyer's remorse.

"You were telling the truth, Jasper. Patty really was in on this."

"You didn't believe me the first time?"

"Well, you did have a motive for taking the heat off you."

"This is hardly taking the heat off me, Bex. I basically just gave you proof that the E-mail was, in fact, faked. Up to this point, it was your word against mine."

"And Francis and Diana's."

"Oh, please, all I had to do in a court of law was call as witnesses anyone who'd ever heard them commentate on air. Those two change their minds in the middle of sentence. Their credibility is less than stellar."

"Are you having second thoughts about helping me, Jasper?"

He sighed. "I just hope Patty understands. . . ."

𝔅ℯ𝔵 hoped that Patty understood, too. Bex hoped that Patty understood Bex was about to nail her for fraud and, if she was lucky, murder as well.

Naturally, she declined to share her sentiments with Jasper.

Instead, she took back the floppy. Jasper may have made a lovely speech about truth, justice, and the Erinphillic way, but that didn't mean he couldn't change his mind at any time and click the delete key again; and, this time, Bex felt pretty certain the incriminating document would not be retrievable. She bid Jasper good-bye, promised him she wouldn't do anything rash, and then went down the hall to confront Patty.

Rash, Bex figured, was in derma of the beholder.

Erin opened the door. She saw Bex. She panicked.

"Bex . . ." she tried to hiss under her breath, apparently convinced that the 24/7 researcher was here to blow her cover and announce her intention to create an up-close-and-personal feature on Erin Simpson's secret love life in time for the exhibition.

"Erin . . ." Bex hissed back, hoping to convey that actually no, she wasn't; she was here for a totally different reason, and if she wasn't careful, Erin would end up giving her own self away.

"Bex?" Erin uncertainly double-checked the telepathic message.

"Erin." Bex answered definitively.

The teen visibly relaxed.

Bex was glad they had this talk. Maybe next time, they could use verbs.

"Erin?" Patty's voice sailed out from the corner. She approached the door. Her face soured. "Bex."

Yup, a verb was definitely called for now.

"Hello, Patty," Bex said cheerfully. "Could you spare a couple of minutes to talk to me? It's really important."

The shadow of a dozen obscenities flicked in the creases of Patty's frown. Alas, she could utter none of them in front of Erin. As a matter of fact, even using pleasant words, Patty couldn't really reveal why she didn't want to talk to Bex in front of Erin.

And so she took the easiest path out. Patty told Erin, "It's time to go to bed, sweetie pie, you've got a huge day tomorrow. I'll just step out and chat with Bex in the hall."

Erin shot Bex a look. "Bex."

"Erin." Bex stared at her forcefully to convey that no, this wasn't about the boyfriend, chill out, kid.

"Okay," Erin said. "Good night, Mom. Good night, Bex."

Bex and Patty stepped out into the hall. Bex said, "I don't think you want to talk about this in public. Let's go to my room."

"Fine," Patty snapped. "But make it quick. I really don't have anything to say to you."

Bex took the disk out of her pocket and showed it to Patty.

Patty didn't say another word until they were safely behind the door of Bex's room.

Only then did she make a lunge for the disk. "That's my property. How the hell did you get your hands on it?"

"Jasper gave it to me," Bex lied with no qualms.

"What for? There's nothing on it. You checked it yourself earlier."

"That's what I thought," Bex agreed. "But then, I talked to Jasper and—did you know that deleting a document doesn't really mean deleting it totally?"

"What are you talking about?"

Bex explained.

Patty stayed silent.

Bex said, "I saw the forged E-mail. Jasper retrieved it and I saw it. It's not an accusation anymore, Patty. It's fact. And I know you were involved."

"How?" Instead of crumbling, crying, and confessing as was indicated in the script Bex had written in her head, Patty seemed even more defiant and energized than before. Back when she was competing, Patty Simpson was known for going out and giving the best performance of her life when it seemed like there was no way she could still win. And, after missing a jump, it was inevitable that her next one would be better than ever. Too late, Bex remembered that this was not a woman who crumbled easily. Or ever.

"How do you know I was involved?" Patty asked.

"Well, Jasper said—"

"His word against mine."

"Francis and Diana—"

"Never saw me. You told me they said *Jasper* gave them the disk."

"But the disk is yours."

"Jasper is my Web master. He has access to my computer, my disks, everything. In fact, I often give him Erin's weekly diary entry on that exact disk. Obviously he dummied up the E-mail, approached Francis and Diana, set everything up, then, when he was caught, he planted it on a disk I'd given him and returned it to me to cover his own ass."

It was an excellent theory. Bex wondered why she hadn't come up with it herself. After all, hadn't Jasper seemed a little too eager to help her out? He'd practically handed her Patty on a silver platter. All the while swearing he was doing it to protect her.

"You think Jasper set you up?"

"I know he did."

"Why?"

"I told you, to protect himself."

"Yes . . . but . . ." Bex was doing that thinking thing she was so famous for, again. And, no matter how reasonable Patty's theory had sounded mere moments ago, she was starting to see a few glitches. "Here's the problem. If he really acted alone in dummying up the phony E-mail, why give me the disk it's on? I mean, without it, I've really got no proof except his word against Francis and Diana's. And they've got their own, excellent reasons for denying that anything ever happened. If I went ahead and made the E-mail public, without any proof that it's phony, it would have just been evidence that Erin truly deserved the gold. Which is supposedly why Jasper did all this in the first place. Why would he go through all this trouble to frame you for the fraud, when it would have been better and simpler for him to just deny everything?"

"Because he's a selfish son of a bitch who doesn't give a damn about anyone's feelings but his own. You're right, if he'd just shut up, he could have helped Erin. Instead, he's trying to get me out of the way, so he can have her all to himself."

Bex asked, "You mean, Jasper has some sort of obsession with Erin? Like, you think he's deranged or something?"

"Obsession with Erin." Patty shook her head. "Yeah, I'd say Jasper has an obsession with Erin. Now, he does, anyway. Now, when it's all medals and championships. But, where the hell was he when she was a baby? When I had to bring her to the rink and leave her in a playpen in the snack bar and beg one of the skate moms to keep an eye on her because I was trying to teach and raise a kid at the same time? Where the hell was Jasper's obsession with her then?"

Bex didn't know what to say. No, wait, yes, she did. It was so obvious, she was amazed she hadn't seen it before.

Bex asked, "Jasper is Erin's father, isn't he, Patty?"

Sixteen

"Well, of course, he is," Patty snapped. "She looks just like him. The blonde hair, the blue eyes, the practically white lashes and eyebrows. I used to look at the two of them together, and I used to think, it's obvious, she's his mirror image, how could people not see it?"

Probably, Bex wanted to say, because she is also the spitting image of you. But, then again, Bex supposed people only saw what they wanted to see. And when Patty looked at Erin, she only saw her father.

Bex asked, "Did you and Jasper meet at Stanford?"

Another connection she'd completely missed until now. Patty nodded.

"And he walked out on you when you got pregnant with Erin?"

Bex couldn't help it. She could feel the sympathy welling up inside her. She could see the TV movie now: Patty was probably so shattered from her perceived failure at the

Olympics that she was easy prey for a sexy, smooth talker eager to add the campus celebrity to the multiple notches on his bedpost. Naturally, said sexy, smooth talker had no interest in Erin. It was a classic seduced-and-abandoned tale.

Patty said, "Are you kidding? As soon as the drugstore stick turned blue, I gave Jasper his walking papers. I didn't need him anymore."

Bex said, "Huh?"

"Did you know Jasper was an athlete? Yeah, hard to believe now, he's got that computer nerd thing down. But, Jasper was a jock in college. Swimming, skiing, cross-country . . . couple of other things. Who remembers now? As soon as I saw him, I knew any kid of his would get fabulous sports genes. He was exactly what I needed."

Bex blinked. It was the only part of her body not currently frozen with confusion. She said, "So, uhm, you—you . . . bred, Erin? Like—" Bex was about to make a reference to Adolph Hitler's Lebensborn program, but then remembered that this was a skater she was talking to and went with something simpler, "Like a show dog?"

"I wanted my daughter to have the best," Patty said simply. "I knew I could give her the training she needed to become a champion, but good genes are the most important thing. Don't believe what people say about hard work and desire being all you need to succeed. Hard work and desire are vital—but only as long as you've got the right body. I mean, you, Bex, you could want to be a basketball player more than anything in the world. You could practice every day and do drills until your hands bleed. You're never going to be a basketball player, Bex."

"Thanks for the tip . . . So Jasper had nothing to do with raising Erin?"

"I wouldn't let him. He would have only gotten in the

way. Jasper would have never understood how important skating is to Erin. I realized that from the first. Jasper was a natural athlete; I don't think there was a sport he ever tried that he didn't excel at. He could have been a champion, but, get this—he only wanted to do it for fun. Fun! Have you ever heard of anyone going to medical school for fun? Or law school? He didn't get that skating was as serious as any of those things. More serious, actually, because you have to start so young."

"But you let him be your Web master? If you didn't want him around Erin . . . "

"He popped up again two years ago. We didn't hear a word from him for seventeen years, and then suddenly there he was, on the phone, telling me he saw Erin on television and he wanted to be involved. How could he help? I told him he could do her Web site."

"But he couldn't tell her he was her father."

"Erin," Patty said pointedly, "doesn't have a father. And she doesn't need one. She did, however, need a good Web master and Jasper was ready, eager, willing, and I *thought* he had her best interests at heart. After this, though, after this, I know I was right the first time. He doesn't understand. And he's a threat to Erin's career. That's why he made up this whole thing with the E-mail. He wants me out of the way so he can have Erin."

"Erin is hardly six years old. This isn't *Kramer vs. Kramer*, here."

"He wants Erin. That's why he's saying all those things about me."

"So you deny everything? The phony E-mail, the scheming with Francis and Diana, the E-mail ending up in Silvana's purse . . ."

"Yes," Patty said confidently, about as far from the

breaking down and crying that Bex expected as she, Rebecca Elizabeth Levy, was now from solving this crime. "I deny everything."

"You know," Bex said, "At some point during your 'I saw Erin Simpson on TV and decided to change my life' story, you might have mentioned that you were also Erin's father."

Jasper asked, "Patty told you?"

"I guoooed. And then she told me."

"How did you know?"

"What do you mean?" Bex echoed Patty sarcastically. "The girl looks just like you."

"Patty told me she didn't want anyone to know."

"Does Erin know?"

"Of course not. Patty won't allow it."

"Patty claims you made up the story about Silvana and the phony E-mail because you want Patty locked up and out of the way, and Erin all to yourself."

At this point, Jasper's eyes did not actually pop out of his head cartoon-style, squawk a funny noise, and pop back in with a snap. Bex made that part up. But he did stare at Bex as if she'd just told him his company stock had dropped forty points. He slowly sat down on his bed, shaking his head.

"How could she say that? She knows I would never do anything to hurt her and Erin. How could she say such a thing?"

"Honestly . . ." Bex plopped down on the bed next to him. "I wouldn't blame you." Bex wondered if it was possible to play good cop/bad cop when there was only one of you. And you weren't exactly a cop. "I mean, after everything she did to you, practically using you as an anonymous sperm donor, then cutting you out of your daughter's life, I wouldn't blame you for wanting to get back at her."

Bex figured, if she couldn't get Patty to break down and confess, Jasper would do just as well. At this point, she was willing to pin the blame on herself, as long as it gave her something to write in Gil's report. The one she was supposed to give him yesterday and had yet to start.

Jasper said, "Oh. I see. She fed you that story."

"Story?"

"The, 'I was an independent woman who knew what I wanted out of life. I used Jasper and then dumped him so I could raise Erin to be skating's new great blonde hope.' That story."

"It's not true?"

Jasper said, "When I met Patty, she was a twenty-four-year-old college freshman who'd never spent a night away from her mommy. She'd never eaten alone in a restaurant, never paid a bill, never been kissed. Are you getting the picture?"

Bex nodded, not sure if she wanted to hear more. If this went where she expected it to, it was definitely going to get too sad.

"I would have called her a challenge, if only because she had no idea what she was doing, but virgins are never really a challenge, not when *you* know what you're doing. The other guys on campus saw her as this untouchable celebrity goddess. She wasn't. She was just lonely and scared, utterly inexperienced, and totally *not* a challenge. When she got pregnant, I told her she was stupid and careless. It wasn't until later that I realized she probably was really just clueless. I mean, her mother probably only talked to her about death spirals, not diaphragms. I walked out on Patty, not the other way around. When I heard she dropped out of school,

I thought it was for the best; she couldn't hack the course work any better than she could handle the social life. I was a bastard, I admit it, but I was all about my career back then. I was going to be a millionaire, and Patty plus child most certainly didn't fit into my plans."

Bex said, "Well, you did become a millionaire."

"I did. And everything that I told you happened afterward is true. I did buy stuff and travel and do the whole new-money scene. And, one night, I really did turn on the TV, and there was Erin. I'd never given her any thought. I'd never even wondered if Patty had a boy or a girl. I guess I assumed she did the sensible thing and got an abortion. Do you know what it's like to see your child for the first time on television? I was paralyzed. I couldn't move. There she was. And you're right. She does look just like me."

Uh . . . right, Bex thought. But she figured now was neither the time nor place to quibble.

"So you contacted Patty?"

"I did. And I got her to agree to at least let me do Erin's Web site. I couldn't tell her I was her father, but I could at least get to know her. Hang out a little bit. We're friends, now, Erin and I. We're friends. That's really great."

"Why would Patty lie to me? I mean, your version makes her more sympathetic. In her version, she comes off as a total bitch. Why would someone go to the trouble to make up a story to make herself look worse?"

"Because Patty thinks it makes her look better. She's been telling it for years. It's part of Erin's official lore, just like the cock-and-bull story about how her first word was 'ice.' Think about it, Bex; for a woman like Patty, what would be worse, having other people think she's a bitch or pathetic?"

Bex saw his point. And she said, "Sounds like Patty is

quite the accomplished liar. And—joining our story already in progress—it looks like she's not about to confess to anything. That means you're my only witness."

Jasper sighed. "She won't confirm anything?"

"She says she didn't even know the phony E-mail was on her disk, much less that she was the one who initiated it in the first place."

"I don't understand . . ."

"What's not to understand? Patty killed Silvana."

"No. No, I don't believe you."

"Okay. Then you killed Silvana."

"You know I didn't."

"Just tell your story to the police, Jasper, and let them investigate Patty. They'll get to the bottom of this. In case you haven't noticed, I have no idea what I'm doing, here."

Jasper said, "No."

"What, no? No, what?"

"If Patty isn't going to come forward on her own, I'm not going to drag her into this."

"What?" At this point, Bex's eyes actually did do the cartoon pop, complete with sound effects. She wasn't even exaggerating. "What do you mean? What happened to 'I don't want this hanging over Erin's head'? What happened to 'I'm doing this to protect both of them'?"

"Patty would never hurt Erin. If she isn't confessing to having created the E-mail, that means she must have some other, better plan to protect her. I can't screw that up. I can't, Bex. You understand. If I go to the police with what I know, I'll lose my daughter."

Bex wanted to cry.

She usually tried very hard not to. Even though, unlike

"There is no crying in baseball" (thank you, Tom Hanks), there actually was a great deal of crying in skating (tears of joy, tears of sadness, tears of pain, tears of thank-God-this-is-finally-over), her policy was that Bex did not have to be a party to it. But, as she sat in her hotel room, laptop open, fingers poised over the keys, no longer able to procrastinate writing her report for Gil, Bex wanted to cry. Very, very badly. She had nothing.

After all her hard work, after all her lost sleep and stress and lies and close calls and talking to people she really otherwise had no interest in talking to, she had nothing.

She had the E-mail.

Which was printed on the 24/7 computer. Or on any other computer on the planet that she had yet to get to.

It was printed by Francis and Diana. Unless they denied the whole thing. And if they denied the whole thing, she couldn't link the E-mail to Jasper. Or Patty.

She had Patty's disk. Which Patty and Jasper would now both deny ever having seen before. Heck, at this point, the most incriminating thing about the disk was that Bex even had it. Would it be too far-out for some overzealous conspiracy theorist to suggest that maybe Bex had dummied the E-mail herself, printed it at the 24/7 production truck, then planted it on Silvana's body after she killed her? Bex even had a motive for the crime: 24/7's exclusive on the cheating coach's death. After the scandal, Gil expected huge ratings for the exhibition show. Bex was simply being a good employee.

Bex opened her research binder, pulling out all of her notes from the past few days. As she reached for her copy of the event protocol, Silvana's receipt fell out. Bex picked it up and was about to stuff it back inside the folder, figuring even Gil at his most desperate would never consider this

worth photographing for his special, when the list of purchased items caught her eye. Bex had read it already a million times. She read it again. And this time, she actually paid
attention for a change.

According to the receipt, Silvana had purchased some
lemon-flavored hard candy.

Check. Bex remembered the half-eaten roll she'd briefly
considered testing for poison.

A bottle of ibuprofen and a bottle of aspirin.

Check. Check.

And a travel-sized packet of tissues.

Bex read the list one more time.

And then she grabbed the receipt and ran for the production truck.

It was there on the practice tape.

Presumably, it had been there all along. Bex had no idea
how she'd missed it the first time. By the time she'd first
watched the tape, she already had all the evidence she
needed. And still she'd missed it.

But, it didn't matter anymore. She finally had her proof.

And, tomorrow afternoon, during the live exhibition
broadcast, Bex would use it to expose Silvana Potenza's
killer.

Seventeen

Bex didn't tell Gil what she was planning to do. She was too scared of screwing it up. If there was one thing Bex had learned over the past few days, it was that clever plans that seemed perfect inside her sleep-deprived head had a tendency to go haywire once actually implemented. For that to happen live and on the air would be most bad.

And so, all Bex told Gil was that sure, she'd adequately prepped Francis and Diana for the live interview with Patty and Erin Simpson scheduled to take place before Erin's coronation—oops, sorry, second gold medal ceremony. What she didn't tell Gil was that the list of questions Bex provided the Howarths bore little resemblance to what Gil was, in all likelihood, expecting. But, hey, that's what made live television the sport of kings, no? She'd also neglected to tell Gil that she had, for all intents and purposes, black-mailed Francis and Diana into asking her questions instead of his by threatening to expose their culpability in the

E-mail scam. The way Bex saw it, Gil really didn't need to know what his employees did with their free time.

Erin and Patty Simpson reported to the 24/7 interview room inside the arena exactly at their appointed time, both grinning broadly in preparation for their close-up. They kept right on grinning as they shook hands with Francis and Diana, exchanging pleasantries and agreeing that it really was marvelous of the ISU to admit their error and award Erin her deserved gold medal.

And then Patty saw Bex.

And her grin noticeably faded.

Alas, there really was nothing she could do about it.

Even before her eyes turned into slits and her furrowed brow began to resemble a picket fence, the soundman was plopping Patty down in the interview chair and running a microphone wire up her shirt, while the cameraman was shining bright lights in her eyes and waving around a large, silver reflecting sheet.

Even though she was planning an ambush, Bex had gone ahead and set up the room to look like a typical interview. She had two sets of two chairs facing each other at an angle, like a widely spread triangle, with Diana and Erin sitting closest to each other, and Patty on Erin's right, Francis on Diana's left. Two, bucket-sized lights, suspended from black iron poles, shone down upon them all, making the entire room unbearably hot. The cameraman was positioned directly in front of the talent, hunched over, peering through his lens and, periodically, at the monitor by his feet, which was broadcasting the same picture as his camera, only in color, rather than black-and-white. The soundman sat cross-legged on the floor, earphones on his head, staring intently at the dancing levers that indicated good sound levels. Which left Bex to crouch precariously next to the camera, squatting uncomfortably in the one spot of the entire room where she could both be seen by Francis and Diana in case she needed to signal them, and yet be invisible to the camera. She wore an earpiece so she could hear Gil's countdown in the truck.

"Five, four, three . . ."

Bex raised her arm and pointed at Francis and Diana, indicating that they were now live on the air. At her cue, all four sat up straighter in their chairs and commenced smiling brightly.

Francis welcomed the viewers at home to 24/7's exclusive, live coverage of the world championship's exhibition, then tossed to Diana, who introduced the Simpsons. Together, they summarized the events of the last few days.

Patty voiced how shocked they both were by the results of the ladies' competition.

Erin thanked all of her wonderful fans for their support.

Patty mentioned that www.ErinExcitement.com was selling exclusive, Erin-autographed merchandise for a short time only.

Erin reiterated that the results didn't really matter. Her silver medal truly was the silver lining on her cloud, and she was very happy and proud to have represented her country at these championships and all she cared about was doing her country proud.

If Bex weren't perched so precariously, she might have rolled her eyes. But, considering that any excess movement might send her sprawling, she settled for signaling Francis to wrap up the love fest and start with the questions she'd given him.

Francis said, "Erin, Patty, we have a tape of your Friday

morning practice session right here. Do you think you could look at it with me?"

For a split second, Patty looked this close to asking, "What the hell for?" Luckily for her, she remembered in the nick of time where exactly she was, and exactly how live she was. As a result, her sunny smile only ended up wavering for a moment. "Sure, Francis!"

Francis clicked the button to turn on the monitor in the room while, back at the truck, Bex could hear Gil screaming, "What the hell? Did I say we could have video roll-in, in this thing? Who said we could have video roll-in, in this thing? Is the video rolling? Are they rolling video? Are we rolling video? Roll it, damn it, roll it!"

The video rolled.

"Here you are, Erin," Diana said.

And, indeed, there Erin was. Arriving for practice at the arena, waving to the fans, lining up her talismans along the boards, taking off her skateguards, and stepping onto the ice. As she was warming up, skating around first forward, then backward, clockwise and counterclockwise, Diana casually asked, as if just trying to fill time, "Erin, you know, I thought I read somewhere once where you never get off in the middle of a practice session."

"That's right," Patty said proudly. "I believe that since in competition you don't have the chance if things aren't going well to get off, collect yourself, and start over again, it's best to duplicate that environment in the practice."

"But," Francis inquired, "Erin, dear, didn't you, in point of fact, get off the ice during this particular practice that we're watching now?"

Erin and Patty exchanged looks. If deer caught in headlights ever looked at each other, Bex presumed the Simpsons at that moment were what they would look like.

"I . . ." Erin began.

"Xenia Trubin says she saw you making a phone call," Francis offered.

"Xenia Trubin," Patty began, "is a—"

"Who did you call, Erin?" Diana asked.

Erin snuck a peek at Bex, her eyes darted desperately and at the same time, pleadingly, as if she expected Bex to tell her what to say. Bex raised her palms in the air and shrugged.

"I was calling my boyfriend," Erin blurted out.

At that, Patty whipped her head around so quickly, the sound guy winced from the thump it echoed along her microphone.

"Erin . . ." her mother hissed, as if speaking low would somehow prevent all of America from hearing every word.

"Erin," Diana said evenly, ignoring Patty for the time being, "Tell me, dear, is your boyfriend a recorded voice at the New York University registration line?"

Sitting in Erin Simpson's situation, a darker-skinned person might have gone pale. But, Erin was already as white as typewriter correction fluid. So, in Erin's case, she went blue. Bex thought she could see every vein beneath her pale skin. It was hard to miss them. Each one was pumping like crazy. Between the stress and the hot lights, Bex wondered if she'd overplayed her hand, and the poor kid was about to pass out.

"I'm sorry, Mommy," Erin said.

"For what? What are you sorry for? What are they talking about? What boyfriend? What's this about some school in New York?"

"I—I got accepted, Mom. Into NYU. Isn't that great? I didn't think I'd have the grades, but then my SATs were better than I expected, and I guess it was enough—"

"You applied to college? What for, Erin? You know

we've got the tour coming up. It's great that you got in, honey. Really, congratulations, I'm so proud of you. But, what's the point of applying now? You're just going to have to defer for a couple of years, until—"

"I don't want to defer," Erin said. "I'll do the tour this spring and this summer, but next fall, I want to go to school. I already called and registered for my classes. I tried to do it from the arena that morning, but there were too many people around, and I had to get back to the ice. So I had to do it later. In another place."

Bex waited to see if Erin would mention making the call from Bex's hotel room. But the girl stayed silent. At least, on that particular subject.

"Erin," Patty began, but Bex's notes gave Francis and Diana strict instructions that, as soon as Patty was adequately discombobulated from Erin's revelation, they were to immediately change the line of questioning. Because they were coming up to the key part of the tape.

"Patty," Diana said in a voice as smooth as newly Zambonied ice yet as impossible to ignore as a quad done in combination. In the short program. "Erin wasn't the only one to leave the practice that morning, was she? You also left for a little bit."

"Yes," Patty said, her mind obviously not on the question at hand. She kept staring at Erin, as if her daughter had just transformed into some alien, nonskating creature right in front of her eyes. "So what?"

"Why did you leave?"

"What difference does that make?"

"Humor us," Francis said dryly, playing his part to perfection despite the fact that, when Bex first laid out her scenario for him, he'd sniffed, "This, Bex, is most undoubtedly, inane."

"Erin was out of tissues. I went to get her some."

"Really?" Francis pointed the remote control for a second time, pushed pause, and froze the picture. The monitor now showed Erin and Patty in conference over the barrier, next to the little troll doll, skate guards, and a box of tissues. An obviously full box of tissues.

Francis didn't say anything. Diana didn't say anything. They simply sat and waited for Patty to realize what it was she was seeing on the screen.

On Bex's headset, however, she heard Gil say, "Hey, wait a minute. Isn't that a box of tissues already there?"

"That certainly looks like a box of tissues to me, Patty," Diana offered.

But Erin's mother still didn't seem to be getting it.

Patty said, "Okay. So, I missed it. With all the crap on the barrier, I must not have seen it, and thought we were out. I went to get more. What's the big deal, here?"

Francis fast-forwarded the tape. He stopped at the part where Patty returned to the arena, carrying a box of tissues in her hand.

Francis asked, "Where did you go to buy the tissues?"

"I don't know. I don't remember. Probably someplace in the arena."

"So, you didn't leave the arena?"

"No. Why should I have?"

"Because, Patty, the box in your hand, that's the hotel boutique's brand."

Patty looked down at her hands, as if expecting to see the box materialize there. When nothing did, she looked back up. She said, "So, okay, so I must have gone back to the hotel."

"The clerk doesn't remember you."

"The guy sees a million people a day. I'm not so gorgeous, believe me, that I expect to be remembered everywhere I go."

"But the clerk does remember Silvana Potenza stopping by. And buying the exact same brand of tissues that you got."

"Great minds think alike, I guess," Patty snapped.

Diana said, "We have the receipt for Silvana's tissues. Do you have your receipt, Patty?"

"Okay, now you're kidding me, right?"

"Would you like to know the strangest thing, though?"

"Stranger than 24/7 devoting live TV time to discussing my tissue purchases?"

Gil said, "She has a point there, Bex. This better be leading somewhere and really, really fast, too."

Bex wondered why he was speaking to her when he knew that she couldn't respond. But, just in case, she nodded her head.

Francis said, "When the police examined Silvana Potenza's purse, after she died, they didn't find any tissues. Isn't that odd?"

"Maybe she used them all up," Erin piped up. Bex wasn't certain if she was trying to help out her mother or just jumping into what was allegedly still her interview.

"An entire packet of tissues?" Diana asked. "In the morning hour between buying them and her death?"

Erin shrugged and looked at Patty. A sort of mental, "Ball's back in your court, Mom."

"So, Patty," Francis's voice was soothing, avuncular, even. "How do you explain it? You leave the arena to get Erin a box of tissues, despite there being a perfectly good box already there. But you don't go to the hotel boutique. And yet, there you are later, on video no less, showing up with a box of hotel boutique brand tissues. The same size that Silvana purchased earlier. And yet, at the same time, Silvana's tissues go mysteriously missing."

Patty half stood off her chair, "This is ridiculous, I'm getting out of here."

"No," Francis held up his hand, planting it in such a way that, in a room that small, there really was nowhere for Patty to turn. "You're not. Sit down, please."

Patty reluctantly sat down, visibly determined not to answer a single, other question. But, Erin obviously had other ideas.

"Mom!" She grabbed her mother's arm, tugging on her sleeve rather violently. "Mom, what are they talking about?" She turned to Francis and Diana, ready to throw herself in front of Patty's body if need be. "You take it back. You take it back, right now!"

"Erin," Diana said evenly. "All Francis and I have done is present the facts. It's up to your mom now to explain them."

"Then explain them, Mom," Erin commanded Patty. "Explain it to them."

Patty looked at Erin. She looked at Francis, Diana, Bex, even at the cameraman and sound guy. It was a hostile room, and she knew it. There was nowhere to go now.

She looked back at Erin. She said, "You skated so beautifully in the long program. It was your best long this season, don't you think?"

Erin said, "It was okay. I could have been a little faster on the footwork section."

"You deserved to win the gold. Everyone thought so." She looked at Francis and Diana. "Erin deserved the gold. Didn't she?"

Francis said, "It's not just about how you skate. It's about how you skate in comparison to everyone else."

"You don't think I know that?" Patty snarled. "You don't think I, of all people, know that? I know what it takes to win gold. It takes a perfect skate, and it takes an awake judging panel, and it takes political pull. A lot of political pull. Silvana Potenza could have given Erin that gold medal. She should have. She should have voted with the West. It would have been the right thing to do. It would have shown the damn Russians they can't always get away with their games. It could have sent a message."

Francis asked, "Did you kill Silvana Potenza, Patty?"

"She was going to ruin it." Patty nodded her head up and down, confirming the logic of her actions. "She was going to testify in front of the ISU and tell them she wasn't influenced, that the results were fair. The results weren't fair!"

"You killed her," Diana said. "You left the arena, and you used the pay phone across from the refrigeration room to call Silvana's cell and lure her there. You turned off the light and poured water on the floor, knowing she'd have to step into the puddle to pull the switch and that it would electrocute her. You watched her go in and, after she was dead, you went and you planted this phony E-mail in her purse." Diana held it up for the camera to see.

"Holy shit," Gil said.

Bex smiled.

It really was nice to have her work appreciated.

"This E-mail is supposedly from Sergei Alemazov to Silvana," Francis said, "telling her how to vote in the ladies' long program, in Xenia Trubin's favor. Only it's a forgery. Silvana never printed it out. She didn't have a printer to do it on. You put this E-mail in her purse for the police to find. You knew it would be enough evidence for the ISU to strip Xenia of her gold and give it to Erin, instead. And, when you opened her purse, you saw the box of tissues. That gave you the idea to take them and then claim that's why you left. Erin, did your mother tell you she was going to get you tissues before she left, or after?"

Erin's skin was no longer blue. It had gone gray. She sat rooted to her chair, shoulders slumped, eyes glassy with shock. When Francis asked her his question, it took her a moment to recognize that he was speaking to her, and another moment to find her voice.

"I don't . . ." She had to stop, take a deep breath, more of a gasp, really, and start again. "I don't remember. I don't remember what she said."

For her part, except for the fact that she was sitting straight as a board, her hands clutched in her lap, her eyes narrowed and focused, though distant, as if she were trying hard to remember something awfully important, Patty seemed to be in an equal amount of shock.

"It wasn't Erin's fault," Patty insisted. "She didn't do anything wrong. She should still get her gold medal. She skated beautifully. It could have gone either way. It really could have."

"Mommy?" All of a sudden, Erin sounded like she was five years old. But the look on her face suggested someone ten times older. "Are they telling the truth? Did you kill Silvana?"

"I did it for you." Patty seemed convinced that if she could just make Erin understand that one fact, it would make everything okay. "It was the least I could do. I'm your mother."

When she first set this entrapment exercise up, Bex had sincerely hoped that her publicity-hungry policeman/ stand-up comic friend could recognize a good cue when he heard one.

She wasn't disappointed.

As if on schedule, the door opened, and Stace Hale Jr., who'd been just outside, watching the live interview alongside the rest of America, stepped into the room and, after making sure that he was directly in front of the camera—*I'm ready for my close-up, Mr. Gil DeMille*—pulled out his handcuffs and solemnly intoned, "Patty Simpson, you are under arrest for the murder of Silvana Potenza. . . ."

"Holy frickin' Mother of God," Gil's scream was so loud, Bex bet it could be heard not only in her headset but also throughout the entire room. "This, people, this! Are you paying attention? This is what I call good television! Bex, I can't wait to see how you top this, next season!"

Turn the page for a special preview of
Alina Adams's

Missing on Ice

Coming in October 2004 from
Berkley Prime Crime!

"He is the best young skater in the United States," the voice on the other end of the phone receiver unequivocally pronounced. "And you are never going to see him."

As the senior —all right, only—researcher for the 24/7 Sports Network, Rebecca "Bex" Levy was used to out-of-the-blue phone calls praising this or that previously unheard of athlete. What she was not used to, however, was being told that she wouldn't be allowed to see him. After all, the point of said phone calls was usually to convince Bex to convince the 24/7 top brass that said athlete was worthy of a 24/7 up-close-and-personal feature, preferably in prime time. Rarely was the point of the phone call to taunt her about a feature she wouldn't be able to do.

Which was why, rather than following her first instinct, to politely offer, "Well, thank you very much for sharing that with me," and hanging up, Bex, instead, stayed on the line, waiting for the explanation that she could only hope would be forthcoming.

Oh, and Bex had another reason for continuing to listen. The voice on the other end of the telephone receiver belonged to one Mrs. Antonia Wright.

Bex had met Toni a year ago, before Bex started working as the 24/7 researcher, back when she was just another struggling, freelance sports reporter, newly out of college and still barely earning enough to simply get by (granted, she was trying to do the getting-by thing in Manhattan, a borough where "simply" and "get by" couldn't even acquiese to sharing a Central Park bench), much less begin making any sort of substantial dent in paying back her rather substantial student loans.

Bex had written a cover feature for "Black Maturity Magazine" (she refused to let a little fact like being neither Black nor mature stand in her way; Bex's other freelance clients included "Boy's Life," "Parents," and "Cats," and she wasn't any of those things either), chronicling Toni's struggle as the first African-American ice skater to attempt competing within the United States Figure Skating Association (USFSA). It truly was a fabulous and inspiring story, ranging from the first time seven-year-old Toni tried to pay her admission to a local ice rink and was told, "No niggers allowed," to her breaking the color barrier by joining a skating club so that she could perform at a local competition, to her triumphant win of a U.S. pair title with—oh, the scandal of it!—a white pairs partner. Afterward, Toni went on to a rather successful professional career before settling down as a coach at the Connecticut Olympic Training Center in Hartford. These days, she was past sixty years old and still lacing up her skates to get out onto the ice with her students. The woman was a marvel. And, when she talked, Bex

listened. Even if, at the moment, Toni wasn't making a heck
of a lot of sense.

"I have this student," Toni backtracked. "His name is Jeremy Hunt. He is thirteen years old, and he's terrific, a
prodigy. He started skating at eight— most people will tell
you that's too late, I know I thought it was. But, then, he got
all of his double jumps in six months, started landing triples
within a year, passed his senior test at eleven, and now he's
doing quads! Quads, Bex! Good ones, not cheated, fully ro-
tated. The Salchow, the toe loop, and even the loop three
out of five times. A quadruple loop, can you believe it?"

A year ago, Toni's words would have sounded like gib-
berish to Bex. A year ago, she hadn't been able to recognize
an Axel on the ice from the one on her ten-year-old car. But,
in researching and writing the article on Toni, she'd paid
careful attention. And the older woman was an excellent
teacher.

So excellent, in fact, that Bex had no trouble running her
current words through the "Skating Universal Translator"
in her head to come up with the following interpretation:
"While eight years old would still seem to be a rather young
age on most normal planets, in the world of competitive
skating this Jeremy Hunt might as well have been named
Grandpa Moses. Popular wisdom dictates that, in order to
succeed at the sport, the potential Olympic and World
Champion ought to begin his serious, daily training by the
age of preferably eighteen months, private lessons by age
three, and lessons with a top-ranked coach by no later than
five. A boy who only takes up the discipline at age eight
might as well scrape "loser" onto his forehead with a rusty
skate blade and prepare for a future as Eeyore's fuzzy rear
end in the European company of "Disney on Ice." However, it seems that Toni's student, Jeremy, has beaten the

prognosticators by being somewhat of a talented fellow, and precociously mastering his double jumps—meaning he could take off from the ice, rotate twice in the air, and come down on one foot without his other foot, hand, chin, or chest also slamming into the ground beside him. Mastering the double jumps—Salchow, toe loop, loop, flip, lutz, and especially double Axel, which, in spite of its name, actually required two and half revolutions in the air—was a process that some skaters took years to perfect. The fact that Jeremy did it in under six months was impressive. But, not as impressive as the fact that he then went ahead and mastered all his triples, as well—meaning he could take off from the ice, rotate three times in the air, and come down on one foot without his other foot, hand, chin, or chest also slamming into the ground beside him. Mastering all of the triple jumps—Salchow, toe loop, loop, flip, lutz, and especially a triple Axel, which, in spite of its name, actually required three and half revolutions in the air, was a process that took some skaters—well, never. Most skaters never mastered all of their triple jumps. And they especially didn't do it in one year. At the age of eleven. Of course, when it came to quadruple jumps, there were only a dozen men in the world who could actually land one successfully, much less land two-almost-three of them (and at least half of those who claimed to be landing quads cheated them somehow, either taking an extra half turn on the ice before they jumped, or after they'd landed). When it came to men doing clean quads, that is, four full revolutions in the air—no cheating—there were only a handful. And none of them were thirteen years old, that was for sure.

"Oh, and Bex, this is the best part," Toni sounded almost religiously ecstatic as she unveiled her pièce de résistance. "He can actually skate!"

Come on, Universal Skating Translator—Bex cheered on her brain—do your stuff! And sure enough, after a moment, it kicked in with the code breaker. What Toni actually meant to say was: "When Jeremy Hunt gets on the ice, he doesn't look like he is trudging from place to place through gravel, and he doesn't just perform like an acrobatic monkey, he actually knows how to stroke, to glide with a semblance of smoothness, to float the way you're supposed to if we're to keep this sport from becoming tumbling on ice, instead of the art it was always intended to be."

All right, so maybe Bex embellished a little on that last part. But, it was exactly what Toni meant. She could tell from the excitement in her voice.

Still, Toni wasn't as over-the-moon excited as Bex would have expected a coach to be when talking up a supposed find of this boy's caliber. There had to be a catch. Something Toni intended to tell her, but couldn't quite find the right words.

Bex tried to guess, offering up her version of "Skating Twenty Questions." She asked Toni, "So, what's the problem? Does he leave it all on the practice ice?"

In human language, what Bex meant was, "Is he good in practice, but then can't deliver in competition?"

"Not at all," Toni assured. "If this boy can do it, he can do it, doesn't matter when or where."

"Meaning he doesn't freeze up under pressure?"

"Nope. Solid as a rock. Two minutes before competition, he's grinning and waving to his friends and clapping for the competition and jabbering about which little girl he's planning to invite to his eight-grade dance. Nothing fazes him. I swear, when results went up at Sectionals last week and we saw he'd placed first, the smile he had is the same one he'd have had if he finished last."

Translation: Sectionals were a qualifying competition. There were three in the country, divided into geographic regions—Pacific Coast, Midwestern, and Eastern. The top four skaters from each discipline advanced on to the U.S. National Championships. If Jeremy Hunt won his Eastern Sectional, it meant he had a very good chance of winning a medal—even a gold one—at Nationals. And a U.S. National Champion, traditionally, had a very good chance of going on to win a medal at the World Championships, or even at the Olympic Winter Games.

"Not bad for a thirteen-year-old," Bex noted.

"Except that there's a problem."

A-ha! Chalk one up for Bex's instincts. Of course, there was a problem.

"It's Jeremy's father."

Oh, yes, here it came. Bex took mental bets with herself on exactly what sort of cliché "problem" parent Mr. Hunt would prove to be. There was a limited number of types, and none of them were a barrel of monkeys. "What's wrong with him?"

Toni took a deep breath and, in a voice that suggested she couldn't believe it herself, revealed, "Jeremy's father won't let him compete at Nationals."

"What?" Bex sat up in her office chair, rubber wheels scraping the floor with a squeak equal in volume to her dismay.

This was certainly a new one for her. Usually, when one said there was a problem with a skating parent, one meant that Mommy Dearest (and it was usually a Mommy Dearest, though a Daddy or two did sneak into the party once in a while) was beating her Skating Sweetie in the back bathroom with a hairbrush while screaming that Skating Sweetie messed up her combination jump on purpose. Or it meant that Mommy Dearest was keeping her Skating Sweetie on a diet so strict, gaunt Ethiopian children were sending Skating Sweetie humanitarian relief. Or, at the very least, that Mommy Dearest had taken to calling up judges at their regular place of employment to demand an explanation for why Skating Sweetie hadn't qualified for Nationals, when anyone could see that she was the superior child in her flight, if not in the entire world.

Although Bex had only been in the formal research business for a little more than one season (last year had been her first and she was just three months into her second), she'd been writing about sports of all kinds for almost ten years now, going back to her high-school paper. And she'd never, ever heard of parents trying to keep their child *out* of a competition.

"Does the dad say why?"

"He says that he has no problem with Jeremy skating for fun, but he doesn't want it consuming his life."

Oh. Well, that certainly was a new one. Bex almost didn't know what to say. She stammered, "I, well, Toni, he's not exactly wrong in that, is he?" This was truly unprecedented. On the other hand . . . "But why did he let Jeremy enter Sectionals if he wants him to do it just for fun?"

"I asked him the same thing. Mr. Hunt—his first name is Craig—he said that local competitions are still fun. Nationals are where it gets crazy."

Well, he was right and he was wrong about that. From where Bex sat, she'd seen some pretty crazy behavior at local inter-club competitions for skaters between the mature ages of five and five-and-a-half, but, okay, let Mr. Hunt have his opinion.

Bex said, "This Jeremy though, he sounds to me like the

type of kid who can handle big-time competition. Especially if he's got no pressure coming from the home front."

"Personally, I don't think it's that at all. Personally, I
think Mr. Hunt is afraid of Jeremy losing. He dotes on that
boy, he's afraid to see him hurt."

"Again, Toni," Bex, as a civilian, was treading carefully
now. You never knew with these skating people what exactly would set them off. One time Bex watched a skater go
mental because someone mistook his teal costume for being
blue. There were certain things these people took extra-
special seriously. And you'd darn better take them seriously, too, if you wanted them to keep talking to you.

Still, Bex bravely pressed on, "Is that so wrong?"

"When you've got a boy of this talent, yes!" The fervor
in Toni's voice reminded Bex that no matter how generally
reasonable the older woman sounded, she was still a skater
down to the Freon in her veins. Of course, to her, Craig
Hunt was spouting heresy. "Jeremy Hunt is the most talented male skater I've seen since Robby Sharpton. Do you
want him to end up throwing his potential away the same
way Robby did?"

Actually, Bex had no idea who this Robby Sharpton was.
She made a mental note to act out her job description and
go research it. How hard could it be? She already had a
pretty big clue. Apparently, Robby Sharpton never lived up
to his potential.

Toni went on, "What if someone had kept Fred Astaire
from dancing? Or Enrico Caruso from singing? What if
someone had taken away Van Gogh's paintbrushes?"

"He might have ended up with better hearing?" Bex was
being flip, she knew she was being flip. But, she just
couldn't help it sometimes. Not when it was this easy.

Toni said, "This boy could be the star of the next Nationals. Doesn't 24/7 want to be the first ones to tell his story?"

"Not if he's not going to be there, Toni, which, right now, it sounds like he's not."

"I need you to do something for me, Bex."

Ah, only sixteen digressions later, and here they were finally arriving at the point of this conversation. Bex immediately felt more comfortable. This was an arena where she was the star, where she knew what to do. As 24/7's only researcher, anyone who had a story to pitch had to come to her first. Only after Bex decided whether or not it had any merit or dramatic potential would she take it to her executive producer, Gil Cahill. If Gil agreed with her assessment, he would dispatch a producer to shoot the story, based on her research notes. If Gil disagreed with her assessment which was usually—he made her feel like she was exactly three centimeters tall and ready for the birdbrain remedial classes.

Bex did not enjoy that sensation. Which was why, before Gil had a chance to shoot down the ideas she brought him, Bex took the time to shoot down most ideas herself. She was a sort of Gil in training. God, but that was a horrifying thought.

Still, Toni wasn't just any coach trying to sell Bex on a story. She was a classy lady who deserved to be listened to and treated with respect. Before she was shot down.

"What can I do, Toni?"

"I think you should send a camera crew here to the training center to shoot Jeremy practicing. Once Mr. Hunt sees that a major sports network like 24/7 thinks his son has enough potential to be profiled as an up-and-comer, I think he'll realize just how truly exceptional Jeremy is, and he'll agree to let him live up to his full potential."

Unlike, apparently, this Robby Sharpton person.

"I.e, he'll let him go to Nationals?" Bex just wanted to make sure they were all on the same page here.

"Where he'll steal the show, I guarantee it. And 24/7 will have gotten the first exclusive with him."

Leave it to Toni to do her homework. She was up on all of her TV buzzwords. Still, Bex truly doubted that Gil could be talked into shelling out the expenses for a producer and two-man crew, camera and sound guy, to travel to Connecticut to shoot footage of a boy who, in all likelihood, wouldn't even be at Nationals. And, even if he was, Bex still suspected Toni was doing a bit of the over hype dance. No thirteen-year-old boy could be as good as she claimed this one was. Jeremy Hunt may have had a ton of potential he was in danger of not living up to, but Bex doubted a thirteen-year-old at his first major competition had a chance in hell of qualifying for the top five at Nationals. And, as far as the always compassionate television world was concerned, if you weren't in the top five, you were never even entered in the event.

Toni must have sensed Bex's hesitation. Because, before Bex had the chance to purse her lips in anticipation of, politely but firmly, offering up a "no," Toni interrupted to say, "How about if I send you a tape of Jeremy skating? You can see for yourself how special he is. Just watch him skate for a couple of minutes. Then tell me whether or not you'll go to Gil Cahill with the piece."

She'd been all set to say "no." But Toni was a sixty-year-old ice-skating pioneer. Bex was just a twenty-four-year-old sports researcher with no guts.

"Sure," Bex sighed, knowing that she was merely putting off the inevitable task of saying "no" for a few days at most, and feeling both like a first-class coward and yet oh so relieved at the same time. "Go ahead, Toni. Send me the tape."

"It's already in the mail, honey."

Oh, great, now Bex was not only gutless and a procrastinator. She was also predictable.